"LORD NIGHTINGALE, DO CEASE LARKING ABOUT AND PAY ATTENTION."

"I shall shiver your timbers if you do not pay attention immediately," Serendipity declared. "You are to learn to sing, sir, and I am to teach you. You will oblige me by paying attention."

" 'Tention!"

"Exactly. Now, we shall begin with our scales." Serendipity began to sing the first of the scales, "La-la-la-la-la-la-la-la."

Lord Nightingale went to the pianoforte. C he played and F and then D and E together and then he moved into the minors and back to the majors.

"Zounds!" exclaimed Wickenshire as he opened the door to the chamber. "What a musician he is! I thought for a moment it was you who played so very badly, Miss Bedford. I must apologize for making such an unwarranted assumption."

Dear Reader,

Welcome to the world of Lord Nightingale. *Lord Nightingale's Debut* is book one of the Nightingale Trilogy. It will be followed by *Lord Nightingale's Love Song* and *Lord Nightingale's Triumph,* and the series will conclude with *Lord Nightingale's Christmas.*

But that's *four* books, you say? Yes, I do know that a trilogy is a series of three books. That's what the Nightingale Trilogy originally was—a series of three books. A real trilogy.

Then my editor called. "How about a Christmas book?" she asked hopefully.

"How about a vacation?" I asked even more hopefully.

"Sure," she said. "As soon as you finish the Christmas book."

And that's how the four-book trilogy came about, with *Lord Nightingale's Christmas* bringing the series to a close. If you enjoy *Lord Nightingale's Debut,* you won't have to wait long for more of Lord Nightingale's (mis)adventures. The series will be published in four consecutive months.

In this, his debut, Lord Nightingale travels west to the ramshackle estate of Nicholas Chastain, the Earl of Wickenshire, where, producing a bit of mayhem and ignoring a brush with villainy, he unites the self-conscious earl and the sadly abused Miss Serendipity Bedford in that most perfect of unions by singing for them a joyous hymn to Spring.

LORD NIGHTINGALE'S DEBUT

JUDITH A. LANSDOWNE

Zebra Books
Kensington Publishing Corp.
http://www.zebrabooks.com

ZEBRA BOOKS are published by

Kensington Publishing Corp.
850 Third Avenue
New York, NY 10022

Copyright © 2000 by Judith A. Lansdowne

First Printing: August, 2000
10 9 8 7 6 5 4 3 2 1

Printed in the United States of America

To Rebecca Turney—

Thank you for always being there.

ONE

"Ouch! Thunderation!" roared the Earl of Wickenshire, sticking his finger into his mouth and beating a hasty retreat. "Deuced bird," he mumbled around his bleeding digit. "Be a parrot pie by the end of this day, I promise you that."

"Yo ho ho!" squawked the green-winged macaw raucously, in a voice so reminiscent of her beloved brother that Wickenshire's mama felt a stab of tears.

"He is merely a bird, Nicky," the dowager Lady Wickenshire said. "And you are a stranger to him."

"Yes, well, does he make a habit of biting every stranger who comes within his reach?"

"No, dearest. You are the very first stranger to ever get within his reach, I think. Most people are not inclined to approach Lord Nightingale so readily."

"No, not many," offered Mr. Trent from his place behind the shining oak table in the study of the Spelling mansion in Hertfordshire. "He is a rather intimidating fowl, but you cannot have him made into a parrot pie, Nick."

"Wait and see," muttered Wickenshire.

"No, Nicky, you cannot," repeated his mama. "If you had been here when first William read your Aunt Winifred's will to us, you would not make such a suggestion, even in jest."

"Is that so?" asked Wickenshire, lowering his long,

lean form into the chair provided for him. "Aunt Winifred actually wrote in her will that her nephew, Nicky, is not allowed to make a pie of the deuced parrot? How omniscient of her."

Mr. Trent could not help but laugh. He covered his mouth with his hand, but the laughter came regardless, though as a snort through his nose rather than an ear-splitting guffaw.

"What is so extraordinarily funny, Will?" asked the earl with a cock of his left eyebrow. "I assure you, Aunt Winifred knew me well."

"And treasured you, dearest," added his mama, "though she did abhor your profound sobriety. She always asked me, when she came to visit at Wicken Hall, if you did ever laugh like other boys and go larking about just for the fun of it. But she loved you, dearest, as did your Uncle Albert."

Wickenshire took the dowager's hand comfortingly into his own as she sat restlessly in the chair beside him. He knew well how sad his Uncle Albert's death had made her. And now to lose Winifred, who had treated her as though she were a true sister and not merely a sister-in-law—his mother's grief was immense. "Deuced bird did sound like Uncle Albert, did he not?" the earl murmured helplessly, not knowing what to say but knowing he must say something.

"Which is one of the reasons your Aunt Winifred treated Lord Nightingale as though he were King George himself," she replied softly, smiling through unspilled tears. "Spoiled that creature rotten, Winifred did. Whenever Nightingale spoke in Albert's voice after—after—well, there was nothing Winifred would not give him."

"And so she gave him you, Nick," added Mr. Trent quietly.

"Gave him *me?* What the deuce do you mean by that?"

"William," Lady Wickenshire commanded, her tears fading and a smile enveloping her countenance, "do

cease teasing Nicky and explain it all to him at once or
he will go off into one of his pouts and there will be no
reaching him."

"I do not pout, madam," responded Wickenshire. "I
ceased to pout when first I donned long pants."

"So you think," his mama responded, which set Mr.
Trent to snorting again.

Wickenshire attempted to glare at his boyhood friend,
but he could not prevent a glint of humor from lighting
the odd forest green of his eyes. "Will, really, such a
noise. Not at all professional."

"I kn-know," laughed Mr. Trent. "Father would be ap-
palled at me. And on such a solemn occasion, too."

"Nonsense, William. Your papa would be proud of
you. Always was," declared the dowager. "If your papa
were in your place, he would have boxed Nicky's ears
an hour ago and told him to sit still and be quiet. After
all, you do have other things to attend to, and Nicky has
kept you waiting forever."

"Only because the lowlands at Willowsweep flooded
and there were things to be done at once," Wickenshire
said. "I would have come for the funeral else. You know
that I would have done, Mama. I have always liked Aunt
Winifred."

"Yes, dearest, I know. But there were cows to be
pulled from the mud and sheep to be rescued, and likely
as not that disgrace of a barn near the stream filled with
water up to the loft and you had to move everything in
it beyond the north pasture."

"Indeed," frowned Wickenshire, remembering. "I
needs must work harder and faster or Willowsweep will
fall entirely to ruin right before our eyes."

"I and some of the staff from Wicken Hall are coming
to Willowsweep at the end of the week to help you with
the house, Nicky. And your Cousin Eugenia comes with
us. Eugenia has had a rather trying winter, dearest,
and . . ."

"I do not mind at all that Eugenia comes," Wickenshire interrupted. "I shall be pleased to have her with us."

"And you will be able to hire more men to help with the fields and the cattle soon," Lady Wickenshire assured him confidently. "Only be still, do, and let William read the parts of Winifred's will that pertain particularly to you."

Wickenshire stood as his mama left the room. Then he raised his quizzing glass disdainfully to his eye and glared at the green-winged macaw that strutted arrogantly upon its perch before the study window. "And just what am I expected to do with him?" he drawled, glaring at Lord Nightingale with considerable contempt. "Explain that part to me again, Will."

"Scuttle the blackguard!" squawked Nightingale.

"Ah, a mind reader," said Wickenshire, allowing his quizzing glass to fall to the end of its riband and sticking both hands into his breeches pockets. "How intelligent of you to read me so well, you feathery curmudgeon. Will, cease snorting and answer me. What am I to do with the wretched thing? I do not think that I can have heard you aright."

"It says here that you are to get him to sing," laughed Trent. "Though your Aunt Winifred does not say how you are to get him to do it."

"Sing." Wickenshire cocked an eyebrow. "But sing what?"

"It don't say, Nick. Just when. You must get Lord Nightingale to sing a verse of a song by June the first of this year, but it don't say what song. Your Cousin Neil and I are to bear witness to the fact that you have succeeded, too."

"Surely it is some sort of jest. June the first? We must begin the shearing then or I will miss the best of the market prices. I cannot be mucking about attempting to get a parrot to sing. Of what significance can June the first be to—"

"Your Aunt Winifred don't say. Only that Neil and I must witness the song on June the first or you lose all."

"Every bit?"

"Indeed. And it is a significant sum, Nick."

"Enough to pay off all the mortgages and more," Wickenshire nodded. "I have been attempting to do that since I was thirteen, you know, and I am gaining ground, but this—"

"—would turn everything around for you."

"Yes, everything. I could cease spending all my time working on the estates and actually have a life. I could open the London house and take my seat in Lords. By gawd, I could afford to cut a dash in town and . . ."

"And?"

Lord Wickenshire blinked his odd forest green eyes at Mr. Trent in the most ridiculous manner and his lips tilted upward in a most charming smile. "And perhaps, Will, this frog could learn to court the ladies and find himself a magical princess who will kiss him, turn him into a real earl and take him for a husband. That would be something, would it not? Mama would leap for joy. But I cannot think of supporting a wife and children without Aunt Winifred's bequest. Not for another ten years or so, I cannot."

"I hate to say it, Nick," sighed Mr. Trent, "but thank goodness that your papa had the good grace to tumble down those stairs and break his neck before he ruined you and your mama completely."

"Yes, well, you have got the right of that. One more year on Papa's part and Mama and I would have been forced to remove to the cottage in Worcester and depend entirely upon Uncle Albert's and Uncle Ezra's largesse. But we were not forced to do so and I have made a deal of progress since then. I cannot think why Aunt Winifred has bequeathed me such a sum now."

"Perhaps because it existed and she thought Neil to have inherited quite enough already."

"Even so, there are Marjorie and Desmond and Eugenia—no, not Eugenia. She is upon Papa's side."

"Yes, but Marjorie has gotten all of the jewels, Desmond this house and Neil everything that was his father's, including the house in London. But do not forget, Nick, you do not get the money unless the parrot sings by the first of June. If the parrot does not sing, Neil inherits Lord Nightingale and the money. And nothing untoward must happen to Lord Nightingale, mind, or the money goes immediately to the Sisters of the Resurrection. Must have been an odd woman, your Aunt Winifred. Never read such a will before in all my life."

"You have only read three," replied Wickenshire primly.

"I have read more."

"Yes, over your father's shoulder. Nothing against you, Will, but I do wish your father had not died just when I need him most. He might actually know why Aunt Winifred insists that that rackety old mop of feathers should sing—and on June the first."

"Might know. Father penned this document for her. But he did not pass on the knowledge to me."

Wickenshire sighed and leaned with both shoulders against the mantelpiece. "How could he pen such a thing?" he growled. "I always thought your father liked me."

Miss Serendipity Bedford glowered at the passing traffic upon Little Bridge Street. Oh, how she detested London with all the noise and the dirt and the hubbub. One could barely hear oneself think. Not that she wished to hear herself think, because she did not. She was at wits' end and her thoughts were not worthy to be listened to even by her own self. Drat! What a horrible day it had been. And just when her hopes had been on the rise, too.

Well, she ought to have expected it. That was all. She just ought to have expected it.

Now what am I to tell poor Delight? she wondered as she trudged tiredly toward Marlborough Street and Upton House, which she and her sister had taken to calling home. "Not that we shall call it home much longer," she muttered under her breath. "Mr. Henry Wiggins comes to town within a fortnight. Wherever will we go once he has arrived? There must be some place, someone who will have us."

It did not bear thinking on. Serendipity could not believe that Mr. Henry Wiggins could be so cruel. But he was, and that was that. To think that her own father must leave his viscountcy and his houses and all but a perfectly paltry sum to that—beetlebrain! And to think that Mr. Henry Wiggins would take all of it, too, and not make one provision for herself and Delight, that he would think nothing of sending his very own third cousins out into the streets of London starving and homeless. Really, the man ought to be horsewhipped.

"Are you all right, Miss Serendipity?" asked a quavering voice beside her, immediately diverting her attention from thoughts of the wretched Henry Wiggins.

"Pardon, Bessie? What did you say?"

"I asked were you all right, miss."

"Oh. Yes, I am perfectly fine. Why?"

"You were—were—making the oddest noise in your throat, miss. You were—growling—sort of."

Serendipity's frown crinkled into a smile instantly. "No, was I?" she queried, her bright blue eyes alight with laughter as she gazed at the little abigail trudging doggedly along beside her. "I expect it frightened you, did it not? But you are not to worry, Bessie. I was thinking of Mr. Henry Wiggins, merely."

"That devil," muttered the abigail. "I would growl too, Miss Serendipity, thinking about that devil."

"You must not call him *devil*, Bessie. Really, you must not. And I must desist in thinking of him as Mr. Henry

Wiggins, too. He is Lord Upton now and we must both remember that."

"Aye," nodded Bessie. "And he is coming to London to toss us out of our own house, too, just like he tossed us out of Upton Manor, ain't he?"

Serendipity nodded. Not that the man had literally thrown them out of Upton Manor. But a virtual stranger and a bachelor, he had made no attempt to provide for any sort of chaperonage. And she and Delight could not possibly abide with a bachelor they did not know without tossing all propriety to the wind. Now, Mr. Henry Wiggins wished to inhabit the house in London as well. It had come to him in the entail. She and Delight had no cause against him. They must remove from Marlborough Street at once.

"You are not to worry, Bessie," Serendipity said as comfortingly as possible. "I shall obtain some sort of position soon; Delight and I will rent a set of perfectly respectable rooms; and we will make a way for ourselves in the world. I am certain of it. I must only try a bit harder. I have written to my dearest friend, Miss Eugenia Chastain, to request that she find a position for you in her household. You shall be well taken care of, I promise you. I have explained all. Eugenia will not fail to offer you a position."

"I ain't about to look after no Miss Eugenia Chastain," declared Bessie roundly. "I have been with you and Miss Delight all of my years, and I will remain with you and Miss Delight whether we live in a house or a set of rooms above a bakery, and that's a fact."

The very indignation upon the abigail's face turned Serendipity's heart to mush. Tears started to her eyes, and though she did her best to fight them back, they began to fall one by one to her wind-rosy cheeks. She halted in mid-stride and searched hurriedly through her reticule for her handkerchief.

* * *

Wickenshire stood, hands on hips, and studied the enormous cage that absolutely overwhelmed the Gold Saloon at Willowsweep. Four feet by four feet and rising to a height of six feet at the tallest part of the sloping top, the cage filled the corner of the room in which it sat and then extended outward a considerable distance onto the worn carpeting. "It sets the entire room akilter," he mumbled, cocking his head to one side in consideration of its placement.

"Awwwrk!" squawked Lord Nightingale from within the safety of his familiar framework of bars, flapping his wings and fluffing his feathers. "Awwwrkk!" Which he followed with an ear-splitting whistle.

The sound set Wickenshire's teeth to aching. "How anyone, even Aunt Winifred, could have put up with such noise for years on end, I cannot guess," the earl grumbled. "And why Uncle Albert ever brought you home in the first place is completely beyond my ken. But now that I have got you, we are going to come to an understanding, you and I, my Lord Nightingale. We are going to lay down some rules."

"No bite birdie!" the macaw exclaimed in a perfectly deafening tone. "No bite birdie," he repeated in a mutter. "No bite. Birdie. No. Birdie. Birdie. Birdie."

"Just so," nodded Wickenshire. "First rule: Do not bite. You do not bite me, sir, and I will not bite you. Fair enough? Eh?"

The parrot cocked its head and peered at Wickenshire out of one large amber eye.

Wickenshire cocked his head and peered back at him out of two fine green ones. "You are flustered, are you not? Poor old bird. I cannot say that I blame you. Bad enough that you should have lost Uncle Albert, but now to lose Aunt Winifred, too. And then to be carried off in a coach and tumbled and tossed all over creation—and to wind up in this ramshackle excuse for a house with the likes of me. I will lay odds that you are confused beyond measure and frightened to death."

Lord Nightingale bobbed his head up and down as if in answer and then let himself slip forward over his perch until he was hanging upside down, where he proceeded to cling with one foot while scratching his fine red head with the other.

Wickenshire grinned in spite of himself. He had never before had a pet, much less a parrot. Oh, there were cows and sheep and the shepherds' dogs roaming about Willowsweep, just as there were cows and chickens and ducks at Wicken Hall and at Farthermore, but they were none of them welcomed inside the houses. They were none of them pets. They were farm products like the crops in the fields, to be harvested and sold when the time came.

"Knollsmarmer," offered Lord Nightingale conversationally, returning himself to an upright position and gnawing at his perch with some vehemence. "How de do. Beg pardon."

Wickenshire's grin broadened. Taking an apple from the bowl upon the sideboard, he slipped a ten-penny blade from his jacket pocket and quartered the fruit. Then he walked slowly to the cage, cut a piece from one of the quarters and offered it to the parrot through the bars. "You are not such a fierce old bird, are you, Nightingale? Come on. Come get it."

Lord Nightingale ceased to gnaw upon his perch and cocked his head. Then he pondered deeply. Then he shuffled sideways toward the bit of apple. He halted a moment, shuffled one more step and nuzzled at the fruit.

"There. Good old bird," whispered Wickenshire. "We shall learn to be friends, you and I."

"Mend yer bellows," declared Lord Nightingale loudly, and took a nibble of the apple and then another.

"I must merely learn how to deal with you. I warn you, sir, I have not the least experience, but I shall make the attempt."

"Tempt. Tempt. Temptest fugit," mumbled Lord Nightingale, taking another bite of the apple.

The earl laughed very quietly, so as not to frighten the bird. "Not quite, old man. It is tempus that fugits."

The parrot's enormous bill was very near Wickenshire's fingers now, and the earl had the greatest urge to drop what was left of the piece of apple to the cage floor, but he called himself a veritable poltroon to even think of such a thing, steeled himself for another fierce bite and held on. The bite did not come. Instead Lord Nightingale rubbed the side of his face softly against the tips of Wickenshire's fingers, then straightened and very carefully took the last bit of apple from between them.

Miss Eugenia Chastain allowed the door of the Gold Saloon to close fully and stepped off down the corridor with a smile. Eugenia rolled when she walked like a sailor upon the deck of a man-o'-war in high seas. Her left leg was a sight shorter than her right and had been since she had broken it at the age of six. She had rolled for so very long that she, herself, barely noticed it. She would roll rather than walk until the day she died, and that was that. She refused to allow it to disturb her, though it had proved over the past few years to send any number of eligible bachelors running in the opposite direction.

"Oh, you should see them," she announced as she entered the rear parlor and took up a place before the window. "Nicky is feeding Lord Nightingale an apple, Aunt Diana. And Lord Nightingale is behaving like a perfect gentleman."

"Thank goodness," sighed the dowager Lady Wickenshire. "If only he continues to do so, Nicky may well develop a fondness for the creature. There is a missive arrived for you, Eugenia. It is there upon the table beside you. Your papa sent it on to you from Billowsgate."

"It is from Serendipity Bedford!" Eugenia exclaimed, slitting the wafer with her thumbnail and gazing first at the signature. "I have not had a word from Serendipity in almost a year. I wonder what can have prompted her to write at last." Eugenia gazed down at the dark, steady lines which crisscrossed the page. She smiled, then frowned, then tilted the page and frowned more deeply.

"My goodness, what is it?" queried the dowager. "I have not seen such a look upon your face, Eugenia, since you were two and Nicky convinced you that he had lost all his teeth and could not find them anywhere."

"Serendipity requests that I find a position for her abigail at Billowsgate. She gives her the most glowing recommendation. Oh, Aunt Diana, something dreadful has happened."

"What, child?"

"Her papa, Viscount Upton, has died and left Serendipity and her sister orphans! She says that she is presently seeking a position and that keeping Bessie now is quite beyond her means."

"Upton? Your friend's papa was Viscount Upton?"

"Yes, and he has always provided most excellently for Sera. She had the most beautiful dresses and the loveliest bonnets of any girl at school. I cannot believe that he put nothing away for her in expectation of his death. Surely he has bequeathed one of the houses or . . ."

Lady Wickenshire cocked a finely drawn eyebrow. "You say that her mama is dead as well?"

"Yes, years and years ago. There were only His Lordship and Sera and her sister."

"No sons," murmured the dowager sullenly.

"What, Aunt Diana?"

"I said, he had no sons."

"No, not a one."

"Some male relative has inherited the title, then, and all the entailed properties. Her father depended upon the kindness of his heir to provide for the girls, I expect, and the heir instead proves to be most unkind. If she can no longer support so inexpensive a servant as an abigail, things must be dire for her indeed, Eugenia."

"Dire for whom?" queried Wickenshire, wandering

into the room and coming to a halt before the hearth with his arm stretched out along the mantelpiece.

"Dire for Serendipity Bedford," Eugenia sighed. "She was my dearest friend at school, Nicky. She gives me a London direction and asks that I answer her as soon as possible, Aunt Diana. I will take the maid, of course, but I do wish that I could do more. Something for Sera and Delight."

"Serendipity? What sort of a name is Serendipity?" asked Wickenshire.

"A perfectly good name," his mama responded. "Now, please cease interrupting. Who is to come into the Upton title, Nicky? Do you know?"

"Yes, madam. But you have requested that I cease to speak."

"No, I requested that you cease to interrupt. You may speak when spoken to, and well you know the difference. Really, Nicky, some days there is no getting on with you at all."

"I gather this is one of them," nodded Wickenshire, a faint smile twitching at his lips. "A Mr. Henry Wiggins has become the new Lord Upton. One of Neil's cronies. Had a line from Neil about it way back in November, crowing about his luck in being chums with the next Viscount Upton."

"One of Neil's cronies?" gasped Eugenia. "Oh, it cannot be!"

"Well, but perhaps they are merely acquaintances, dear," offered Lady Wickenshire. "You know how Neil is, always claiming close bonds with prominent people."

"No, not this time. They are definitely bosom bows," Wickenshire asserted. "One just as vile as the other, I should think. Why?"

"Because Eugenia's friend is the old Lord Upton's daughter and the new Lord Upton has tossed her out upon her ear without one farthing," declared his mama vehemently. "Oh, how I detest the entails. If a man has not got a son—"

"Yes, Mama, I know," interrupted Wickenshire immediately, having heard his mama rail against entails and properties leased for life so many times that he could not bear to hear it again. "But you *do* have a son, you know, and so you will be safe until your dying day."

"Only if you do not die before me," his mama replied. "All will go to your Uncle Robert else. Unless you—"

"I will, Mama. Do not say it again. I will marry and produce a son before I die. I vow it. Not that Eugenia's papa would refuse to provide for you. And he would do so in a much finer fashion than I have been able to do, let me tell you. But we began by discussing this Miss Serphnipity, ah, Serinphinity—"

"Serendipity," provided Eugenia, almost drawn into a smile by Wickenshire's teasing mispronunciations. "And it is not humorous, I think, Nicky. She does not say, but I expect that your mama is correct. Things must be simply terrible for her or she would never have written me such a note as this."

Wickenshire, who had not the least idea what the letter actually said, nor who, exactly, Miss Serendipity Bedford actually was, nor why any of it should descend upon his shoulders, nevertheless knew, when both his mama and his cousin looked up at him pleadingly, that upon his shoulders it had descended. "Does she say that she is seeking a position or that she has found one?"

"Seeking one," provided Eugenia, a tinge of expectation in her voice.

"Does she sing better than you do, Eugenia?"

"She has the sweetest contralto."

"Write and tell her that she has found a place, then. Say that my wretchedly sprung old traveling coach will arrive at her door next week Tuesday."

"She has a younger sister," offered Eugenia, tentatively. "And an abigail who has served her forever."

"Tell her to bring them both."

"But if she should suspect it is charity—"

"It is not charity. Tell her that I am in need of a singing

teacher, and as soon as possible. Say that I shall give them all room and board, and we shall discuss her salary when she arrives. I cannot afford an inordinately large sum, but—"

"Nicky, you are a dear!" Eugenia exclaimed, leaping from her chair, rolling over to him and giving him an enthusiastic hug.

"A precious gem," agreed his mama, smiling.

"Nothing of the kind," protested Wickenshire gruffly. "You do neither of you think that, with my voice, I am going to attempt to teach Lord Nightingale to sing? The poor old boy would die of fright at my very first note."

TWO

Serendipity stepped down from the Earl of Wickenshire's traveling coach and gulped. She ought to have guessed, from the advanced age of the vehicle sent to gather her up, what awaited her at the end of her journey, but she had been so very grateful to be offered a position that she had not given her destination the least consideration. Now she stared in disbelief at the enormous jumble of stone and timber before her.

The house stood a full four stories high beneath a patched roof of red slate dotted with precariously leaning chimneys. And all of the windows along the fourth story were boarded up. Not simply shuttered—anyone might shutter their windows—but covered over with rough-hewn boards in the most haphazard fashion, as though someone had made a hasty and desperate attempt to board something or someone inside. *Which is utterly ridiculous,* thought Serendipity with the tiniest shudder. *My imagination runs wild. The Earl of Wickenshire is most likely as ancient as his coach and his house and he does not see that either is falling into disrepair. And the windows are boarded over because—because—*

"Sera!" an excited voice interrupted her thoughts, and Serendipity's gaze lowered immediately to discover Eugenia Chastain rolling merrily toward her down the two front steps of Willowsweep. In a moment Serendipity was thoroughly hugged and kissed. "How wonderful to see you again, Sera! We thought you would never arrive. My Cousin Wickenshire has been pacing the floor muttering about sorry roads and ancient axles for two whole days, and Aunt Diana and I have been washing and dusting and sweeping right along with the servants to have all ready for your arrival. We expected you yesterday. But there, that is nothing. Did you not bring Delight? We expected you to bring Delight and your Bessie as well. Did I not make that clear in my letter?"

"Yes, of course you did," Serendipity replied, peering back over her shoulder at the Wickenshire traveling coach, which stood motionless with one door open and the steps let down. "Delight, dearest, come out and meet Eugenia. Bessie? Come out. Why do you linger so?"

"I cannot get Miss Delight to come, Miss Serendipity," called Bessie, sticking her head out the coach door. "She will not move from her little corner.

"Is she so very shy, then?" asked Eugenia, bustling toward the vehicle.

"Frightened, I think," Serendipity responded with a shake of her head. "We were forced to move to the house in London not a month ago. And now to move again to another strange place . . . And she is not . . . like other children . . ." Serendipity's voice trailed off as she followed Eugenia to the coach.

"Delight, dearest, do come and meet me," urged Eugenia kindly, standing on tiptoe to peer in through the coach window. "I have been wishing to make your acquaintance for ever so long. Will you not come into the house and have some lemonade and ginger snaps? Cook has made ginger snaps expressly for you. She did so the very moment she learned that you were coming."

"Delight, do come out, dearest," prodded Serendipity, climbing back inside the coach. "There is no need to be afraid. No one here will hurt you or make sport of you. Do you not remember what I told you? We have come to the Earl of Wickenshire's house so that I may teach Lord Nightingale to sing. A gentleman who wishes to teach his—his—a lad—to sing must be a perfectly nice gentleman himself, do not you think?"

Eugenia giggled. She had purposely not informed Serendipity of Lord Nightingale's relationship to her cousin, and especially had not mentioned that Nightingale was a parrot. She intended for Wickenshire to do that.

"You will be very pleased with Lord Nightingale, Delight. I assure you," Eugenia said. "The two of you will get along famously. But you will never meet him if you do not come out of the coach, my dear."

Still Delight did not budge. She hid in her corner of the coach, her face turned away from Eugenia and Bessie and Serendipity, and sighed the saddest little sigh.

Lord Wickenshire stood upon the third rung of the ladder which leaned precariously against the side of the stable and stared bemusedly down at his coachman. "She will not exit the coach? Surely you jest, John."

"No, m'lord. I ain't be jestin'. Afeared she be. Wants a bit o' coaxin'.."

"Well, her sister and Eugenia—"

"Be tryin', m'lord. An' m'lady has come out herse'f ta try an' make the child step down, but she willn't budge, the little miss. She willn't even look at any of 'em. Jus' be sittin' in the corner a-hidin' of 'er head, m'lord."

"I'll be damned," mumbled Wickenshire, dropping the hammer he held to the ground and climbing down. With long strides, he made his way up the hill to the house and then hurried around to the front drive, pausing only briefly to pluck a yellow jonquil from the edge of the long-neglected vegetable garden near the rear door. Sure enough, Bobby Tripp held the team in check while Lady Wickenshire stood upon the coach steps and Eugenia clung to one of the windows, holding herself up upon her toes.

Wickenshire strode directly to the window opposite

Eugenia's and peered inside. A pretty little straw bonnet with a cherry riband shuddered right beneath his nose.

"I do not believe that I have ever seen such a bonnet in all my life," he declared softly. "Of all things, a bonnet with a flower growing right up out of the very top of it."

Serendipity looked up from the seat beside her little sister to see one large, rather dirty hand reach in through the window, set the stem of a flower into the bonnet's woven straw and then disappear again. How odd, she thought, that one of the earl's workmen should come to persuade Delight to exit the coach. What a strange establishment this must be. "Oh!" she exclaimed then in feigned surprise. "Delight! This very nice man is correct. There is a jonquil growing right up from the straw in your bonnet. However could such a thing have happened?"

"A jonquil?" asked the little girl, her voice muffled.

"Yes, dearest. A pretty yellow flower."

"The most beautiful flower in all the world," confirmed the man beyond the window, his face all planes and angles and his dark curls blowing in the wind. "Is it magic, do you think, this flower? Well, it must be. It could not grow right up out of a bonnet else."

"M-magic?" asked Delight, turning her face the slightest bit away from the squabs and toward the window where Wickenshire stood.

"Only take off your bonnet and see for yourself."

A pale blue eye glanced shyly up at Wickenshire, and then the child turned her head fully in his direction. The earl's heart stuttered a bit at that first sight of Delight's face, but he did not look away. He did not so much as allow his brow to wrinkle or his eyes to blink in surprise. He grinned instead—his verimost charming grin which he had practiced in front of the mirror for four whole days once, when he was seven. "No wonder the jonquil has chosen your bonnet to grow upon, my child," he managed without the least catch in his voice. "If I were a magic jonquil, I should wish to grow precisely there myself."

"Why?"

"Do you mean to say that no one has told you? Why, you are a most exceptional person."

"Me?" asked the small voice, the pale eyes widening.

"Indeed. Exceeding special. You have been kissed by Glorianna, the Queen of the Faeries, little one."

Wickenshire did not hear his mama's tiny gasp at his words and so he did not look to see what might have startled her, though Eugenia, Serendipity and even Bessie did.

"Has no one thought to tell you so?" he continued softly. "Magic jonquils always long to linger with persons beloved of Glorianna. Here, let me show you how pretty your flower is," and reaching inside, he untied the cherry riband from beneath Delight's chin and eased the little straw confection from off a mass of golden curls. "Only see how tall and straight it stands because it is so very proud to have discovered you," he declared, holding the bonnet from which the jonquil sprouted in his large, rough hands.

Delight touched the soft yellow petals and made a sound very much like the chiming of faeries' bells, which made Wickenshire's heart stutter in his breast again.

"Are you afraid to step out of this coach?" he asked quietly. "You need not be, you know. Especially now that you have a magic jonquil to protect you."

Delight raised her eyes from the flower to the man and smiled the sweetest smile. "An' you," she said shyly.

"Oh, indeed. Not only does Glorianna's kiss recommend you to me, but you have smiled upon me as well. You have won my very heart, and I vow to protect you always. I am your servant, miss, for as long as I live."

Serendipity watched, astounded, as Delight scrambled from the seat and pushed open the coach door on the man's side. How kind he is, Sera thought as, without so much as a glance at anyone else, he lifted Delight gently to the ground, took her hand into his own and, twirling her bonnet about in his other hand, led her around the vehicle, right up the step and in through the front door of Willowsweep.

"I am called Nicky," murmured Wickenshire, giving the bonnet to the butler and kneeling down upon one knee before Delight to unbutton her pelisse. "And you are called Delight, I hear."

"Who tole you?"

"Do you know, I cannot remember. It seems to me that it was the breeze which blew across the meadow last Thursday afternoon. Or perhaps it was one of the leaves upon the chattering oak beside the stables. It was one or the other of them, I am certain." He stood and handed the pelisse to Jenkins, then retrieved the jonquil from the bonnet and, extending his hand, led the little girl down the long corridor toward the very rear of the house.

"Magic or not, your flower must have water," he said. "You shall choose whichever vase you like from among all the vases in the pantry, and then we will place your flower in it and take it up to your room to sit upon your windowsill in the sunlight."

Serendipity heard as she entered the vestibule and looked after them, wondering that a hired man from the fields or the stables or the garden should feel so free as to wander about his master's house, even up into the bedchambers. What a peculiar person the Earl of Wickenshire must be, she thought.

"Nicky will see that she feels welcome here, I promise you," Eugenia whispered. "I did not know about Delight, Sera. You did never tell me."

"N-no," stuttered Serendipity in some confusion. "I did never think to say—"

"You need say nothing at all, Miss Bedford," declared the dowager Lady Wickenshire, allowing Jenkins to divest her of the shawl she had seized for her excursion out into the April day. To think that Nicky should remember after all these years the few stories of Glorianna that his papa had seen fit to tell him. And to think that he should make such fine use of them on behalf of a child. Lady Wickenshire's heart swelled with pride for her son.

"You need say not a word, unless, of course, you wish to do so, Miss Bedford," she repeated then, with a shake of her head. "You and your sister are as welcome here as you would be in your own home. Do come up to the drawing room and take tea with us. Jenkins will look to your luggage, and Nicky, I assure you, will bring Delight to us as soon as they have placed her flower upon her windowsill."

Lady Wickenshire led the way up the staircase to the first floor and down the corridor to the drawing room. Eugenia, managing the stairs with an aplomb grown from years of coping, urged Serendipity up ahead of her.

"I did not so much as hope that you would be here to meet us, Eugenia," Serendipity whispered. "I thought you to be at Billowsgate."

"Yes, well, I am visiting with Aunt Diana for a time. She has just removed from Wicken Hall to here, and I have come to help her make this old place as habitable as it once used to be. At least, that is my excuse."

"Your excuse?"

"Shush. Aunt Diana will hear you. She has not the least idea that there is an ulterior motive to my visit."

"And the Earl of Wickenshire? Is he in residence?"

Eugenia and Serendipity gained the first-floor corridor, and Eugenia grinned, only that moment tipping to Serendipity's mistake. Of course Nicky had not looked at all like an earl. Anyone might have . . . "Indeed the earl is in residence," she replied, "and you will be most pleasantly surprised when you make his acquaintance, I assure you."

"And Lord Nightingale? When shall I meet my pupil?

I expect he is merely a lad, Eugenia? Well, and I could not think that a grown man would desire singing lessons. But I cannot think why a lad should wish to have a singing teacher, either. I did never think that young gentlemen were interested in learning such things. Of course, I did never actually know a young gentleman."

"Oh, Lord Nightingale is not at all interested in learning to sing," offered Eugenia. "It is Lord Wickenshire who wishes him to learn. He is determined that Lord Nightingale shall warble like a—well—like a nightingale."

Serendipity looked toward the threshold at the sound of approaching feet and stared. The gentleman who entered the drawing room with Delight's hand held protectively in his own could not be same who had coaxed her sister from the coach, but he was remarkably like—so much so that Serendipity's jaw lowered for just a moment in amazement, causing Eugenia to laugh softly and whisper in her Aunt Diana's ear.

Wickenshire's dark brown hair, which had been tossed and tumbled by the wind, now lay in well-combed waves, and the old woolen jacket he had worn had been replaced by waistcoat and morning coat. A small diamond glittered from a conservatively tied neckcloth, and his down-at-the-heel high top boots had become elegantly polished Hessians.

"Miss Bedford," said Lady Wickenshire with great goodwill sparkling in her eyes, "may I properly present my son, the Earl of Wickenshire. I fear that I forgot to do so at the coach. Nicky, dearest, you have not as yet said so much as 'how do you do' to Miss Delight's sister."

"How do you do, Miss Delight's sister," responded His Lordship, bowing with such a flourish that it set Delight to giggling. "You are welcome to Willowsweep. May we join you, Mama, for tea? Delight and I are very thirsty."

"In that case, you must join us," nodded his mama. "And I do believe that if you will give the bellpull a tug, Nicky, a pitcher of lemonade and a plate of ginger snaps are like to come waltzing in."

"All by themselves?" asked Wickenshire with a cock of his eyebrow, setting Delight to giggling again. "Really, Mama."

Nicky! Serendipity's eyes widened. This was the kindly workman who had come to Delight's aid, except that he was not a workman. He was Lord Wickenshire himself. How odd that he should have come to the coach so raggedly dressed. Serendipity bestowed upon him a dazzling smile and then patted the sofa upon which she sat, bringing Delight to sit beside her. "I must thank you," she said quite properly as the earl took up a chair midway between herself and Eugenia. "I must thank you for offering me a position in your household, my lord. It was most kind of you." Though not nearly as kind, she added silently, as the manner in which you have made my sister welcome.

"You are a friend of Eugenia's," Wickenshire responded, taking a cup of tea from Eugenia's hand and leaning back in his chair, crossing one long leg over the other. "And Eugenia informed me that you would make an excellent teacher. What more incentive need I have to employ you? But it may prove an impossible task."

"Impossible? No, I do not think it can be so, my lord. Why, everyone can learn to sing."

"Not I," offered Wickenshire. "And quite possibly not Nightingale. But then, I place my faith in you, Miss Bedford. If it is possible for him to learn, I am confident that you will be just the person to teach him."

"Exactly the person to teach him," nodded Eugenia.

" 'Zactly," murmured Delight shyly.

Serendipity tucked an arm around her sister and gave the child's shoulders a squeeze. "And Delight has promised to be on her very best behavior for as long as we are here. We do thank you for including her in your offer, my lord."

"An' Bessie," Delight added.

"Yes, and Bessie as well."

"You are quite welcome," drawled the earl. "Enough now of thank yous. You will earn whatever salary we agree upon, Miss Bedford. Do not doubt it."

Serendipity gazed from the window of the bedchamber that she and Delight were to share for this one night until a new mattress could be brought from the village for Delight's bed. The night sky beyond the glass glistened with stars. Her legs drawn up beneath her upon the window seat, her arms wrapped lovingly around a sleepy Delight, Serendipity whispered a prayer of gratitude to the heavens. They had escaped the house in London on the very day that Mr. Henry Wiggins had been expected to arrive. Thank God that they had. Thank God that Delight had not been forced to make that particular gentleman's acquaintance, for he would have treated the child abominably. Serendipity had no doubt of that. Mr. Henry Wiggins had taken over the viscountcy without the least consideration for anyone, and he would have handled Delight in the same heavy-handed fashion. "You would have suffered most terribly, my darling, from his insensitivity, and you have had far too much of suffering."

"Hmmm?"

"Nothing, dearest. Close your eyes again. I am merely speaking to myself."

They had been given time to refresh themselves and to nap a bit and then had been treated to a fine dinner. And Delight had not been sent off to the nursery as Serendipity had warned her to expect, but had dined with them at table. Afterward, they had all retired to the drawing room, where Lady Wickenshire had requested that

Serendipity sing for them while Eugenia played upon the pianoforte.

Serendipity smiled to herself. Eugenia had never been a virtuoso upon the pianoforte when they had been at school together, and she had not improved one bit. But she had played with such enthusiasm. That was what the earl had called it, once their performance had come to an end. "Miss Bedford, you sing like an angel. And Eugenia, you play, as always, with such enthusiasm."

Really, he seemed the sweetest and most patient of gentlemen, this cousin of Eugenia's. And all within his household had taken note at once of the manner in which he treated Delight and treated her likewise. Not once had a question been broached or the wine-red splotch which covered her sister's right cheek been alluded to all evening. No matter what sort of person Lord Wickenshire should prove to be in the days ahead, the precedent he had set in regard to Delight had won for him a permanent place in Serendipity's heart.

Have you had experience, my lord, with such a one as Delight? she wondered as her sister's head fell back to rest upon Serendipity's shoulder and Delight's palest of blue eyes closed at last in true sleep. If you have not, you are a man among men to cajole her into smiles without so much as a blink of your eye at your first sight of her countenance. A man among men.

Perhaps, she thought, as she carried Delight to the cot beside her own bed and tucked her in beneath a pile of quilts, perhaps little Lord Nightingale is somehow disfigured as well. Perhaps that is why no one remarked upon Delight's misfortune.

It did seem odd that she had not met Lord Nightingale. She had been hired to teach the boy to sing, after all, and she had thought to be introduced to him first thing. And yet, after acknowledging over tea that her task might prove nearly impossible, neither Lord Wickenshire nor Eugenia nor the lovely Lady Wickenshire had referred to Lord Nightingale again. Nor had the lad come down to dinner, or appeared in the drawing room after dinner. And no one had suggested even once that she go up to the nursery to meet her pupil.

The nursery. If this house were like most of the country houses with which Serendipity was acquainted, the nursery would be on the top floor—that floor on which all of the windows had been boarded over in such a hodgepodge manner. Serendipity gulped as a thought fluttered through her mind. Was there something wrong with Lord Nightingale? Something terribly wrong? Had Eugenia's cousin locked the boy away in that fourth story and boarded over the windows? Was Lord Nightingale even a boy? She had merely assumed him to be one because no one had gainsaid her when she had first referred to him as a lad. But perhaps he was not a lad at all. Perhaps he was a grown man and mad, and the earl hoped that learning to sing—that sweet music— would calm him or bring him to his senses once again.

"Balderdash," mumbled Serendipity, climbing between her own sheets and lowering the lamp upon the bedside table. "I have much too much imagination for my own good. There is no madman locked away on the fourth story. No, nor is there an ill-used child either. A gentleman like Lord Wickenshire would never permit such a thing to happen to anyone.

"Unless Lord Wickenshire could not discover any other alternative," she whispered into the night. "Or unless I am his only hope. Am I his only hope?" She gulped again, and then she berated herself for not having requested to meet Lord Nightingale straight out.

Serendipity tossed and turned for a good half hour before she drifted into sleep, only to be awakened by the most dreadful screech. She sat up at once, hugging the bedclothes to her bosom, and waited in silent dread for the horrible screech to be followed by another even more terrifying sound. But it was not. The house fell silent around her and remained so. Beside her bed, Delight lay upon the cot breathing softly and easily and smiling in her dreams.

Did I imagine it? Serendipity wondered. My goodness, how could I have imagined such a screech as that? Why it sounded as though—as though—someone were being murdered.

"I knew I ought not to have depended upon you to keep your peace," grumbled Wickenshire, tossing one of his Aunt Winifred's old knitted shawls over Lord Nightingale's cage. "To sleep, rascal. Night is upon us. No, do not peer out at me through that hole. I know my lamp is still lit, but it is not by any means morning and I do not wish to hear anything more out of you but a snore, sir. You will wake the child. Most likely frighten her so badly that her hair will stand straight up on her head. And Lord only knows what Miss Bedford will think of your racket if you wake her as well."

The earl returned to his chair before the fire, took his brandy glass back in hand and gazed into the flames for a moment. Then he sighed and lifted a raggedy piece of foolscap from the table beside him. As he studied the handwriting that covered it, his brow creased.

"There is something familiar about it," he murmured to himself. "I know that I have seen this writing somewhere before. Long before these notes began to appear, too. But where?"

Aye, that was the question. Where? At whose script was it he stared, and how had it come to be tacked to the door of the stables this very morning by a ten-penny blade?

"It is some fool prank," he muttered. "It must be. But it makes not the least bit of sense." Wickenshire sighed and took a sip of brandy. He leaned his head against the high back of the chair and stared into the fire again. "Why the devil would someone write notes warning me to beware of witches and those who dwell with witches?

This is the twelfth one since January. What the devil do they mean by it?"

Wickenshire closed his eyes. He ought to toss the thing into the fire and take himself off to bed. It had been a long day. He and Jacob Smith and Robert Walder had been out at seven in the morning to replace the rotten boards they had stripped from the stables with the new lumber that they had milled yesterday. And then Miss Bedford had arrived and he had been forced to abandon the job and put on his company face and manners, which was a good deal more work and took a great deal more energy than repairing the stables. And now he could not take himself off to bed because the wretched note plagued him, though he had managed to wipe it from his consciousness for a goodly portion of the day.

"Witches," he muttered. "Of all things. Why should anyone think to warn me against witches?" And then he smiled. Better to have warned me against the stuttering of my heart in the presence of Miss Delight Bedford and her sister. Lord knows I was never expecting such a blue-eyed vision as Miss Bedford to be in dire straits. Thought she would be prim and plain and—spinsterly, like Eugenia. Why, Miss Bedford might crook her finger and marry any one of fifteen fortunes tomorrow. She need not suffer from the loss of her father's lands to some Henry Wiggins.

Likely it is the child, he thought then. Likely she hopes to find a gentleman who will allow her sister to abide with them and cannot discover one willing to take on the responsibility. Or perhaps they cry off for fear that Delight's birthmark might travel through Miss Bedford's blood to their own sons or daughters. Humbug, that. Miss Bedford does not bear the mark; why would her children? And what if they do? What if they do? There are some of us carry worse marks than that about with us, only they are not noticeable because they are etched on our very souls.

Wickenshire finished his brandy, set the glass aside

and stood. With a shrug of his broad shoulders, he stuffed the annoying piece of foolscap into the pocket of his coat and, taking the lamp in hand, whispered good night to Lord Nightingale and left the Gold Saloon for the comfort of his bed.

He fell asleep the moment his head touched the pillow. Small witches with red blotches upon their cheeks cawed and cackled through his dreams, but a lovely young lady with sky blue eyes and hair of spun gold distracted him from the witches and kept him from waking in terror. As she smiled up at him, Wickenshire drew a deep breath, turned upon his side, ceased to murmur of foolscap, ten-penny blades and singing lessons for nightingales, and whispered instead, "Serendipity? What sort of name is Serendipity?" into the darkness of his chamber.

THREE

The scream echoed through Willowsweep, so piercing, so strident that Serendipity, alone at the breakfast table, sprang straight up from her chair and sent it crashing against the wall behind her. Her hand went to her breast. She gasped for air. Her heart pounded wildly. "Heavens!" she gasped. "Oh, my heavens!"

It came again and again, so shrill, so discordant that it sent shivers up her spine and set her hands to shaking. She spun first one way and then the other, thinking to run out the doorway and down the corridor, thinking to escape through the French doors to the unkempt lawn beyond, thinking, at one point, to hide beneath the table. But then she took a very deep breath and called herself to order. "I am *not* a coward," she whispered raggedly. "Someone requires assistance. Perhaps it is not as bad as it sounds. Who would think to murder a person, after all, at six-thirty in the morning?"

Straightening her shoulders, though her hands still shook, Serendipity stalked from the breakfast room into the corridor in search of the initiator of the incredible screeching. Her slippers whispered along the worn carpeting in the corridor at a wonderful pace as she hurried toward the staircase. Certainly the cries must come from the frightfully boarded-up fourth floor. Certainly they must.

But they did not. No sooner had she reached the staircase and placed one foot upon the step than another screech set her nerves to vibrating, and this one came, quite noticeably, from the opposite end of the corridor she had just traversed. Serendipity spun about and hurried back, passing the breakfast room, running now, certain that, whatever had happened, someone's blood had been spilt. Visions of the gentle Earl of Wickenshire stretched his full length upon the floor of some isolated chamber, a knife puncturing his heart, stabbed at her brain, and tears started to her eyes. "No," she gasped. "Never. Not so kind a gentleman as he!"

The screech came one more time, from behind a closed door just to her left, almost deafening her. Serendipity seized the knob and yanked the door open, stumbling into the room, her vision blurred by tears, her breath coming in great heaving gulps, her hands shaking with fear.

"Dunderhead," muttered a gravelly voice.

"What? What? Who?" Serendipity turned one way and another seeking the vision she feared to find, her cheeks flushed, her pulses pounding.

"Featherbrain," muttered the same voice. And then, "Miss Bedford?" said another. "There, I knew he would alarm either you or Delight if you were awake, but I could not get him to cease. He is always so very enthusiastic the first thing in the morning."

Serendipity stared open-mouthed at the scene before her. She raised the back of her hand to her brow and brushed aside the curls that had slipped from their pins. She took one deep breath after another. "What is . . . Are you . . . Oh, thank heavens you are not . . . A bird?"

"Indeed," nodded Wickenshire as the parrot took the last of a bit of turnip from between his fingers. "Come, Miss Bedford, and sit for moment." Wickenshire stepped toward her and took her arm in his firm grasp, leading her to a wing-back chair. "You look as though you have seen a ghost. Several ghosts."

"A bird?" repeated Serendipity, sinking down onto the chair but never hearing a word he said. "A bird made those dreadful sounds? What were you doing to it, tugging its feathers out one by one?"

"No, not at all, Miss Bedford. I simply removed the cover from his cage, opened his door so that he might come out and fed him some turnip. But he gets a wee bit rowdy in the mornings. First thing in the morning and the last thing at night, he will screech." Wickenshire attempted to appear nonchalant as he took up a place before the empty mantel in order to stare down at her with some degree of savoir faire, but he could not quite get his feet into just the right position or his arm to rest comfortably or find anything at all suitable to occupy his hands.

"Knollsmarmer," said Lord Nightingale.

"Knoll what?" asked Serendipity, her bright blue eyes flashing between exasperation and laughter.

"Knollsmarmer. Do not ask me to translate, Miss Bedford. I have not the least idea what it means. There are times when Nightingale does not quite get his words right."

"Nightingale? Do you mean to tell me that this—this—"

"Parrot."

"This parrot is Lord Nightingale? *The* Lord Nightingale whom I am expected to teach to sing?"

"Quite," nodded Wickenshire.

"You are making sport of me, my lord."

"No, I am not. Did not Eugenia mention that Lord Nightingale was a parrot when she wrote to you of my offer?"

"Not one word."

"Well, perhaps she thought that you would not take the offer seriously if she did."

"And I am to take it seriously, my lord?"

"Oh, yes. It is of the utmost importance that Lord Nightingale learn to sing. Eugenia did say that you would be just the person to teach him. Are you about to tell me that you are not just the person to teach him, Miss Bedford?"

The sudden worry in Wickenshire's tone and the frown that began to pucker his brow stilled Serendipity's first angry response. Perhaps this was not some plot devised by Eugenia to offer her charity disguised as a position. "I only question whether it is necessary, my lord," she said after a long pause. "Birds do sing, after all, quite naturally on their own."

"Yo ho ho!" squawked Nightingale loudly, finished with his turnip and his muttering and at once craving Wickenshire's attention. He stretched to his full height on the very top of his cage and flapped his wings with great enthusiasm. "Knollsmarmer! Knollsmarmer!" he called at a most disturbing volume, and then he sidled cavalierly in Serendipity's direction and jiggled his head up and down at her. "Knollsmarmer," he said, gazing at her with one bright amber eye.

"No, she is not called Knollsmarmer, you villain," declared Wickenshire soberly. "She is called Miss Bedford, and if you do not behave, she will leave us and you will never learn to sing. He does not sing naturally, Miss Bedford. I have lived with him for two long weeks now and not heard one note out of him. And besides, he must learn to sing a song—with words—and—and—a melody. And I cannot—and Eugenia cannot—and if I should advertise in the papers, I expect I should become a laughingstock—and—" Wickenshire gazed down at his old top boots, which would insist upon slithering about beneath him as though they were not attached to his legs, and sighed. He was making a total muck of it. He sounded more like a whining schoolboy than an earl, and he knew it. He wished that he could just disappear right down into the cinders on the hearth.

Serendipity could not for the life of her understand why the parrot's learning to sing should be so very important to the man, but obviously it was. She had been mistaken about the position being charity, then. She was relieved that she had not spoken on that assumption. "I doubt you could ever become a laughingstock, my lord," she said. "But I shall not force you to discover whether you would or not. I have never attempted to teach a bird to sing before, but—"

"You will?" asked Wickenshire, his gaze meeting hers.

"I will attempt it, yes."

The light that came to sparkle in his odd, yet wonderful, eyes was all the thanks that Serendipity required, and she smiled in acknowledgment of it. "Might we move the pianoforte into this room, do you think, my lord? It would help to have a pianoforte."

"Then you shall have it," nodded Wickenshire. "Whatever you require, you need only mention it. Jenkins and John and I will move it in here for you within the hour."

"Why does he glare at me so?" Serendipity asked, watching Lord Nightingale watching her.

"He is not glaring, Miss Bedford. He always looks at one out of one eye or the other like that. Cannot see you out of both. On opposite sides of his head, his eyes. Not made for looking at things together."

"Of course," murmured Serendipity, studying the bird out of the corner of one eye much as he continued to study her. "I had not thought. Of course he cannot look at me straight on. I was being foolish."

Wickenshire thought her anything but foolish. Desperate, perhaps, and kind, too, to take on such a task. Ill used, to be sure, to be sent out into the world with a younger sister to care for and not one relative to whom she might turn for assistance. Even courageous, to come to a strange house in the country trusting in Eugenia's word alone that all was upon the up-and-up.

Because things are not always upon the up-and-up, Wickenshire thought, watching as Miss Bedford stood and walked toward the bird, whispering nonsense to it. Especially they are not always upon the up-and-up where vulnerable young women are concerned. Neil would be set upon compromising such a pretty thing as Miss Bedford from the very moment he set eyes upon her. Did she take up a position in Neil's residence, she would not be safe from him for one moment.

But Miss Bedford is quite safe here, Wickenshire told himself. And though that thought ought to have filled his heart with unreserved pride, it did no such thing. Instead it brought a scowl to his face and caused him to shove his fists deep into his breeches' pockets. It is not a great thing, he thought soberly, to be always known as a safe and sober gentleman.

It was precisely then that his heart began to throb and ache as it had not done in a number of years. Safe and sober. Yes. Precisely. But not a gentleman. A farmer merely. A man who has worked with his hands for so many years that the calluses will never go away. A man who knows the plow and the harrower, the raddle and milk bucket and the loose boards upon the stables intimately. Not a gentleman; not a nobleman despite the title.

Wickenshire ceased to watch Miss Bedford whispering to Nightingale and stared down at the worn carpet and the slightly warped floor of the Gold Saloon. These things—the carpet, the floor—were still to be done, were very far down upon a very long list of things still to be done.

I have not taken my seat in Lords or gone to fight Napoleon or offered my services as envoy or employed myself in any way at all befitting my title, the earl thought bitterly. I am a farmer and have been a farmer since first I donned long pants. I do not deserve to be called "my lord" or anything like. There is no lordship at all about me.

"Oh, he is beau'ful!" cried a little voice then, awaking Wickenshire from his reverie. A tiny hand tugged his hand from his pocket and clasped it tightly. "Is he magic, too, Nicky, like m'flower?" Delight was smiling confidently up at him, her wine-stained cheek fearlessly displayed and not a bit of hesitation in her pale blue eyes.

"I have never seed such a bird as that one," she continued. "He is so very big. An' he looks like a rainbow."

"Do you think so? A rainbow?" Wickenshire's hand closed completely over Delight's. "His name is Nightingale. Lord Nightingale. And your sister is going to teach him to sing."

Serendipity turned from her scrutiny of the parrot at that, about to make it perfectly clear to Lord Wickenshire that she would attempt to teach the parrot to sing, but that she could not promise—and then she saw his hand clasping Delight's and an unfaltering confidence upon Delight's countenance that she had never seen there before, and every word she intended to say was halted by the large lump that abruptly developed in her throat.

Mr. Neil Spelling peered at the kippers on his plate in profound disgust. It was not that he loathed kippers, but that a vision of his Cousin Nick had lurched into his mind, eliminating any enjoyment he might have gained from his breakfast. "Are you certain?" he asked the gentleman across the table from him. "How can you be certain, Upton?"

"M'butler told me," replied the new Lord Upton, slicing into a rare beefsteak with enthusiasm. "Got to the town house, you know. Asked where the blasted girls had got to. Place called Willowsweep, Lansing said. Butler's name is Lansing. Must remember that. Different butler in town. Pity, too."

"What is a pity?" asked Spelling. "That you have a different butler in town? Easily cured. Simply bring the other from the country, Upton."

"No, no, pity that the blasted girls have gone off to this Willowsweep place. Devil of a thing. Never did think that Miss Bedford could secure a position anywhere. Counted upon it. Intended to let them see how easily I could put them out on the street. Want Serendipity to have a taste of what life could become, just so that she would be fearful enough to leap into bed with me at a waggle of my finger. Devil of a thing! She ain't fit for any position that I can think of. Not a one."

"One, obviously, or she would not have gone off to Willowsweep."

"B'longs to your cousin, don't it? Willowsweep? One of his?"

"Indeed. Got the other two estates running on a paying basis now. Went off to Willowsweep to see could he do the same there. Nothing but a hovel by this time, Willowsweep. He has all but ignored it, you know, for years."

"Yes, well, he is there now. And Miss Serendipity Bedford is there as well. Likely intends to take advantage of the chit, your Cousin Wickenshire."

The mere mention of his Cousin Nicky in connection with the words "taking advantage of a chit" dispelled Spelling's bad humor and elicited a rumble of laughter from deep in his chest. "Nicky? My Cousin Nicky? Take advantage of your Miss Bedford?"

Lord Upton, the former Mr. Henry Wiggins, stared at Spelling in confusion with a piece of beefsteak partway to his lips.

"Yes, well, stare if you like, Upton. I cannot help myself. The thought of Nicky—too humorous, dear boy— stiff, sober, honorable Nicky molesting your Miss Bedford? The sun would fall from the sky at the shock of it. If you have got it into your head, Upton, that Wickenshire lured her there for some nefarious reason, you had best toss that thought right out. There is something or someone else at work here. Devil it, but I should like to pay Nick a visit. Yes, and I should like to snatch Lord Nightingale right from beneath his nose, too. Carry the blasted beast off to some cave until June the second. That would fix Nicky's wagon. Shan't get Nightingale to sing by June the first if he cannot find him."

Upton, his keen blue eyes fastened upon Spelling,

nearly choked on a mouthful of ale. "Abduct a lord and stow him away in a cave? You would hang within a day."

"Lord Nightingale is a parrot, you dolt. I told you about him. If Nicky can get him to sing by June the first, he will inherit an enormous sum from my late, lamented stepmama. I would prefer to strangle the danged bird; bury it in the garden; give out the tale that it had flown off somewhere, but I would never get the money then. Not a chance of it. Bird dies an untimely death, or disappears without a trace, and my stepmama's fortune goes immediately to the Sisters of the Resurrection. Feather-brained, my stepmama was."

Lord Upton snickered as the mask of civilization tilted a bit upon Spelling's handsome face to reveal the wolfish countenance of greed that lay beneath. "Wickenshire would be a fool to allow you across his threshold. A fool or a madman."

"Oh, a fool by all means," nodded Spelling thoughtfully. "Nicky was born a fool. No trick at all for me to gain entrance to Willowsweep. Go knock on the door and be welcomed quite properly. Excellent manners has my cousin, I assure you. Most loyal to the family. Nicky would never do the least thing contrary to his code of honor."

Upton's eyes flashed. He patted his thin lips with an edge of his napkin. "Surely you jest, Spelling. He would welcome you with open arms when he knows that you would profit by preventing him from teaching the bird to sing?"

"Of course he would welcome me. Prim and proper and never raises a dust about anything, Nick. Would not be at all happy to see me, mind you, for we have never gotten on together, but he would not think to turn me away."

"Let us do it, then," urged Upton quietly, containing his eagerness with great effort.

"No. Why? He will never get the bird to sing regardless. Damnable parrot. Sang for m'father once or twice, but squawk is all it has done since Father died, all it will ever do. The money will be mine come June."

"Are you so certain of it, Spelling?"

"The money will be mine. It must be mine. She had no right to leave it away from me, the old hag!"

"Yes, well, you could make quite certain to have it," Upton suggested lazily, pushing himself back from the table. "All you need do is to linger about this Willowsweep and keep an eye on things. Not let your cousin gain too much ground in teaching the parrot, eh? And I, of course, should be more than pleased to accompany you."

Neil Spelling's dark, brooding eyes met the new Lord Upton's earnest blue ones across the crockery and Irish lace of the breakfast table. For the longest moment, neither spoke.

Then, "I do rather long for a breath of fresh country air," Spelling drawled. "At least a week's worth, I think, or perhaps two? That should give me time enough to see that Nicky fails in the task my stepmama set him."

"Yes," mused Upton, his lips turning upward in a smirk, "and I cannot but feel it m'duty to check upon the safety of Miss Bedford and her sister. Ain't made a servant of her, your cousin, do you think? Well, ought to check and see. Called upon to do it. Cannot have the chit compromised, after all, can I?"

"Definitely not. Not by anyone but yourself," snickered Spelling.

"Pretty trinket. Devil of a lightskirt she would make. Always despised Bedford and his chicks." Upton licked at his lips thoughtfully. "Ruin the gel first, then cast her off when I grow weary of her. Let the tidbit taste how bitter fortune and power can be when she don't have none and I do."

"Yes," agreed Spelling softly. "An opportunity for both of us at the end of a fortuitous drive. You get the gel and I get the bird, and the fortune that flies with him."

* * *

Lord Nightingale was not at all interested in learning to sing. Once the pianoforte had been brought to the Gold Saloon, all the spectators had been expelled and Serendipity at last struck middle C upon the keys, Lord Nightingale gave an ear-piercing shriek and flew once around the room.

Serendipity ducked as he passed over her head, and she struck middle C again, more forcefully.

Lord Nightingale landed upon the shawl which covered the top of the pianoforte and attempted to sidle toward her. His claws caught in the material, and he squawked and flapped his wings and rose into the air once more, taking the shawl with him.

Serendipity giggled and ducked as the parrot and shawl both soared over her head this time, the tufts on the shawl brushing her cheek. "Lord Nightingale, do cease larking about and pay attention," she managed through her giggles. "You are being most impolite."

The shawl, loosed at last, fell to the floor, and the parrot landed with a clicking thud upon the top of his cage. "Shiver me timbers!" he cried raucously.

"I shall shiver your timbers if you do not pay attention immediately," Serendipity declared. "You are to learn to sing, sir, and I am to teach you. You will oblige me by paying attention."

" 'Tention!"

"Exactly. Now we shall begin with our scales." Serendipity began to sing the first of the scales, accompanying herself upon the pianoforte. "La-la-la-la-la-la-la-la," she sang in a lovely contralto.

Lord Nightingale ambled to the very edge of the cage top and stared at her with one huge amber eye. As she reached the final "la," he bobbed his head up and down twice, then raised his left foot to his beak and began to peck at his claws. He used the claws to scratch at his magnificent red head. Then he shook himself all over, beat his wings against the air and took flight, coming to rest upon the bench beside Serendipity, where he stepped carefully into her lap and began to peck at the edge of the pianoforte beneath the keys.

"No, it is not something to eat," laughed Sera.

Nightingale ceased to nibble and stepped onto the keys. He was just heavy enough to make the hammers touch the wire strings inside the instrument and force the notes to jangle into the room. C he played and F and then D and E together, and then he moved into the minors and back to the majors, dancing proudly upon the ivories and fluffing out his feathers and bobbing his head in obvious joy at the discordant song he played.

"Zounds!" exclaimed Wickenshire as he opened the door to the chamber. "What a musician he is! I thought for a moment it was you played so very badly, Miss Bedford. I must apologize for making such an unwarranted assumption, but I never thought to see a green-winged macaw dancing upon the keys of my pianoforte."

He was dressed as he had been hours before, dressed for the outdoors in leather breeches and high top boots and an ancient woolen hunting jacket. His dark curls tumbled over his brow, his strange eyes glowed in the sunshine from the windows, and for some odd reason, the very sight of him filling the doorway sent a flash of heat up into Serendipity's cheeks and caused her to gasp the tiniest bit.

"Did I frighten you? I did not intend it," he said, noticing the gasp. "I merely heard the racket and wondered what had gone wrong. Wretched bird. Never behaves properly. You are not frightened of him, are you? I never thought to ask that."

"No, no, he does not frighten me at all."

"No. Good. I shall be on my way then and allow you to continue with—your lesson?" His eyebrows arched in such a way as to send a giggle bubbling into Serendipity's throat, though she did not allow it to escape into the air between them. "I can put him inside his cage and close the door, if you would rather," Wickenshire added as an afterthought, lingering at the door. "Perhaps he will pay you more heed if he is confined."

"No. We are merely getting to know one another, I think."

"Oh. Be careful then, will you? When Nightingale and I came to know each other, he bit a hole clean through my finger."

"He never did!"

"Well, perhaps not clean through."

"I should hope not."

"No, well, I had best get on with my day then and leave you to yours, Miss Bedford." But he did not move. Oh, he tugged a glove—a very dirty, rough-looking glove—onto one hand, but he did not move to leave her. Instead, his gaze wandered over her as she sat upon the bench, surveying her from top to toe and back to top again. "S-spring hesitates just beyond our reach at the moment," he murmured. "But it will arrive in all its glory soon enough. You are not cold, Miss Bedford, in that gown? I can send one of the boys in to add fuel to the fire."

"Cold?" Serendipity could not think what brought such a question to his lips when the sun was shining brightly into the room through a bank of windows and could have warmed the room to a nicety without any fire at all, though a small one did burn upon the hearth now. "I am not at all cold, my lord," she responded, fiddling with the delicate net gloves she wore. "Why should you think—? Oh, because my gown looks just like sprigged muslin and sprigged muslin is very light. But it is not really muslin. It is merely a pattern woven into a light wool."

"Wool. Yes. Sheep. Waiting upon me. Must go," said Wickenshire all at once. And then, for no reason that Serendipity could guess, his cheeks began to turn a delicate pink. He nodded to her, turned about and exited the room, closing the door tightly behind him.

"Yo ho," called Lord Nightingale after him. "Yo ho ho. Knollsmarmer. Batten yer hatches." He fluttered to the slick top of the pianoforte, skidded like a drunken ice-skater across it and gazed with one gleaming eye at the empty space where Wickenshire had stood.

"Yes, well, I cannot think what that was all about either, Nightingale," Serendipity said softly. "And why should he color up as he did? He said nothing at all to be embarrassed about."

"Fool," Wickenshire muttered as he mounted the bay and turned her head toward the largest of the sheep barns that huddled between two hills near the north pasture. "Bedlamite. Frog." He laughed a bit then. Frog, yes, that was it. Once again that word summed him up quite nicely. "No, do not protest, Grace," he said to the mare as she fought him for a moment. "I know you do not care for the sheep, but we are lucky to have them, you know. It is their wool pays the taxes on you, my darling. It is they who fertilize the fields to grow your food. And we must get them raddled, Grace, and send them off to the riverbank and the cornfields quickly or we shall have a sad crop of corn to lay by when the time comes, let me tell you."

The mare beneath him whinnied and tripped upon a stone, but recovered nicely. Wickenshire grinned. It was the reason he had named her Grace—she was forever tripping over something. But the grin faded as quickly as it had come when he remembered the spectacle he had made of himself only minutes ago in the Gold Saloon. "What a Bedlamite she must have thought me," he whispered to no one, "hemming and hawing about in search of conversation like some tongue-tied farm boy who has never spoken to a young lady of Quality in his entire life.

"I truly am a frog," he sighed, giving his head a shake and sending his curls bobbing about in the most extraordinary manner. "I am a frog longing to be kissed so that I can see if I will turn into a charming earl or not. Though I am most afraid that I will not, Grace. Frogs often become princes in fairy tales, but very rarely does a frog become an earl in real life."

As they reached the track that led down into the north pasture and to the sheep barn beyond, Wickenshire urged the mare into a run. It was a dangerous thing to do with Grace, allow her to run full tilt while you were upon her back. Even when the track she traveled was well kept and smooth, she was like to stumble and send a man soaring over her head. But for some reason, this day, Wickenshire did not care whether he went soaring over her head or not. He would just as soon do it, as a matter of fact. That way, he would never be forced to face Miss Bedford again.

I cannot think what it is about her that turns me into such a dullard, he mused as Grace carried him forward into the wind, her golden mane flying up around his gloved hands. It is not as though I have not made pleasant conversation with any number of females in my lifetime. I have. And enjoyed it too. Of course, they did none of them ever look at me in quite so attentive a fashion as Miss Bedford does. Well, they would not, because they did none of them ever wish to hear what I had to say. Does Miss Bedford actually wish to hear what I have to say? Thunderation! And what did I say? Nothing but half-witted phrases about fingers and weather and sheep.

"Lord! Did I actually mention sheep? To a young woman who is a guest in my own household? No, I did not. Said the word once, that was all. Nothing untoward in that. Sheep. That was all. Did not talk about the raising of them or anything. And she is not a guest," he consoled himself. "She is one of my employees. Lord, now I sound as if I have more employees than I can count upon my two hands," he mumbled. "Besides, she is not truly an employee. I hired her simply because she is a friend of Eugenia's and in dire need. It is not as though she actually works for me like a housemaid or a cook or something."

He wondered then how the conversation would have gone had Miss Serendipity Bedford actually been Janie, the little farm girl who came in daily to help about the house. And he discovered the outcome to be most lowering. "I am hopeless," he grumbled. "More comfortable speaking with the likes of Janie than with the daughter of a viscount, and not at all good at pretending to be something I am not. I am a man with the aspirations of an enchanted frog and the conversational skills of an ancient coachman. Damnation, but I wish Miss Bedford had not turned out to be so very beautiful. Why could she not be a plain little thing like Eugenia?"

FOUR

Alone in her bedchamber that evening, Eugenia waited most impatiently until the entire household had settled down. At midnight she stepped into the corridor, a pale cloak covering her dinner dress and stout walking shoes on her feet. She stood very still for the longest time, listening. Not a sound came to her. Good. Very good. Nicky would be fast asleep by now. He had spent most of his day raddling the sheep and driving them back down into the recently flooded lowlands to graze near the river. And there had been the hurdles to erect as well, so that the ewes and lambs might be safely penned in the cornfields for the night. There would be no need to particularly check Nicky's chamber. An exhausted Nicky could be counted on not to linger at his window, stargazing, far into the night.

She was not quite so certain of Serendipity, but as she began to move down the corridor, a veritable specter in the light of the single lamp—Nicky always kept one lamp lighted upon each floor and in the stairwells—she paused outside her friend's chamber and listened, her ear to the door. Nothing.

Delight had been moved from Serendipity's chamber to the adjoining bedchamber when the new mattress had been delivered that afternoon, and Eugenia paused there as well, heard a tiny snore and smiled. Only her Aunt Diana remained. Lady Wickenshire's chamber door, though it was made of good, stout British oak, had suffered more than the others through the years of neglect and no longer hung properly. Spaces at the top and side allowed the glow of candles to shine through. Tonight, no light appeared.

Eugenia gave a sigh of relief and increased her pace, rolling along the remainder of the corridor like a harried captain at sea. She descended the main staircase in admirable silence, only two of the ancient old steps creaking beneath her feet, and turned, as she reached the ground floor, toward the rear of the house. She passed the library and Nicky's study and the farm office and turned into the kitchen where the muted light from the lamp in the hallway could not pierce, but where the banked coals from the eternal fire in the ovens flickered sparsely, allowing her to find her cautious way to the kitchen door. This she opened carefully and slipped out into the chill night. Shards of moonlight scattered around her, breaking over the pale cloak as she raised its hood to cover her hair. Perhaps, Eugenia thought, perhaps my little journey will prove to be in vain. Perhaps no one will come. But she could not trust in perhaps, and so she set off down the hill in the direction of the near empty stables.

Serendipity could not guess what had awakened her—a thunk, a squeak, the whisper of a footstep? She lay still, tucked warmly beneath the quilt, and listened intently. Nothing. Her imagination. Or the ancient house gasping and groaning, as ancient houses always did. She was almost falling back to sleep, her eyelids fluttering, when a scurrying, scuffling sound high overhead brought her fully awake with a start.

Something on the fourth floor. Something awake and scurrying about on that boarded-up fourth floor. Something most sinister. Serendipity gulped. Delight and I have been here almost a week, she thought, and never has anyone invited us to see the fourth floor. No one so much as mentions it. What—or who—can it be they hide there? Why board up the windows? So that no one can see in—or out? Her heart pounded with excitement, with anticipation, with a deep sense of forboding. Oh, but in a way it was delicious.

And then a single fact surfaced through the ocean of fantasies playing about in Serendipity's mind. Her bed-chamber lay upon the second floor, and so the noises above her head likely did not come from that intriguing fourth floor at all, but from the third floor, where she knew that the few servants who lived upon the premises were housed.

She felt a settling of her pulses and a sinking feeling of adventure forsaken. "Am I a complete ninnyham-mer?" she whispered into the night. "Do I not have enough to worry about? On the first of June, whether Lord Nightingale sings or whether he does not, I will be again without means to support us. Delight and I will be truly homeless then."

But she could not help herself. Beginning with her days at Miss Haverleigh's School for Young Ladies, she had developed the most ravenous appetite for Mrs. Rad-cliffe's gothic novels, and Mr. Lewis's and Zachary Spiniker's and every other thrilling volume by every gothic author she could lay her hands upon. And some-where, deep down inside, lay just the tiniest urge to con-front the dangerous, the dreadful and the supernatural.

"But not tonight," Serendipity told herself with a quiet smile, laying back down and tugging the quilt up to her chin. "It is Mr. Jenkins or Cook or John Coachman or perhaps even Bessie. Though why they are not all abed at this hour, I cannot guess."

Serendipity's eyelids began to flutter closed once more. But because her chamber lay at the rear of the house, directly opposite Eugenia's, she could not help but hear soft footsteps making their way toward the ser-vants' staircase, nor could she help but wonder as they descended, haltingly, with barely a squeak of the ancient wood, where they were bound. Tossing the bedclothes aside, she hurried into robe and slippers and stepped out into the corridor, softly, very softly, and crossed to the baize door which separated the servants' staircase from the remainder of the house. She opened that baize door as quietly as she could and heard a door open and close far below her, most likely upon the ground floor.

Eugenia shivered in the darkness, but not from the cold. Not from the cold at all. The chills that swiveled and swirled up and down her spine had nothing to do with the temperature of Willowsweep in early May. They had to do with what she feared to discover at the stables, in the dark of night. Pulling her hood more closely about her face, Eugenia stepped cautiously to the stable door. Nothing. Either she had arrived in advance of the person she sought or that person would not arrive at all this night. Well, she thought, I will slip inside the stables and wait. At least the wind will not bite at my nose there. And if he does not come by the time I have grown so cold as to feel it in my bones, I will simply return to the house and try again next Tuesday. It is always on a Wednesday morning that Nicky finds them. And always somewhere in the stables.

Eugenia was unaware, as she entered the stables and searched for a place to make herself comfortable for a time, that dark, brooding eyes had caught sight of her pale cloak in the broken moonlight. She had not the least idea that a figure composed of mist and murk and a touch of shadows had watched her at a considerable distance all the way down that long, lonely hill. Unaware, she yawned widely and settled into a pile of hay at the far right of the doorway. How considerate of you, Nicky, she thought, to leave the hay in such a convenient place.

So intent was the shadow with the dark, brooding eyes upon keeping Eugenia in sight that he failed to hear so much as the kitchen door open and close behind him, much less notice that he, himself, was being observed.

Serendipity absolutely shivered as the chill breeze whipped straight through her dressing gown despite the enormous wool shawl she had hastily wrapped around herself. She squinted into the night that was lit by a million stars but only sporadic moments of moonlight. Yes, there was someone ahead, just descending the hill on the path that led toward the stables. Serendipity could not distinguish much about the person. But whoever it was, he was being exceedingly careful about keeping to the shadows.

Serendipity's heart chattered with delicious fear. At last, it appeared, her dreams of gothic heroineship might well come true. But then she scolded herself silently. What a peabrain you will feel, she thought, when you follow this dark stranger all the way to the stables only to discover that it is John Coachman gone to check upon some ailing animal.

Still, the shadowman before her did not bear the least resemblance to John Coachman, who was monstrous tall, with shoulders the width of a ceiling beam and legs and arms to match. As best Sera could tell, the shadowman she followed was of medium height and medium build, though she could not be certain. Perhaps he was thin, and the little bulk she made out from time to time was his greatcoat billowing in the breeze. Or perhaps the shadowman was a woman? Certainly, if a woman went so far as to don a pair of breeches . . .

And what woman at Willowsweep would even consider to don a pair of men's breeches? she chided herself. Pure foolishness. Of course my shadowman is a man.

Serendipity gave the tiniest groan as she discovered that, in all of her thinking about the figure before her, she had quite lost sight of him. Had he noticed that someone followed behind him and stepped off the path? No, how could he have noticed? Her slippers were soft and silent upon the heavily packed dirt path. Perhaps he had glanced for a moment to the rear and discovered her there, deep in thought, looking at nothing in particular and pondering his identity?

Or perhaps, she thought, he has increased his pace and has already reached the stables—his most likely destination—and stepped inside. With a little shake of her head and a deep breath, Serendipity set off again down the hill.

The longer she waited, the more thankful Eugenia was for the hay. Truly, even though Nicky had replaced much of the wood, the stables continued to be cold and drafty. Worse than that, they smelled potently and unalterably of horse. Eugenia was not fond of the scent of horse. Over a prolonged period, it engendered in her a strong tendency to sneeze explosively. Abruptly remembering that, she began to question the sagacity of the hiding place she had chosen. Perhaps there was a more practical and more comfortable place? Well, of course there was. There was the little well house just at the corner of the stables. It was solidly built and, though perhaps damp, would not be near as drafty. And it would definitely not smell of horse.

With eyes beginning to itch and the queerest feeling in the back of her throat, Eugenia abandoned her nest and was just brushing the hay from her skirt when the latch upon the stable door tilted upward with a squeak. Eugenia froze. In the very last stall, Grace whinnied, and in the stalls across and to the side of the mare, the carriage horses nickered and pawed at the wood flooring in expectation.

The door opened inward, slowly, spastically, a bit at a time. Eugenia brought herself to order and dodged into the deepest of the shadows, where she pressed herself against the side of the building. This cannot be him, Eugenia thought in confusion. He would not be opening the stable door in such an awkward manner, would he?

She gulped and held her breath and brushed a cobweb away from her face with trembling hands. The door opened farther and farther; Eugenia gasped and gasped again and then she sneezed the most tremendous sneeze.

"Heaven save me!" Serendipity shrieked, while nearly jumping out of her slippers. Her heart flew into her throat and her pulses roared in her ears.

"Sera? Is it you?" gasped Eugenia, stepping away from the wall and squinting toward the door. "It is you! What in heaven's name are you about to be sneaking into the stables in the middle of the night?" Eugenia's nose itched, and she scratched at it and sniffed and sneezed again.

"Eugenia?" Serendipity could not believe her ears. But her eyes were of little use in the darkness of the stables, and so she must believe her ears or nothing. Then Eugenia stepped farther out, into a beam of moonlight which entered through the open door. "Eugenia, it is you. But—but—what are you doing here?"

"Well—I d-do have a reason. But you do not," pointed out Eugenia defensively. "I thought you to be asleep long ago. What are *you* doing here?"

Having spent five entire years as Eugenia's closest schoolmate, Serendipity had heard that tone before and took note of it. Eugenia was not about to confess her reason for being in the stables. One might beg and plead. One might twist her arm or force her to eat green peas, but she would never tell. "I—I heard someone sneaking out of the house. I followed to see why anyone would do so in the middle of the night," Serendipity confessed without any further effort to demand an explanation from Eugenia.

"You could not have heard me. I was very quiet. Merely two of those wretched steps on that unfortunate staircase squeaked at all. And the carpeting—"

"There is no carpeting upon the servants' staircase, Eugenia."

"I did not say a word about the servants' staircase. I

am referring to that unfortunate grouping of steps at the front of the house."

Serendipity nodded. She had known it to be so. It had not been Eugenia whom she had followed down the hill. She could not have mistaken Eugenia for a man, and especially, she could not have mistaken Eugenia's distinctive, rolling gait. "The person I followed, Eugenia, went down the servants' staircase and out the kitchen door and was most likely a man—at least, it was someone wearing breeches and a greatcoat."

"And he came in here?" Eugenia asked, astounded. "Sera, he could not have come in here. I have been sitting right there in that pile of hay and no one has entered but yourself."

"Well, I only guessed that he had come in here, Eugenia. Where else would he have gone? He was on the path and then he was not. I was woolgathering a bit, and he just disappeared. So I thought—well—was it someone for whom you waited, Eugenia? I think, now, that he saw me trailing after him and dodged into the shadows near the trees. Will he come if I go away? I am so very sorry if I have—disrupted an—assignation."

"What?" asked Eugenia. "An assignation? It is nothing at all like that. I—well, I cannot tell you. I promised Papa not to say a word to anyone. But it was *not* an assignation, I assure you. The man saw you, you say?"

"He may have."

"Well, he will be leery of the place for a while now. Come, let us go back to the house, Sera, and find our beds. I cannot think that he will appear again tonight, and I am frightfully chilly. I should think you would be frozen," she added, for the first time taking note of Serendipity's bedroom slippers and the shawl pulled tightly around the dressing gown. "Come, we will stop in the kitchen and make a pot of tea to warm us up and then be off to bed."

The two young women abandoned the stables and set off up the hill, crossing in and out of the shards of moonlight, Eugenia at first thoughtful and then growing quite giggly as they reached the house. Serendipity, shivering with delicious anticipation of a mystery in which her friend appeared to be involved, and the particulars of which she would subtly pry from Eugenia if it took the next three months, grew giggly as well. "I thought I was going to choke on my very own heart when you sneezed," she said, her voice a happy gurgle. "I do not know what I expected to find in the stables, but it was not you, sneezing."

"I should think not," laughed Eugenia. "And when the stable door began to open so very slowly, I thought I should die of fright. I could not imagine who would make such a cautious entrance. Oh, my, but I thought to see a murderer or something."

Eugenia reached out to the latch on the kitchen door. She jiggled it up and down. "What the deuce?" she muttered. "Oh, do pardon me, I ought not to have said *that*. Papa would box my ears. Sera, it is stuck somehow and will not open."

"What? How can that be? Of course it will open." Serendipity took the latch into her own hand, jiggled it up and down, attempted to jiggle it from side to side, muttered under her breath and jiggled it again. And then she laughed. It was a most unaccountable thing to do and she could not think why she did, but she laughed and laughed. "We are—we are—l-locked out, Eugenia. In the middle of the n-night."

Her laughter brought a smile beaming across her friend's face. "And you in your nightclothes," Eugenia giggled. "Whatever shall we tell Aunt Diana in the morning?"

"We cannot possibly remain out here until morning," snickered Serendipity. "We will both freeze into icicles. Only picture the look upon Cook's face when she opens the door to go to the pump and discovers us frozen." At which point Serendipity posed in imitation of an icicle in the moonlight, which sent Eugenia into suppressed whoops. "Do you think, Eugenia, that it was the person I followed who did it?"

"What? Did what?"

"Do you think that I frightened whomever it was and he dashed back into the house and locked the door after himself?"

"Oh, no," responded Eugenia half groaning, half laughing. "It might have been. It very well might. Come on, Sera." Barely restraining her giggles and staring at the ground, without one word of explanation, Eugenia took Serendipity's hand and tugged her around the side of the house.

"Eugenia, hush. You will wake the entire household," Serendipity urged, unable to smother her own laughter completely. "What are we looking for?"

"Pebbles."

"Pebbles?"

"Do you see that window, Sera? That is Nicky's window. We are going to throw pebbles at Nicky's window until he wakes up and comes down and lets us in."

"Oh, you cannot mean it. What will we tell him? He will think I am mad to be following men about in the middle of the night. And you—well—you will not even tell *me* what you were doing at the stables."

"He will be so amazed to be awakened by two such beautiful damsels as ourselves that he will not even think to ask what we are doing out here," declared Eugenia in droll accents. "He will simply rush to our aid and feel privileged to do so."

He was six years old and peering out into the darkness from the nursery window at Wicken Hall. Lightning strobed across the skies followed by great dragon roars of thunder. He might have hidden under the bedclothes for fear the dragon would spy him and blow his fiery breath in precisely his direction, but he did not. He did not care whether the dragon's fiery breath came down upon him. He only cared that his papa had come home again and that, though he could hear his papa clearly—had been able to hear him clearly for hours as he declaimed and proclaimed and generally shouted at everyone and everything—still he had not been called down into that gentleman's presence. "Don't you never want to see me, Papa? Not never?" he whispered, one neglected tear making a lonely trail down his cheek.

And then the wind came, rushing out of the east, driving the rain before it, the raindrops crashing so hard against the glass that he thought certainly the window would break. But it did not break, and the crashing persisted and persisted and persisted until Wickenshire's eyelids fluttered open. "What the devil?" he mumbled, rubbing at his eyes.

An entire handful of pebbles bounced against his windowpane, and he sat straight up in bed. It did not sound like rain. Not at all. "Dreaming about the rain," he muttered, slipping from between the sheets. He made his way in the darkness to the window, only stubbing his toe once on the nightstand and taking a moment to howl softly and dance about because of it. Then he listened curiously beside the closed draperies. No, no rain. Something else entirely, for nothing was hitting the windowpane now. He thought for a moment that he heard stifled laughter and whispered phrases, and he rubbed his eyes with both fists. "Faeries flouncing about upon the lawn," he told himself with a grin. His papa had told him only two stories in his entire lifetime—both of them about Glorianna and her faery legions. And Wickenshire had never forgotten them. Could not forget them to this day. They were, in fact, the only joyful memories of his father that he had to hold in his heart, and he held them there faithfully, recalling them now with a grin.

A single pebble bounced off the glass. This was followed by the rackety-clackety ping-ping-ping of a handful of pebbles. Wickenshire pulled the draperies aside, unlatched the latch and swung the casement outward, to be rewarded for his efforts by one last pebble bouncing blithely off his nose.

"Ouch!"

"Oh, I say, Sera. Excellent shot!" Eugenia cried, giggling madly and then staring up at her cousin with hands upon her hips. "Where have you been, Nicky? We have been throwing pebbles at your window for hours."

"You don't say?" responded Wickenshire, rubbing his nose. "And may I ask why?" *Great heavens, they do look like faeries cavorting about upon the lawn in the shatterings of moonlight,* he thought, gazing down upon the young ladies. *I wonder if I am dreaming still? No, cannot be. Nose hurts much too much to be a dream.* "Eugenia, Miss Bedford, speak to me. What are you doing down there? What is it you require?"

"Merely that you come and open the kitchen door for us, Nicky, so that we may get in. We are locked out, you see," Eugenia said very prettily.

"Yes, and we are f-freezing," offered Serendipity in a voice so pitiful that it set both young ladies to giggling again.

The Earl of Wickenshire ran his fingers through his hair, knocking his nightcap completely off his head without so much as noticing. *How the devil had they gotten locked out of the house? And at this hour, too.* "What time is it?" he asked then.

"It is close to one, I think," Serendipity replied. "Does that make a difference?"

"Indeed. Nicky does never come down to open doors for people after one o'clock," droned Eugenia madly. "Not even for the very best people."

"Balderdash," commented Wickenshire. "I am coming down right this minute, Eugenia. And if I discover that you have unearthed Bobby Tripp's stash of home-brewed in the well house and have been nipping at it, I shall take a switch to the both of you."

Serendipity and Eugenia gazed in amazement at each

other as the earl's long, lean form disappeared from the window.

"Home-brewed?" murmured Eugenia.

"Stashed in the well house?" Serendipity giggled. "Eugenia, you do not think it was that poor little groom, Bobby Tripp, whom I frightened off the pathway? Is the well house near the stables?"

"Right beside," nodded Eugenia. "Right beside. Come on, Sera. If we are not at the door awaiting him, there is no telling but that Nicky will think it was all a dream and go back upstairs again without letting us in."

"No, he would not."

"I should not wager upon it," laughed Eugenia. "I should not bet one penny. Bobby Tripp. Can you imagine?"

FIVE

Jenkins was most inclined to close the door directly in the gentlemen's faces, but he could not, not by his own authority. "If you will be kind enough to wait in here," he droned, leading the way into a tiny, ill-furnished antechamber, "I shall inform my lady of your presence."

"You do not mean to say that Aunt Diana has taken up residence in the gawdforsaken place, Jenkins? Glory, what a thing! Has Nicky completely lost his mind to force his mama to reside in a bundle of sticks and stones likely to crash down around her ears at any moment?"

"I shall inform my lady of your presence," repeated Jenkins, not deigning to answer such an audacious question, especially from such a personage as Mr. Neil Spelling. "If I may have your cards . . ."

"For goodness' sake, Jenkins, just say it is her nephew Mr. Spelling and a friend."

"Very good, sir," nodded Jenkins, stalking away with his nose tilted just a bit higher into the air than usual. He climbed the stairs as slowly as he possibly could and walked haltingly down the first-floor corridor, pausing to straighten a painting upon the wall and place a cricket table more appropriately. He noted a bit of a spot on the ancient wallpapering, took his handkerchief from his pocket, gave it a lick and rubbed at the spot carefully until it disappeared. Then a hole in the carpeting near the door to the Gold Saloon caught his eye. He stepped into the Gold Saloon and gazed at Lord Nightingale who was busily swinging upside down upon the swing that His Lordship had made for him. Jenkins took a ladder-back chair from the Gold Saloon and set it carefully over the offending piece of carpet in the corridor. All in all, the butler managed to allow Spelling and his friend to cool their heels in the antechamber for a good five minutes before he even reached the Striped Saloon where Lady Wickenshire and Miss Eugenia, with Miss Bedford's able assistance, were busily making a list of the things in the house that could be restored to former glories and the things which must be given up for lost and thrown away.

"Yes, what is it, Jenkins?" asked Her Ladyship, taking note of the butler who stood silently upon the threshold.

"Visitors, my lady."

"Visitors? Who on earth? You do not mean to say that someone from the neighborhood has had the audacity to come calling when they know perfectly well that we are not in the least prepared to receive them? Certainly they are all of them sagacious enough to realize that a house which has stood empty for twenty years and more cannot be ready to receive guests in less than a month."

"It is Mr. Spelling, my lady, and another gentleman."

"Neil?" asked Eugenia with a frown.

"Indeed, miss."

"That boy," sighed Lady Wickenshire, annoyed. "I always loved Winifred, and goodness knows that Albert was my pride and joy, but that child has grown to be as much of an annoyance as was his mama! Why Albert should have married Aurora first and left Winifred until second I cannot understand. I expect you must send them up, Jenkins."

Eugenia sighed the most dreadful sigh, causing Serendipity's gaze to fall questioningly upon her.

"Well, never mind, Eugenia," Lady Wickenshire said. "Perhaps Neil is visiting with the other gentleman somewhere in the neighborhood and has just stopped in to pay his respects. We shall receive them in the sun room. You will both accompany me, will you not? Yes. And tell Cook, Jenkins, that we shall be five for tea. And bring the tea as soon as possible. They must leave once we have finished with it. It is the polite thing to do."

She dismissed Jenkins with a harried wave of her hand and began at once to straighten her gown. "If we do not linger over tea, my dears, we shall have them on their way before Nicky even thinks to return to the house."

"Are you certain that you wish me to take tea with you, my lady?" Serendipity ventured as the three hurried up the corridor to the sun room. "I am merely an employee, after all and—"

"Nonsense! You are in rather lowering circumstances at the moment, but merely because your mama did not see fit to have a son," proclaimed the dowager. "You are the daughter of a viscount, not some serving girl from the village, and you shall take tea with us just as you ordinarily would."

"Hear! Hear!" exclaimed Eugenia.

"There is no telling who accompanies my nephew. Perhaps the gentleman is an eligible bachelor. One never knows."

"No, one never does," agreed Eugenia with a broad wink at Serendipity. "Eligible bachelors do appear at the most unlikely moments. Aunt Diana has been hunting one for me for years now. But he has not appeared as yet."

"He will," declared the dowager. "It is merely that he must be a particular type of gentleman, Eugenia."

"One who does not abhor a young woman who blushes at the least cause, has no conversation, walks like a drunken sailor, and cannot dance without falling upon her—"

"Enough! I will hear no more disparaging remarks made about yourself," commanded the dowager. "You are quite as adept as Nicky at listing your liabilities,

Eugenia, and equally as incapable of realizing your assets."

"Yes, Aunt Diana. That is just what I was about to say—a young woman who cannot dance without falling upon her assets."

"Eugenia!" giggled Serendipity.

"Ha!" laughed Lady Wickenshire. "There! One of your assets rises to the occasion even as we speak!"

Serendipity blanched; Eugenia's jaw dropped right open; only Lady Wickenshire appeared not to notice the significance of the title, Viscount Upton, when Jenkins announced the gentlemen. They entered the sun room, both of them smiling broadly. Spelling crossed to the sopha upon which his Aunt Diana sat and bowed quite properly over her hand. "And my dearest Eugenia. What a surprise to discover you here," he drawled, taking his cousin's hand into his own and strategically missing the back of it with a kiss. "And who is your lovely companion, may I ask?"

"M-Miss Bedford," Eugenia managed, tugging her hand away from Spelling.

"Your servant, Miss Bedford," Spelling greeted, taking Serendipity's hand in turn and this time not missing the back of it with his lips. "May I present to you, ladies, my dearest friend, Lord Upton."

Serendipity's heart stuttered in her breast as the loathsome beast's gaze fell upon her. He came to bow over her hand, but she snatched it away from him and hid it behind her back. "You are—Mr. Wiggins," she gasped.

"No, no, I assure you, Miss Bedford. I am Lord Upton now," he responded. "How are you, my dear? I have not set eyes upon you for years. You have grown into a most lovely young woman. And Miss Chastain, you are quite as charming as Neil assured me you would be. My lady," he said, bowing quite properly to the dowager. "I hope we have not come at an inopportune time. I did suggest to Spelling that he ought to write first and not just appear upon your doorstep."

"I thought to discover no one but Nicky here, Aunt Diana," drawled Spelling, taking a chair and waving Upton to one as well, "and so I dispensed with the niceties. Just three old bachelors getting together, you know. Thought it would be a nice surprise for Nicky. I do hope you will accept my apologies for not once anticipating your presence."

The dowager nodded. "Have you a house in the neighborhood, Lord Upton?" she inquired.

"Me? Here? I should think not. I have never been so very far south of London in all my life. It is quite— unique—here, is it not? One may hear the sea pounding against the rocks, I imagine, on a still day."

"We are hardly that close to the sea," responded the dowager. "Though we can, in fact, smell the sea on days when the wind blows sharply. Do you mean to tell me, Neil, that you have come here expecting Nicholas to put you up?"

"Actually, yes. No inns hereabout, Aunt Diana."

"There is an inn on the post road at Swiftinwhold. I am positive of it," offered Eugenia with lowered eyes. "A mere twelve miles as the crow flies, Neil. I should drink my tea quickly, if I were you. Since you are not a crow, you know, it will prove a distance farther for *you*. Horses never fare as well as crows."

"How kind of you to point that out, Eugenia. However, we did not come on horseback. We came in my new traveling coach. And, I dare say, the coach horses cannot be pushed any farther until day after tomorrow at the earliest. Besides, we have come to visit Nicky, not to drive back and forth most of the day between here and Swiftinwhold. No, no, I think it best if we remain at Willowsweep. Nicky will think so as well, I expect. Where is Nicky, by the way, Aunt Diana? It is nearly four in the afternoon. Do you not keep country hours here at Willowsweep?"

"We dine at six," nodded the dowager. "And since you have come all this way for the express purpose of visiting Nicky, I expect he will discover chambers for you somewhere for tonight. Though you must be aware, Neil, that they will not be in the best of condition. Nicky has only begun upon the restoration. Still, if you do not mind a bit of inconvenience, you and Lord Upton are quite welcome to dine with us," she added, ignoring a muttered comment from Eugenia and a tiny gasp from Serendipity. "Did you think to bring your valets with you, gentlemen? I must admit that Nicholas has no one in residence at the moment capable of serving you in such a capacity."

"It is of no import, Aunt Diana. We shall do without."

"Good. Ah, tea! How delightful. Jenkins, Mr. Spelling and Lord Upton are to remain with us overnight."

"And perhaps longer," inserted Neil quickly.

"You will be good enough to tell Nicky that he must discover chambers for them, will you not?"

"Yes, my lady," Jenkins responded as he set the tray upon the table before her.

"Yes, and of course their horses must be stabled and their coachman must be given a place to sleep."

"We are sorry to cause you so much trouble," drawled Lord Upton quietly, his blue eyes hooded in the most seductive manner and gazing upon Eugenia. "We did not imagine it to be quite so far from civilization, Willowsweep."

Eugenia tilted her head upward and studied Lord Upton fully for the first time. The blue of his eyes dazzled her and the gold of his hair glistened in the sunlight that flowed into the room through a veritable wall of windows. His lips were narrow, but tilted upward in quite a charming smile. And his countenance as a whole, though not as dazzling as his eyes alone, was nevertheless openly appealing.

"I am so pleased to discover that you are here and quite safe, Cousin," he said then, shifting his gaze from

Eugenia to Serendipity. "When I reached London to discover you gone, I could not think what to do, my dear. Is your sister here as well?"

"Yes," replied Serendipity flatly.

"Good. Good. We have had a misunderstanding, I think, you and I. I did never intend that you should go off upon your own, m'dear. Certainly there is a place for you and your sister both in my household."

"We have no need to depend upon you," frowned Serendipity.

"Of course you do, m'dear. You cannot impose upon your friends forever."

"Serendipity is not imposing upon us," declared Eugenia softly, taking her gaze from Upton and choosing to study the carpet instead.

"No, she most certainly is not," agreed the dowager. "Eugenia, come pass the gentlemen their tea. Miss Bedford's presence here is a great favor to us, Lord Upton. You must know that we could not do without her at present. She does my son the favor of teaching Lord Nightingale to sing."

Mr. Spelling's eyebrows came near to flying up into his curls, and Serendipity, annoyed as she was that Lord Upton should find his way into this establishment, nevertheless found Mr. Spelling's reaction to the dowager's statement most amusing. "Oh, yes," she nodded. "I have offered my services on Lord Nightingale's behalf, and he is doing splendidly. Do you know Lord Nightingale, Mr. Spelling?"

"Unfortunately, yes," mumbled Spelling. "Dratted bird. M'father had him before he had me."

"Did he? Well, he is in fine feather and quite the most delightful student. I expect he will have his first song down within the week." Serendipity could not think what had possessed her to say such a thing. Lord Nightingale's idea of a singing lesson was to stalk about upon the keys, nibble on the edge of the pianoforte and turn himself upside down in her lap to have his stomach rubbed. Still, she was adequately rewarded for the tiny lie as Mr. Spelling's eyebrows flew even higher and his jaw dropped for an instant. But he pulled himself together immediately with praiseworthy aplomb. "How delightful for Nicky," he drawled. "Apparently he will find himself free of debt at last. Wonderful. Wonderful."

Serendipity could not think what Mr. Spelling meant by that. How could a parrot free a gentleman of debt? Still, it did give more credence to Lord Wickenshire's statement that her position was not a charitable one, that teaching Lord Nightingale to sing was most important. "I do think," smiled Sera, stretching the lie a tiny bit farther, "that Lord Nightingale is the very best student I have ever seen. Why, he learns far more quickly than any of the girls at school did, does he not, Eugenia?"

Eugenia, quiet laughter lighting her eyes, joined in this subterfuge with enthusiasm. "Oh, he is quicker by far than any of us ever were, Neil. It is lowering to think oneself a fine student and then to see a parrot, of all things, outstrip one, but such, apparently, is to be the case."

Late that afternoon, Delight came prancing happily into her sister's bedchamber, her little hands flapping excitedly, her dress muddied, and with a rather large hole in one of her stockings. "Giddyup, giddyup, giddyup, whoa!" she sang, galloping about the room. "Lef' is lef' an' right is right an' both is stop an' go! Giddyup, giddyup, giddyup, whoa! An' Grace knows 'tis so!"

Serendipity could not think what had happened to fill the child with such energy and enthusiasm. And such a song! She had never before heard anything like it. "Delight, dearest, do come to a halt before you fall and hurt yourself," she smiled. "Whatever are you singing about?"

"I have had the bestest time of all m' life!" exclaimed Delight, jumping up onto the window seat and bouncing excitedly about. "The very bestest time of all my life. I have rode a horse all by myself. Giddyup, giddyup, giddyup, whoa!"

"You look more as if you have fallen from a horse," Serendipity observed. "However did you get so very dirty?"

"I have been helping Nicky."

"You ought to call him Lord Wickenshire, dearest. That is his proper title."

"No, he said I was to call him Nicky. He is my dedicated knight, you know, an' I am his faery princess."

"No, are you?"

"Uh-huh. An' I have rode his very own horse all by m'self! I have chased the sheep, too, an' helped to pen 'em in the hurdles. That is what Nicky calls the little fences, the hurdles. Me an' Grace chased all our sheep right where Nicky wanted them, just like the shepherding dogs did. Oh, we were wonderful! An' we did not fall but one time."

"You rode Lord Wickenshire's horse? You and Grace fell? Who is Grace? You did not both fall from the horse?"

"Grace is Nicky's horse an' she is not a dumb ol' pony neither. An' I did not fall off her. Grace felled. But I did not make a sound when she did, you know, because Grace was soooo embarrassed an' I did not wish to make her feel any worser."

"The horse fell with you on it?" Serendipity could not contain a creeping horror. "You might have been killed!"

"Not I! I knew 'zactly what to do. I practiced an' practiced all morning."

"Practiced what?"

"Jumping. I jumped from the rocks an' I jumped from the stiles, an' I jumped from a tree, an' I jumped from the very top of a fence. All morning long I jumped an' jumped an' jumped. An' when it came time to jump from Grace, I was not afraid at all an' I did it perfect!"

"But—but—"

"Oh, it was so verimost wonderful, Sera! And Nicky says as I may do it again tomorrow if I wish."

The knock upon Serendipity's door that interrupted this positive gush of enthusiasm was somewhat hesitant. Serendipity, with one more long glance at Delight, crossed to the door and tugged it open. "Lord Wickenshire. Good afternoon. You are just the gentleman I wish to see."

"Nicky!" Delight cried from the window seat. "I have tolded Sera all about Grace!"

"You have? All?" Wickenshire's eyes met Serendipity's a moment; then his gaze flickered to the floor. He shifted uneasily from foot to foot, cleared his throat and then cleared his throat again. "I thought I ought to— She is a bit raggedy looking and you might— She was never in any danger—"

"Oh, no, of course not, my lord. Any seven-year-old young lady might jump from a falling horse without the least danger."

"Well, no, that is not true at all," Wickenshire responded, his eyes meeting hers. "But I was certain that Delight could do so without hurting herself. I made her practice jumping all morning and most of the afternoon, too. I knew Grace would stumble and—"

"You knew that your horse would stumble?"

"Yes, she almost always does, though she does not always go down. She only goes down once in a great while. Still, it is safer to know how to jump off when you are riding Grace, so I made quite certain, you know, that Delight—that she—"

"And I expect you set her upon the horse's back astride as well, did you not?"

"I—well, yes. Delight and I rode double out into the meadow. I could not have done so had I put a sidesaddle upon the beast. Ought I not— I mean, Eugenia rode astride with me when she was no more than seven— I begin to comprehend from the way you are glaring at me that it is something not ordinarily done?"

"Not ordinarily."

"Oh. Well, I will not do it again, then."

"But, Nicky, you promised," cried Delight, bouncing off the window seat and running to throw her arms about his waist. "You did promise," she insisted, staring upward with the most pitiful look upon her face.

"Yes, well, we shall locate Mama's old sidesaddle and—but they are so very dangerous, Miss Bedford," he said, his gaze roaming up and down between the sisters. "And Delight is so very small. And Grace is so very large—and clumsy."

"Delight has never been upon so much as a pony before in all her life. Papa did never think to—"

"Yes, so Delight told me. That is why I taught her the rhyme, you know. So she would remember how to tell Grace what she desired with the reins. At any rate, I did come to say that I am to blame for the state of Miss Delight's clothing and I shall see that she has a new dress and new stockings the very next time I ride into the village. And I also came to say that—that I am extremely sorry—but Neil and Lord Upton apparently intend to remain here for a week at least and I could not throw them out upon their collective ears, though I did think of it."

The mention of Mr. Henry Wiggins, who had usurped her papa's title and lands, drove all thought of Delight's adventure from Serendipity's mind for the moment. She frowned up at Wickenshire, a tiny pucker between her brows. "I cannot think it happenstance that brought Lord Upton here," she said softly. "He only just arrived at the London residence hours after we departed. He has had little enough time to enjoy himself in town. Why should he come so hurriedly into the country?"

"You think that perhaps he learned of your whereabouts and then petitioned Neil to bring him here? Why would he do that, Miss Bedford?"

Serendipity shrugged. "I cannot think why."

"Well, they have been friends for a number of years, the new Lord Upton and Neil. I know that to be a fact.

And while I have certain suspicions about why Neil should arrive on my doorstep at this precise time, perhaps it *is* just happenstance that Upton accompanies him. At any rate, I am sorry on your account that they intend to remain. If there is anything I can do to make things more comfortable for you—"

"No, no, there is nothing. Delight and I shall survive this bit of unpleasantness, I assure you. Oh, I did not explain to Lord Upton that I am in your employ."

"No, Mama said as much. Better that you allow the man to assume you are a guest here. Eugenia's friend, you know. Nothing odd in Eugenia inviting you to linger with her in the country for a while."

"Just so," nodded Serendipity.

"Indeed," nodded Wickenshire. "We gather in the drawing room before dinner as usual," he added, tearing his gaze from the glorious blue of Miss Bedford's eyes and smiling down at Delight who had gone from holding him around the waist to jiggling up and down with his hand held in both of hers. "And I shall expect you, my princess, to be turned out in top form for dinner. Mud gone; hair combed; and wearing that very pretty blue dress that makes your eyes light up uncommonly bright."

"An' you will wear the green velvet coat," giggled Delight. "Your frog coat."

"Indeed," chuckled Wickenshire and, freeing himself from Delight's grasp, he bade Serendipity adieu and went off down the corridor to his own chambers.

"The green velvet frog coat?" Serendipity asked Delight, curious.

"Uh-huh. Nicky says he is just like a enchanted frog an' if he is kissed quite properly by the very perfectest princess, perhaps he will turn into a charming earl."

"Lord Wickenshire told you this?"

"Uh-huh. But he don't hold out much hope for it."

"For being kissed by the perfect princess?"

"No, silly, for turnin' into a charming earl. He says that he will likely croak and hop away does it ever happen. I tole him he already is a earl, but he said as he is a earl just on paper an' don't know how to be a real one. Really he is a frog. Why does he say he is a frog, Sera?"

"I have no idea," murmured Serendipity thoughtfully, tugging at the bellpull for Bessie. "How very sad that such a charming gentleman should call himself a frog."

SIX

Upton stared about him, his eyes wide with wonder. "And I thought my chambers abominable," he drawled at last. "Really, Spelling, is your cousin mad?"

"No, impoverished."

"Perhaps, but still, he is an earl. Look at these rooms. By gawd, Spelling, there is not a piece of furniture in them not held together by hope and spit."

"I expect that Aunt Diana has not got around to re-furnishing as yet. Come, Upton, it is not as bad as you think. We are at Willowsweep, are we not? And your little bird is here, just as you were told. Yes, and my little bird as well. Surely you can withstand the loss of a bit of elegance for the opportunities that await us."

"The loss of a bit of elegance, yes. But this!"

"And Nicky did not toss us out upon our ears," added Spelling with a wicked smile. "I told you that he would not. A paragon of propriety, my cousin."

"Perhaps if we open the draperies, a bit of sunlight will make everything look—Spelling!"

"What?" asked Mr. Spelling, pressing lightly upon the hastily made-up bed with the tips of his fingers.

"Spelling, your chamber windows are boarded over!"

"Surely not," murmured Spelling. "The shutters are closed."

"No, no, there are no shutters. There are boards nailed

over the windows. Some of the nails have come straight through the window frames."

"Devil, if you ain't right," Spelling grumbled, crossing to the window to see for himself. "Now what do you suppose—"

"Cost too much," interrupted Wickenshire, coming to a halt in the open doorway. "Three floors full of them was quite enough, thank you."

"What?" asked Spelling and Upton in concert.

"Windows. Taxes. Two pounds eight shillings apiece. A mere two pounds less than what I pay the government to keep Jenkins. Got rid of all the fourth-floor windows. Kept Jenkins. Apologize for putting you way up here, Neil, Upton, but the only other chambers available have—are—well, the chimneys are not working properly and soot tends to pour out of them into the rooms at the most inopportune moments. A great deal of soot. Thought you would not like it."

"Yes, and you thought correctly, too," nodded Upton.

"Just so. I wonder, if you do intend to remain, Neil, will you lend me a hand?"

"Well, of course we intend to remain, Nick. Not have come all this way, else."

"Just so. But you did not know about the windows then."

"Keep the draperies pulled," sighed Upton. "Won't notice. What sort of help are you in need of, Wickenshire?"

"Hands to bring your trunks upstairs."

"Surely your servants—" began Upton.

"Do not tell me there is only Jenkins," mumbled Spelling.

"No, there is Cook and John Coachman and Bobby Tripp, and Miss Bedford's abigail, Bessie, and little Janie and the men who come out from the village to lend a hand during the daylight hours, but no one can be spared at the moment. So I thought that you and I, Neil, and

Upton here— Jenkins is not so young as he once was, and the trunks are rather heavy—"

"None of your servants can be spared to bring us our trunks?" Upton asked, aghast.

"Not if you want dinner, no."

"Explain to me, Nicky, what the coachman has to do with dinner?" queried Spelling, lifting his quizzing glass to his eye and surveying his cousin thoroughly.

"Milking cows. Cook needs the milk. He cannot abandon the cows in favor of trunks, Neil. Cows must be milked when they are ready to be milked and not much later."

"Well, my coachman or the men from the village, then. They cannot have departed already. The sun is still up."

"They are gone."

"Gone? Gone? In heaven's name, where?"

Wickenshire shrugged. "Off with Bobby Tripp. M'bull broke through the fence and set off for Squire Hadley's. Needs must be rounded up at once. Extremely expensive animal."

"Oh, all right," Spelling sighed, allowing his quizzing glass to drop. "Come, Upton. Two trunks. Two men upon each trunk. Take a moment merely."

And it might have taken merely a moment, too—well, perhaps two or three moments—except that the trunks had been strapped to the roof of Spelling's new traveling coach and Jenkins had climbed to the top to unfasten them.

"Jenkins, do be careful," Wickenshire called. "I will not have you falling and breaking something."

"Never, sir. Here is the first. Will you take it?" And with no further warning, Mr. Jenkins balanced one end of the trunk upon the rail that made a full rectangle of the rooftop and gave it a mighty shove. Wickenshire held out his arms to catch it, took one glance upward as it hurtled toward him and stepped hastily out of its way.

The trunk crashed to the stable floor, one brass-encased corner of it splitting the pine planking.

"Devil it, Jenkins," drawled Wickenshire.

"Sorry, m'lord. Will not happen again. Slipped."

"Help me tug it out of there, eh, Neil?" Wickenshire said. "Here, you take the handle. I will grasp it by the hasps and . . . on three. One, two, three!"

The corner of the trunk arose from the hole in the planking with such force that it knocked Spelling backward. His shoes slid; his body wobbled. Visions of himself pinned beneath his own trunk caused him to release his hold, and just as he shoved the trunk aside, his posterior hit the ancient and none-too-clean stable floor with a magnificent *ka-thwack!* The hasps in Wickenshire's hands opened with considerable force as the trunk flew past him and landed on its side at Upton's feet.

"Not to worry, Neil," Wickenshire offered, following after the trunk. "All is well. Only one jacket and a neckcloth have actually touched this filthy floor." Whereupon Wickenshire went to set the trunk upright, tripped over his own feet, caught at one of the stall posts to keep himself erect and sent the trunk sprawling a second time, spilling its entire contents.

"Oh, well done, sir," whispered Jenkins from the top of the coach. "Well done, indeed." Not one of the gentlemen heard him.

Upton broke into whoops; Spelling sputtered; Wickenshire merely shrugged his shoulders and took refuge behind a most apologetic countenance.

"It is not humorous, Upton," Spelling pointed out with some asperity. "What the devil am I to do now? I have ruined the clothes I am wearing, and everything I brought is covered with dirt and straw and gawd knows what else."

"Horse manure," provided Wickenshire helpfully. "Bobby has not got around to mucking out the place after your team passed through, I expect."

"Oh, gawd!" groaned Spelling.

"Not to worry, Neil. I shall give you the loan of some

of my clothes, eh? Of course, they will not fit you perfectly."

"They will not fit me at all, you beetlebrain. I shall look a perfect clown."

"Well, then. I will give you the loan of a nightshirt and robe and you shall have dinner in your chambers, and by tomorrow your valet—"

"I did not bring my valet!" Spelling shouted.

"Oh. Jenkins, then. By tomorrow, Jenkins will have done something to make these clothes presentable again, will you not, Jenkins?"

"Indeed, my lord."

"Just so. Best come and stuff things back in here, though, Neil. No telling but they will get spread all over the place else. Pass the other trunk down, Jenkins. Carefully."

Lord Upton stepped forward to get his own trunk to the floor without incident, catching the lowered end as Jenkins eased the other into Wickenshire's hands. "There we have it," smiled Wickenshire affably. "All safe and sound, eh? Have you got yours closed, Neil? Good. Climb down, Jenkins. Climb down. Step over and take an end of Mr. Spelling's trunk. Need not carry that one far. Drop it off in the scrub room. Set, Upton?"

"Quite."

"Off we go then."

The little parade of trunks and men marched up the hill to the house without the least misstep. In through the kitchen door they went, Jenkins and Spelling turning immediately to the right and disappearing through the archway that led to the butler's pantry, the sinks, and at the very rear, the scrub room, while Wickenshire and Upton went straight ahead and made their way through the kitchen to the servants' staircase.

"Careful on the stairs, eh, Upton? Dreadful old things. Warped," Wickenshire advised, leading the way.

"Um-hum," grunted Upton, wishing he had not

packed quite as much, since the main weight of the trunk rested upon him.

"Ought to put more candles about in this staircase. Would, too, if there were not so many more lucrative things to be made from the sheep fat than candles."

"What did you say, Wickenshire?"

"Sheep fat. Candles. Tallow, you know. I—I— Damnation!"

"What?" The question was immediately answered for Upton as the trunk lurched down at him. It would have sent him tumbling head over heels down the stairwell if he had not had sense enough to release his hold and step aside. As it was, the thing soared over two steps before it actually crashed and began to crack and kalumph and in general make a devil of a noise as it careened down to the bottom of the stairway, its top fracturing, its clasps springing open, and everything that Upton had brought with him spewing out along the way.

"Son of a western sea turtle!" bellowed Wickenshire. "Damnable cat! I'll have its head! Sorry, Upton. Did not see it. Did not so much as hear it. So very sorry. Are you all right? Here, I will gather everything up for you. My fault. All my fault. Ought not to have stepped on the cat."

Upton stared, dazed, at the gentleman who made his way down the steps past him, trampling upon shirts and breeches and drawers even as he attempted to pick them up.

Jenkins, who had just then opened the door at the bottom of the staircase where lay the empty trunk with lid hungrily open, suppressed a smile and hurried to step on as many of Lord Upton's garments as he could before stuffing them back into their box. For shame, my lord, he thought. What will the gentleman do if he ever learns we have not got a cat?

Dinner at Willowsweep that evening was likely to prove a solemn and tension-filled affair, and Serendipity de-

scended to the first floor in the expectation of such, her
nerves steeled against the sight and sound of the infamous
Mr. Henry Wiggins. She had carefully warned Delight not
to address Lord Upton nor to take any notice of anything
that he might say to her, other than to be polite.

I do not care if everyone thinks us rude, Serendipity
thought as she entered the drawing room with one hand
protectively on Delight's shoulder. I will not encourage
Delight to accept that—worm—as a person to be looked
up to. I do not trust the beast as far as I can throw him.
And if he says one thing to send the smile from Delight's
face, I shall slap his own face for him and leave the
room, no matter what sort of row it causes.

But as dinnertime approached and the remainder of
the little party assembled in the drawing room, Mr.
Henry Wiggins did not present himself. Neither he nor
Mr. Spelling, Serendipity discovered, intended to appear
at dinner at all.

"They have requested to be served in their chambers,"
Wickenshire answered when his mama questioned him
about their absence over the mock turtle soup. "Miss
Bedford's Bessie was kind enough to take them up a tray.
Perhaps they are exhausted from the ride and do not wish
to dress for dinner, Mama."

Jenkins, who for lack of a single footman stood alone
behind the earl's chair to attend to all the needs of those
at table, cleared his throat quietly. His fine brown eyes
sparkled and a smile twitched at his lips. Serendipity
suspected that the butler knew exactly why Mr. Spelling
and Lord Upton had not appeared. Yes, and she suspected
that Lord Wickenshire knew as well, because the earl
grinned without the least provocation at the very moment
that Jenkins cleared his throat.

Wickenshire was not grinning, however, as he downed
his breakfast shortly after sunrise the following morning.
Alone at table, he stared at the note he held in his left

hand and gulped his coffee. "You did not see anyone at all, Jenkins?" he asked as the butler placed a plate of shirred eggs and a rasher of bacon before him.

"No one, my lord. Found it lying upon the table in the vestibule first thing this morning."

"So, whoever it is has gained entrance to the house now," whispered Wickenshire to himself. "Damnation, but I cannot think what this can be about. And there has been no further word from Uncle Robert?" he added with a bit more volume.

"No, my lord. None."

That puzzled Wickenshire. He debated the sagacity of writing to his uncle once again about the odd notes that he had been receiving since first he took up residence at Willowsweep a full three months ago. Still, if his uncle had any new ideas to offer, most certainly he would have written again by now. Eugenia's father was never one to withhold information, and especially he would not hold back some secret when he knew that his nephew was being subtly threatened over and over again. Though this note was not so subtle as most had been.

Depart this place, you who cavort with witches, or face the cleansing of the witches' fire, it read in strong, black lines. Wickenshire paused with a forkful of eggs at his lips, closed his left hand into a fist and crumpled the paper into a ball. "Depart indeed," he mumbled, and then proceeded to eat the rest of his breakfast in silence.

Really, it was the outside of enough. He had not so much as set foot in this house in over fifteen years. And he had never before in his life taken up residence here. And now, when at last the other estates had been put upon a paying basis and he had the opportunity to restore Willowsweep to its former glory, someone had the sheer audacity to suggest that he abandon the place.

And this nonsense about witches, he thought, chomping on a piece of bacon. It is nothing but balderdash. Whoever writes the notes wishes me to dwell upon something that has nothing at all to do with the real reason they want me gone. Though why witches? Odd, that. What sort of mind would think references to witch-craft would send me running back to Wicken Hall? A mind without much but air floating about in it, that's what sort of mind.

And am I afraid of such a person? he asked himself silently, helping himself to another slice of bacon. Well, if I were afraid of anyone, I expect it would be such a person rather than a gentleman with a quick mind and clear motives. Fools are so much more dangerous. They do never see in advance the consequences of their actions and therefore do the most extraordinary and unexpected things. Bah! he thought then, draining his coffee cup and wiping at his lips with a napkin. I am not inclined to be afraid of genius or fool. If this note writer thinks he will drive me, shuddering, from Willowsweep, he is sorely mistaken.

With a shake of his head and an exasperated sigh, the earl left the table and wandered silently down the corridor to the Gold Saloon to open the draperies there and uncover Lord Nightingale's cage. It had quickly become a habit with him to visit the parrot directly after break-fast, endure Nightingale's raucous early morning greet-ings and play with the creature a bit before taking himself off to tend to the sheep and the cattle and work on whatever appeared most in need of his attention that day. Jenkins, this morning, depended upon this new habit and, no sooner did he hear Lord Nightingale's first screech of the morning, than he seized the crumpled note from off the breakfast table, smoothed it out, read it, then folded it in quarters and placed it into his coat pocket. Muttering, the butler collected the dirtied china and carried it down to the kitchen, then made his way quietly up the servants' staircase to the second floor and scratched softly on one of the bedchamber doors.

Serendipity would never have heard him at all had she not been unable to sleep through the night and so arisen with the sun, dressed and opened her door to descend to the breakfast room in hopes that, since the earl apparently always arose early, something might be had to munch upon at this hour. As it was, she had barely opened her door when she caught the sound of Jenkins scratching upon Eugenia's.

Whatever has happened? she wondered. Why should the butler attempt to awaken Eugenia at such an hour? Visions of an accident involving Lord Wickenshire flitted through her mind, but then, would not Jenkins be scratching upon Lady Wickenshire's door? Serendipity allowed her door to swing closed until it left her the merest crack to peer through. She held her breath, waiting to see if Eugenia would, indeed, answer Jenkins's summons, and hoping to hear what conversation would take place.

I am being perfectly outrageous, she thought. Eavesdropping! And on my best friend—a friend who saved me when I thought I should be thoroughly lost. But there is something very odd going on with Eugenia. Something very odd, indeed, or she would not have been hiding in the stables in the middle of the night. Nor would there have been a man making his way in her direction either. I did interrupt a tryst. I am positive of it, let Eugenia deny it all she may. Jenkins? Sera thought then, her mouth rounding into a tiny O. Eugenia and Jenkins? No, that is perfectly ridiculous. Why, he is old enough to be Eugenia's papa.

And then Eugenia's door opened and Eugenia, wrapped in a flannel robe, her hair dangling in a braid from beneath a very pretty ruffled cap, whispered something to Jenkins that Serendipity could not make out. The butler whispered back words equally inaudible. Then his hand went to the pocket of his coat and he handed Eugenia what appeared to be a piece of paper. Whereupon Eugenia smiled and nodded. Then Eugenia closed her door and Jenkins turned back toward the servants' staircase. Serendipity closed her door the rest of the way at once. She stood with her back pressed against the door, a finger to her lips, considering.

As unlikely as it seemed, an obvious alliance had been formed between Eugenia and Jenkins—Serendipity could tell by the manner in which Eugenia had smiled upon the man. But the basis of that alliance—could it truly be love? Had it been a love note or a poem comparing Eugenia to the fairest flower that the butler had slipped into her hand? Serendipity was dying to know. On the floor below, Lord Nightingale continued his raucous greetings to the sun and Wickenshire both, but Serendipity was so very deep in thought that she did not take note of it.

Lord Upton, however, took note of Lord Nightingale's serenade to the morning. The very first screech he heard caused him to sit straight up in bed, dazed with sleep. Petrified by the sound, he attempted to leap from beneath the bedclothes, but his feet became entangled in the sheets and he tumbled straight to the worn rug which a considerate Jenkins had placed beside the bed. Unaware that he had clunked his chin hard enough to make himself bite his lip, he hastily gained his footing and in oversized nightshirt and stocking-tailed nightcap, not taking even a moment to draw on the knitted slippers that Wickenshire had loaned him, fled from his chamber and down the corridor, bursting into Spelling's room with such energy that he sent Spelling's bedchamber door crashing against the wall.

Spelling leaped up in bed, much as Upton had just done, and stared at the apparition before him. "Great gawd, Upton! What has happened? There is blood dribbling down your chin."

"People are being murdered," Upton cried excitedly. "Murdered in their beds, Spelling! Hurry, we must get out of here at once. It will not take the villains long to reach this floor and then we shall be in for it!"

"People murdered in their beds? What the devil makes you think—oh, that," said Spelling, rubbing at his nose. "For a moment I wondered if you were moonstruck, Upton."

"Do not just sit there refining upon the thing, Spelling! Up! Up! We must get out at once. Run to the stables, perhaps. There are places to hide in stables—yes, and weapons to be had in them as well. And the coachmen will protect—no, the coachmen are not in the stables, they are apartmented upon the floor below us, are they not? Devil, but this house is ill arranged, ain't it? The coachmen will be dead shortly, I expect, have they not already heard the ruckus. The villains will surprise them in their sleep."

"Do you even know that your lip is bleeding, Upton? Claret leaking down your chin. Got it all over Nicky's nightshirt, too."

"There! There!" shrieked Upton, jumping forward at another screech from Lord Nightingale and tearing the bedclothes off of Mr. Spelling's bed. "Another. They have got another victim!"

Spelling could not bear it. He fell back upon the pillows and roared with laughter. Then he sat up again, looked Upton over from head to toe, pointed one long finger at him and fell back amidst gales of laughter once more.

"Are you mad?" cried Upton, clutching to him the bedclothes that he had tugged right off of Spelling's bed. "Have you lost your mind, Neil? We have only moments left to save ourselves! Get up! Get up!"

"It—it is—N-n-nightingale," laughed Spelling. "It is the b-bird, Upton. My f-father's p-parrot! Murdered in our sleep! In one of Nicky's houses! I—I—c-cannot stand it!" he shouted and fell into outright whoops, tears rolling down his cheeks.

"Bird?" asked Upton, staring at the bundle of laughter shaking on the bed before him. "Your father's parrot? That—that—shrieking comes from a bird? What is Wickenshire doing to the thing? Cooking it alive?"

"If only he w-would," Spelling replied, his laughter fading at last into snickers. "Unfortunately, he cannot afford to cook the beast—alive or otherwise—and neither can I. Someone has merely uncovered Nightingale's cage, Upton. He shrieks like that every morning. Yes, and every night before he retires, too. You will have been too weary last evening to have heard him."

"Great heavens!"

"You will grow accustomed, I assure you."

"Not I," declared Upton, at last swiping at the blood that flowed from his lip and looking at his reddened fingers in amazement. "A civilized gentleman could never grow accustomed to such a racket as that, not in one hundred years."

SEVEN

"I should think, Neil, that you have seen that wretched bird often enough in your lifetime. Why do you wish to see him again? You never did like Lord Nightingale, not even when you were toddling about in leading strings. Attempted to pull out his tail feathers in those days, if I remember correctly," said Lady Wickenshire, taking Spelling's arm and attempting to steer him into the sun room. "And Lord Upton cannot possibly wish to do more than peek in at him, if he wishes even that. Do you wish that, my lord? Or would you rather not?"

"I—"

"Of course he wishes to see Nightingale," interrupted Spelling. "Near frightened Upton to death this morning. Heard him squawking all the way up on the fourth floor, Aunt Diana. I do not know how you bear the racket."

"He has been very good, really," Lady Wickenshire responded, forsaking her attempt to turn her nephew into the sun room and choosing instead to accompany him to the Gold Saloon. "He only screeches so raucously twice a day. Although I do think that Nicky might have chosen not to uncover him quite so early this morning. I was not at all ready to be awakened."

The pianoforte, as they approached the saloon, was clearly audible. "Miss Bedford plays so beautifully," Lady Wickenshire murmured. "And she has the sweetest contralto. I shall not mind for Lord Nightingale to sing in such a voice as hers."

"Have you heard him sing, Aunt Diana?" Spelling asked uneasily. "Is it her voice exactly?"

"No, no, I have not actually heard Nightingale sing. At least, I do not think so. Though, when one is not in the room, how does one know? Perhaps I have heard him and not realized."

Serendipity was crooning a particularly romantic love song when the three entered the Gold Saloon. Lord Nightingale was perched upon the music rack, his head cocked, listening intently. It was, in fact, the very first time that the macaw had deigned to pay attention since Serendipity had begun his lessons a full week ago. She was so intent upon taking advantage of this unexpected event that she did not notice the opening of the door or the entrance of the trio until Nightingale straightened, fluffed his feathers wildly and cried, "Villain! Yo ho ho! Villain. Bite."

"Stow it," mumbled Spelling at the bird.

"Stow it," mumbled the bird back in a childish voice reminiscent of Spelling's.

"Good afternoon, Miss Bedford," Spelling added then, stepping farther into the room. "We do apologize, Upton and I, for taking quite so long to make an appearance, but there was an accident with our trunks, you know, and it was not until an hour ago that we had anything at all acceptable to wear."

"Stow it," mumbled Nightingale again.

"Was that your voice in which he spoke?" asked Serendipity. "It sounded quite like. Good afternoon, my lord," she added, glancing disdainfully at Upton. "Lady Wickenshire, have you come to see what progress we have made?"

"No, my dear," Lady Wickenshire responded. "I did not intend to disturb you at all this afternoon, but Neil would have it that Lord Upton must make Lord Nightingale's acquaintance."

"Awwk! No! No!" squawked Nightingale, making a great show of flapping his wings wildly.

"Do cease and desist you flea-bitten old sparrow," growled Spelling. "If I have heard you cry 'no!' once, I have heard it sixty-five thousand times. What I wish to do is to hear if you can actually sing."

Lord Upton, his eyes grown quite wide at first sight of Lord Nightingale, wandered slowly toward the pianoforte, pausing only as he came abreast of the bench upon which Serendipity sat. "What an amazing bird. How beautiful he is. You never said he was colored so beautifully, Spelling. My gawd, his feathers are like rubies and emeralds."

"Yes, and his beak is exactly like a pincer. Take your finger clean off if you are not extremely careful."

"Knollsmarmer," Nightingale commented, making his way cautiously with claws and beak from the music rack, down over the keys, into Serendipity's lap and then up onto her shoulder where he seized one short golden curl in his beak and chewed upon it thoughtfully, blinking one large amber eye up at Upton.

Lord Upton, entranced with the vision of charming young woman and gloriously plumed bird before him, reached out with one finger toward Serendipity's curls, delicately touching one at the very nape of Serendipity's neck.

Lady Wickenshire's mouth opened to warn him away; Spelling hissed on a great intake of breath; Serendipity twitched from his unexpected touch, and Lord Nightingale's beak clamped down on the tender place between Upton's thumb and forefinger.

"What business had the man to be touching you at all?" Wickenshire stood so close beside Serendipity at the drawing room window, as his guests gathered before dinner, that her shoulder brushed against his upper arm and sent the most enormous shiver through him. "I am glad that Nightingale bit him."

"No, are you?"

"Yes, I am. And I only wish that Jenkins had not been so very efficient in cleaning their clothing. They would not have dared to appear before you or Eugenia, and we would certainly not have been forced to dine with them until tomorrow at the soonest, if only Jenkins could have thought of some more reasons to delay finishing the job."

"Delay, my lord?"

"Yes. You know. Fiddle about. Pretend it was a much more difficult job to redeem their clothing than it actually was. But there was no horse manure upon the stable floor, actually, and so I suspect Jenkins could not fiddle about forever. I said there was horse manure just to keep Neil from attempting to rescue anything at all."

Serendipity gazed up at him, puzzled. "Horse manure?"

"I—did I say—? I do beg your pardon, Miss Bedford," Wickenshire stammered, embarrassed.

"No, no, I do not mind that you spoke of horse manure."

"You do not?"

"I only wonder what it had to do with your cousin and—Lord Upton—coming down to dinner last evening."

"I did not tell you, did I? No, I did not tell anyone. I remember now. Said something about them being exhausted. But I was quite angry. I knew that you had no wish to see Upton, much less dine with the man. And I was wishing Neil to the devil for bringing him here. And so—well—"

Wickenshire, running a finger self-consciously around the inside of his collar, confessed to her how he and Jenkins had joined in a conspiracy to keep Spelling and Upton from table the evening before. Serendipity's wide blue eyes refused to look anywhere else but directly into his and the more he confessed, the wider they grew and the more they bubbled with glee.

"Oh, but you are a rascal, my lord," she said when he had finished. "A veritable prankster. A scamp."

"Yes, I know," sighed Wickenshire. "Most improper of me. Still, I did not invite them to Willowsweep. Neil is the devil of a villain sometimes. I do not want him lolling about when I am so busy that I cannot keep an eye on him."

"You do not think your cousin dangerous, my lord?"

"No. But there is no telling what nonsense he will get into with no one to entertain him properly. The more I think on it, the more I am certain that someone told Upton that you and Delight had come here and Upton convinced Neil to introduce him into this house because of it."

"But why would Lord Upton do such a thing? He wanted us gone. I am certain he did. Gone from Upton Manor, and gone from Upton House in London as well."

"Well, perhaps I am wrong. But I want them gone from here all the same. And if that scoundrel Upton ever touches you again, I hope Nightingale bites his whole hand right off from his wrist."

When the dinner bell rang, Wickenshire offered Serendipity his arm, clasped hands with Delight and escorted them both to the dining room, leaving Spelling to escort Lady Wickenshire and Upton, Eugenia. He then disrupted the entire order of the table by insisting that Serendipity sit upon his right and Delight upon his left. He then encouraged Eugenia to move up, forcing Upton to sit far down the table, despite his title.

"You do not mind, do you, Upton?" Wickenshire drawled. "Not formal in this house. Sit any which way."

Serendipity could not help but see the disbelief in Lady Wickenshire's eyes at her son's rearrangement of the places. "Most informal affair, dinner in the country," the dowager managed to say cheerfully, despite a perplexed frown. "You Londoners are not accustomed to such, I fear."

"Informal, indeed," Upton replied. "That is why such

a young thing as Miss Delight is present, eh? In my day, young lady," he said with an intimidating glare at the girl, "children knew their places and ate their meals in the schoolroom."

"Cannot eat in the schoolroom, Upton. You are sleeping in it at present," offered Wickenshire. "And Neil has the nursery."

"What? You have put them on the fourth floor? Nicky, how could you!" Lady Wickenshire gasped.

"A matter of chimneys, Mama. They will be safe there for now, I assure you," he added with a teasing gleam in his eyes.

On the fourth floor? Serendipity came near to gasping herself. On the fourth floor? And "they will be safe there for now"? There was danger, then, in that place of boarded-up windows? There must be. The earl would not attempt to reassure his mama of the gentlemen's safety else.

The gentlemen did not linger long over their brandy but followed the ladies to the drawing room almost immediately. "Where has Miss Bedford gone?" asked Upton, raising his quizzing glass to his eye and peering about the room. "Do not tell me she has developed the headache."

"Not at all, my lord," Eugenia responded, staring uneasily at her shoes. "She has gone to tuck Delight into bed. The poor child spent the entire day with Nicky and is quite exhausted."

"Spent the day with your cousin?" Upton strolled to the faded red sopha upon which Eugenia sat and settled down beside her. "In the fields, do you mean? What an odd thing for him to do, to take a child with him, and a female child at that."

"He is teaching her to ride," Eugenia offered, the closeness of Lord Upton causing the skin on her arms to prickle in the most annoying manner. "And I do believe he is teaching her to fish as well, for Cook had six nice trout in the kitchen earlier and said that Nicky had brought them."

"There is a stream on the property?"

Eugenia moved farther away from the man under the pretense of straightening her gown. She did wish he had not chosen to sit down beside her. She was not good at conversing with gentlemen. Not at all. "A rather wide stream," she murmured, staring at her slippers. "And we are a deal closer to the ocean than Aunt Diana likes to admit. One may walk to the ocean along the stream in little more than two hours. I have not done so since I was a child. It was the only other time I came to Willowsweep."

"Should you like to do it again, Miss Chastain?"

"Yes, but I do not think it possible now. It would most likely take me forever. I had two equally good legs then."

"Perhaps it would take a bit longer, that is all," said Upton, smiling benignly upon her. "And a gentleman is seldom in a hurry when he wanders along beside a stream with a young lady. Will you stroll with me to the ocean one day? I should like it above all things. We will take Spelling and Miss Bedford with us, of course. And a picnic lunch perhaps."

Eugenia could not think why this splendid-looking gentleman would propose such an outing to her. Any number of times in her life she had dreamed of strolling along beside a stream on the arm of a handsome gentleman. It would be so romantic.

Oh, I am a fool, she thought then. No gentleman with a title and a face such as Lord Upton's wishes to accompany me anywhere. It is all balderdash. "Sera," she cried abruptly as Serendipity returned to the room, "come and speak with me a moment. You will pardon us, will you not, my lord?"

"Indeed," nodded Upton, rising as Eugenia stood and then sinking back onto the couch as she crossed the room to take Serendipity's arm and tug her away toward the French doors.

"Upton, what the devil are you doing?" hissed Spelling, taking the seat that Eugenia had abandoned. "You came here to lay claim to Miss Bedford, not to dally with my cousin."

"Would you be terribly upset if I dallied just a bit with Miss Chastain, Spelling?"

"Yes."

Upton's eyebrow cocked. "You would?"

"Yes. Do you play fast and loose with Eugenia, Nicky will likely kill you and then me just for bringing you near her."

"No. I cannot believe such a thing of—the country squire," snickered Upton. "I doubt Wickenshire has ever seen a dueling pistol, much less handled one."

"He may look the country squire and act the farmer, Upton, but Nicky is an earl, for all that. And he don't require a pistol. Do you play fast and loose with Eugenia, Nicky will strangle you with those enormous, callused hands of his and then cut my heart out with a kitchen knife."

Upton laughed. "What will he do to me, do you think, should I practice my wiles upon Miss Bedford?"

"I should not practice too many wiles upon her, Upton, while she is in Nicky's charge. Just enough to get her to trust you so that you can lure her back to London. Apparently she is Nicky's guest—well, Eugenia's guest—and not an employee at all."

It was a distinct oddity that two young gentlemen should be deep in conversation upon a sopha, and two young ladies on the opposite side of the room involved in a private conversation of their own. Lady Wickenshire could not help but remark upon it to her son.

"Yes, well, I expect it is because I am a poor host, Mama. If I were not, we should all be doing something together at the moment."

"Perhaps, but it is still very odd. I mean to say, it is

generally expected that ladies and gentlemen should come together after dinner, not divide themselves."

The Earl of Wickenshire propped his feet upon the small, square table in the Gold Saloon and leaned back, tilting his chair up on two legs to do so. It was an old, raggedy-looking chair, and once its covering had most likely been gold. Now it appeared a dirty tan with brown stains here and there.

"Many more enjoyable evenings like this and I shall just go out and hang myself," Wickenshire grumbled, lighting a cigarillo.

"Yardarm," offered Nightingale, playing upon the chandelier.

"No, I cannot hang myself from a yardarm, Nightingale. I do not have one of those. A tree will have to do."

"Knollsmarmer."

"And what are you doing up there, by the way? You have no business to be dangling upside down from the chandelier. You ought to be safely tucked away in your cage."

"Knollsmarmer."

"Yes, yes, knollsmarmer. Look what you have done, you goose. You have pulled every one of those candle stubs out from my chandelier and tossed them on the floor. Thank goodness none of them were lighted. Jenkins will have your head when he sees the mess you have made. Come down here at once, you sorry excuse for a pigeon."

Wickenshire could not have been more surprised. Nightingale pulled himself upright upon the chandelier, shook himself thoroughly and then took flight, soaring once around the room and coming to rest on the earl's lazily extended legs.

"By George, you did!" Wickenshire exclaimed.

"Come," declared Nightingale with what Wickenshire judged to be a rightful pride. And then the earl's eyes widened considerably as the parrot, with pigeon-toed steps, shuffled up his legs and came to stand boldly in his lap. Nightingale bobbed his head a number of times, stretched out one clawed foot to play with a button upon Wickenshire's waistcoat and made a most complacent burring sound, as though he were a very contented cat.

Cautiously, Wickenshire moved the side of his hand toward Lord Nightingale and in a moment was lightly stroking his breast feathers. "Do you know, Nightingale, I should like to have had a pet when I was a boy so that I would know better how to deal with you. I do hope Miss Bedford can teach you to sing. If I had Aunt Winifred's money I would be able to—it would not be unseemly of me to—Miss Bedford, you see, is most charming and—"

Wickenshire took another puff upon his cigarillo, blowing the smoke up into the air in perfect rings. "You like Miss Bedford, do you not, old fellow? Yes, well, so do I. It is too bad that she should have been forced out into the world to seek a position. But it is lucky for us that she was, Nightingale, or you and I would be muddling about, both of us attempting to learn to sing. And we should not have had one hope of succeeding at it."

Nightingale, having enough of Wickenshire's stroking, climbed on the earl's hand, waddled up his arm as far as his waistcoat pocket, and began to poke around in it with his beak.

Wickenshire laughed. "Yes, there is something in there for you. Can you not get a proper hold of it? Do cease poking at me, Nightingale. It tickles."

The parrot, after a few more pushings and proddings, tugged a pine nut from the pocket and, securing his hold upon it, made his way farther up Wickenshire's arm to his shoulder, where he perched and ate the treat and then nibbled at Wickenshire's collar. "Knollsmarmer," he said, nudging the earl's ear. "Knollsmarmer. See."

Wickenshire chuckled. "No, I do not see. Knollsmarmer is not a word, you devil. I am quite certain it is not."

The more Serendipity pondered over Mr. Henry Wiggins, the more undecided she became. Have I been mistaken about the man all along? she wondered as she rang the bell for Bessie. Did I misinterpret his enthusiasm for the gaining of a title as callousness and cruelty toward Delight and myself?

It certainly appears as though he is doing his best to be gracious and affable, she thought, removing her slippers. And even Lord Wickenshire believes that he set out to discover our whereabouts and then followed us here. Why would he follow us all the way to Willowsweep if he wished us out of his life? And he did not once remark upon Delight's birthmark. He did not put up the least fuss over sitting lower at table than he ought, either. And he suggested to Eugenia a stroll along a stream and a picnic lunch. Oh, but Eugenia would enjoy to stroll with such a handsome man as he is. If only she were not so very self-conscious around gentlemen.

I did not once imagine that Henry Wiggins would have grown into such a handsome gentleman as he has, Sera mused, as Bessie undid the buttons at the back of her gown. I remember him only as an awkward, spotty-faced lad with abominable manners. But I was little more than an infant at the time. Perhaps he was not at all what I perceived him to be. Perhaps he is not what I perceive him to be now. "Can I have misunderstood his recent actions?" she murmured, tying her robe about her and sitting down before a little vanity table to brush her hair.

"Pardon, Miss Sera?"

"Nothing. Nothing, Bessie. Merely thinking aloud. Bessie, are you comfortable here? I mean, the other servants, are they pleasant to you?"

"Indeed, miss," nodded the abigail. "There are only

Mr. Jenkins and Cook and John Coachman and Bobby Tripp who live on the premises. They are all most kind. And I do not mind to help out, you know, when they are hard-pressed to get something done. I am learning a good deal by doing so."

"You are helping them out, Bessie?"

"Oh, yes, miss. Why, only today I have dusted the drawing room and polished the silver for tonight's dinner, and helped to churn butter."

"Goodness."

"And tomorrow I am to help make ice cream, because His Lordship loves ice cream."

"He does?"

"Indeed. Cook says he loves it so very much that he hired five men from the village this very January to go out and cut ice from the stream and fill up the ice house. There has not been ice in the ice house at Willowsweep for twenty years, Cook says, but it is full now. Do you require anything more, miss?"

"No. You may go, Bessie. I shall just peek in on Delight and perhaps read a bit before I retire. Have you enough light in the servants' quarters to read? Should you like a book? I have brought *The Mystery of Land's End* with me and I have finished the first volume."

"Everyone has one oil lamp and five candles in their chambers, miss," Bessie announced proudly. "But we must be very careful, Mr. Jenkins says, not to take advantage, because His Lordship cannot afford to be always paying for candles and oil for the hired help. His Lordship is not rich, you know, miss. His papa died and left him and Her Ladyship with nothing but falling-down old houses and mortgages and debts."

"His Lordship is poor, Bessie?"

"Oh, yes, miss. He be poor as a church mouse. Will that be all, miss?"

"Yes, Bessie. You do not want the first volume?"

"Perhaps tomorrow night, miss. Sleep well."

"And you, Bessie," Serendipity murmured as the abigail took her leave.

Well, and I knew His Lordship was not rich as Croesus, but poor as a church mouse? Serendipity abandoned the vanity and wandered aimlessly around the room. This estate is certainly in sad shape, but I thought it to be just one of many houses and a long abandoned one at that. His mama speaks of new furniture and carpeting and paint and polish. Lady Wickenshire does not sound like someone who must watch every penny. But Lord Wickenshire does a great deal of work which a lord ought not to do. Delight has even helped him to drive the sheep out of the meadow and into their pens. And his hands are so very worn and callused like a common laborer's.

"Oh, my goodness!" Serendipity exclaimed aloud. "Eugenia has caused me to impose myself upon a gentleman who cannot afford the meager services I offer him, much less afford to take Delight and Bessie and myself into his home and feed us at his own table." Wringing her hands together, Serendipity began to look closely at the ancient furnishings of her chamber.

"Surely the salary he promised me will come from pockets that are very close to empty," she remarked to herself, touching the worn doily which covered her washstand and feeling tears mount to her eyes.

"Every crust of bread and slice of pigeon pie that we consume places Lord Wickenshire in more and more pressing circumstances!" she told herself, noting for the very first time that the wallpaper in her chamber was badly faded.

"I cannot in good conscience allow it to continue. Surely I have been mistaken about Lord Upton. I will ask him first thing in the morning if he will take Delight and me into his keeping." Serendipity settled down upon the window seat and stared out into the night.

"Then I will explain to Lord Wickenshire how I allowed my imagination to run away with me and say that

I am not truly in need of his protection, nor have I any reason to continue on in my present position, and I will cease to take the very food from his mouth at once," she sobbed quietly.

EIGHT

Upton could not believe his luck. He eyed the young woman who stood with her back to him in the morning room with some suspicion. "You would consider abiding in London with me, Miss Bedford? Truly? But that is wonderful! When I discovered that you had left Upton House, I knew that I had somehow given you a very wrong impression. You assumed that I had no intention to take any responsibility for your welfare, did you not?"

Serendipity, her gaze fastened upon a joyous Delight cavorting about the lawn, playing Catch as Catch Can with Bessie, nodded. "I could not think otherwise, my lord, at the time."

"No. I see now that I gave you no reason to think otherwise. I was so absorbed in the business of being approved your father's heir, so very concerned with myself, Miss Bedford—I am ashamed to think how irresponsible, even cruel, I must have appeared in my letters to you. I pray you will forgive me."

"Yes, I do forgive you," murmured Serendipity, though her heart ached at the thought of leaving Willowsweep. But she could not remain. She could not take the last morsel of bread right out of Lord Wickenshire's mouth while he actually paid her a salary to do so.

"We shall begin anew, Miss Bedford," drawled Upton unctuously. "I will hire a governess for Delight, my Aunt

Mary will come to London to provide us propriety and we shall all get on famously as a family ought."

"Your Aunt Mary?" Serendipity asked, turning from the window to face him. "I have never heard Papa speak of a Mary."

"My mother's sister. She is alone in the world and has only myself for family. She will be glad of a young lady and a child to take up her free hours, believe me."

Serendipity studied the gentleman closely and noted a most satisfied gleam in his wonderful blue eyes. She thought how mistaken she must have been about him. Really, her imagination was not at all to be trusted. Surely Lord Upton could not speak so, of family and a governess and beginning anew, and yet be the unfeeling ogre she had imagined him to be. She had misunderstood his letters. He had requested that she and Delight depart Upton Manor before his arrival and suggested that they remove to the London town house. He had said that he would come to London himself, in time.

And then he had mentioned that a bachelor's establishment was not the place for two young females to reside, that such an arrangement could ruin all of their reputations. He had not mentioned calling upon his Aunt Mary to remedy the situation, nor suggested that the four of them form a proper family.

But perhaps he thought I would deduce just that—that an older woman must come to reside with us to uphold propriety, Serendipity thought. He did not write so, but perhaps he merely assumed that I—

"I shall speak to Lord Wickenshire this evening," she began.

"To Wickenshire? But I thought you to be Miss Chastain's guest."

"Oh. Yes." Serendipity had almost forgotten that little bouncer. "Certainly I will inform Eugenia. But I must inform Lord Wickenshire as well. He has come to depend upon me, you see, to teach Lord Nightingale to sing and . . . We may depart by Monday next, may we not?"

Upton had all he could do to keep from rubbing his hands together in gleeful satisfaction. Monday next. Splendid that the chit should wish to abandon this place so soon. He had expected it to take a great deal more time to ingratiate himself with her. He had been prepared to draw Eugenia Chastain fully under his spell—which he had not the least doubt that he *could* do—and then depend upon that young woman to lead Serendipity into his eager and vengeful arms. Now, a fictitious affair with that crippled Plain Jane would prove completely unnecessary.

"We will not remain beyond Monday next?" Serendipity asked again, to be sure.

"I cannot be certain, Miss Bedford. May I call you Sera, do you think? We are third cousins, after all, and you shall be living under my protection."

Serendipity nodded.

"I thank you, m'dear. And you must call me Henry. However, since I arrived with Mr. Spelling, we must abide by his wishes in the matter of departure. You do understand? I have not brought my own coach and so must depend upon his. He may feel Monday next a bit too soon to curtail his visit with his cousin."

"You do not understand, Henry," Serendipity whispered hoarsely. "We can none of us remain much longer. We are all of us a burden to His Lordship. He—well—the thing of it is, he cannot afford to have us linger."

"Not afford to have us linger?"

"Just so. He is poor as a church mouse. And though he does not say a word about it, certainly so many extra mouths to feed must be a great strain upon him. I am amazed that Mr. Spelling does not realize. Lord Wickenshire has kept Eugenia and Lady Wickenshire quite in the dark, I think, because he does not wish to upset them. But the servants all know, and Mr. Spelling ought certainly to be made aware of the earl's situation."

Poor as a church mouse? Upton mulled the phrase over in his mind. Poor as a church mouse? The Earl of Wickenshire? "I shall speak with Spelling about it," he said at last. "And if such *is* the case, well, Neil has the Midas touch much as his father had. He will not discover his cousin to be in deep waters and do nothing, I assure you. Just as I wish to do in regard to yourself and your sister, Spelling will wish to do everything he can to lend aid to the earl. I am certain of it."

Doing it a bit too brown, thought Upton then. Still, it cannot do my case any harm to represent Spelling as a kind and generous man. She knows we are bosom bows. She will believe me to be kind and generous, as well.

"Oh, would you truly? Speak to Mr. Spelling?"

"Of course, m'dear. Pleased to do it."

"Poor as a church mouse?" Spelling's eyebrow cocked considerably at Upton as they lounged in Spelling's chamber before going down to dinner that evening. "Nicky?"

"So she says. She wishes to depart this place with us on Monday next so as to relieve him of the necessity to put food in our mouths."

"She wishes to leave *with us?*"

"Yes. I told you, Spelling. Were you not listening? She has come to see that I am not the ogre she imagined me to be."

"Bosh! You are exactly the ogre she imagined you to be. Nicky may have been poor as a church mouse once, but he is not so any longer. True, he must economize, for there are still debts outstanding, I believe, but he has got the properties turned about and running upon a paying basis now except for this one. And he will succeed with this one, too."

"Well, someone has told Miss Serendipity Bedford that Wickenshire is poor as a church mouse, someone whom the chit believes. And apparently I was so very charming last evening that all her fears of me have been allayed. I expect it was my invitation to Miss Chastain to stroll with me to the ocean that did the thing up properly. A stroke of genius, that! Pondered it; thought it might prove suspicious; but as you see . . . May the four of us depart upon Monday next, Spelling? Now that she thinks Wickenshire poor and has decided to place her faith in me instead of him, I should hate to deny myself her companionship any longer than necessary. The sooner I break her and that ugly little thing she calls a sister to my will, the sooner I will fully enjoy my new position. Monday next is not too soon?"

Spelling leaned back in the only comfortable chair in his chamber and made a steeple of his hands. Then he began to tap his fingers together. "I dare say," he murmured, "that with your help, Upton, I might— What the devil was that?" he exclaimed at the sound of a crash, followed by another and then another.

"Something falling," Upton replied, looking about him nervously.

"What? The entire roof?" Spelling stood and crossed to the door, tugged it open and peered into the adjoining chamber. "Not in here. You did not have something stacked awkwardly in your chamber, Upton?"

"No, but I did have a roof," Lord Upton commented sardonically. "I had best go check on it."

Spelling snatched up a brace of candles and together they strolled out into the corridor and down the permanently dark passage to Upton's chamber.

"Why the devil does not Nicky unboard these windows?" muttered Spelling. "It is like living in eternal night up here."

"Taxes," snickered Upton, gazing about his quarters.

"Yes, well, it does make him sound as though he hasn't a farthing to his name. Everything looks all right in here, don't it? Nothing out of place. Ceiling appears to be still on the ceiling and not on the floor."

"Well, something fell, and it fell somewhere close by," frowned Upton.

"Or someone," grinned Spelling gleefully.

"Someone? What? Tripped over something and

brought part of the house down with him? Such a racket as that was not made by somebody tumbling to the floor."

"No, but perhaps . . ."

"Perhaps what, Spelling? Spill it. You are looking a deal like the cat who swallowed the budgie."

"I have just remembered a tale m'father told me years and years ago. About why Nicky's papa did never stay at Willowsweep beyond a se'night in all his life."

"He feared the house would fall down around his ears?"

"No, Upton. Because of the witch."

"The witch? Oh, come now, Spelling. The witch?"

"The Witch of Willowsweep," Spelling intoned dramatically. "Elaina Maria Chastain. Wife of the younger brother of the second Earl of Wickenshire. Built them this place to live in, the second earl did, because the woman frightened the devil out of him. There is likely a portrait of her about."

"Love to see it," grinned Upton. "Sounds like a woman after my own heart."

Jenkins wiped the sweat from his brow with his handkerchief and exhaled at the sound of the gentlemen's boot heels echoing off down the corridor. Of all things, to trip over his own feet and lose the candle and send the pile of boxes tumbling to the floor right in the midst of their conversation. Well, thank gawd the boxes had ceased to fall before Mr. Neil and his wretched cohort had come dashing into the schoolroom or they would have discovered him and the long-abandoned servants' passageway which wandered hither and thither between the ancient walls. The old entranceways, though not obvious, could easily be recognized amongst the wall panels if one knew to look for them.

Breathing a bit easier, Jenkins stooped down to feel about for the candle he had lost. At last finding the thing, he struggled with his flint and tinderbox in the darkness, muttering to himself for a full three minutes until he had got the candle lit again. Then, very cautiously, he began to restack the wooden boxes one by one.

Really, he ought never to have been forced into such a position. The need to go rambling about in dead black spaces filled with cobwebs and who knew what else, disgusted him. Still, he was glad that he had been in just that place at just that time, because he had—without ever planning to do so—overheard the most interesting tidbit.

Break Miss Bedford and little Miss Delight to my will, Lord Upton had said. Jenkins frowned. I do not know precisely what he meant by it, but I am not stupid, he thought. His plans for those young ladies are not good. Not good at all. His Lordship must be told.

He did wish that he had heard more of the conversation, but he had come only to locate a particular jewelry box that Her Ladyship remembered had been stored away somewhere. It had not been in the attic, and Jenkins had remembered the stacked boxes at the top of the staircase.

With the jewelry box in hand, Jenkins made his way back through the silent and virtually unused passageways that honeycombed the ancient house until he arrived at the subtly disguised panel in the butler's pantry, where he stepped out into daylight again. It did prey upon his mind to have overheard even that particularly important tidbit of someone else's conversation. Jenkins was not fond of those who sneaked about and spied upon people. Still, eavesdropping was a minor thing compared to the situation he had found himself involved in since January, and so he shrugged his shoulders and determined not to tell his employer how he had come by the knowledge concerning Lord Upton, only to inform him of the gentleman's words.

"He will believe what I say. I have looked after that boy since his birth. He always believes what I say. If only he would take heed of those notes he receives, as well, and leave this place," Jenkins told himself quietly, wiping the dust from the jewelry box. "It cannot matter if Willowsweep falls to ruin for a bit longer. It is his pride, merely, keeps him here. If only he would take the parrot to Wicken Hall and teach the bird to sing there, everything would be all right again."

Jenkins truly did wish for the earl to inherit the monies his Aunt Winifred had left behind her and would have sat with Lord Nightingale day and night himself to teach the bird a song. "And if Miss Bedford leaves us, I may well be called upon to do just that," he whispered to himself. "But she will not leave us. Once I tell His Lordship what I have overheard, Miss Bedford will not be going anywhere with this Lord Upton fellow."

"She thinks that I am what?" Wickenshire ceased to tie his neckcloth and stared at Jenkins's reflection in the looking glass with undisguised amazement. "Where the devil did Miss Bedford get such an idea as that? Do we not have food upon our table and clothes upon our backs, Jenkins?"

"Indeed, my lord."

"Yes. And if Mama does not dress in the very height of fashion, her dresses are not shiny from wear or so outdated as to be embarrassing, are they?"

"No, my lord."

"No. And my shirts are not turned at the cuffs and collars or my breeches patched at the knee?"

"Certainly not, my lord," Jenkins concurred heartily, though he did pause a moment before doing so, when, in the first years after the old earl's death, this gentleman's cuffs and collars *had* been turned and his breeches *had* been patched—over and over again.

"Just so," growled Wickenshire. "I am far from poor as the proverbial church mouse and I will tell Miss Bedford so, you may believe that."

"And you will not allow her to—to—"

"Of course not. Though how you should come to over-hear Neil and Upton disclosing such private information as apparently you have, I cannot think, Jenkins. You have not taken to pressing your ear against doors, have you?"

"Never, my lord."

"No, of course not. I apologize for even suggesting it," declared His Lordship. "There is no butler in any-one's employ more proper than you, Jenkins. Confound it, I cannot tie this thing!" he exclaimed abruptly, drop-ping his hands to his hips and scowling at himself in the looking glass, then crossing to his washstand and glaring at a piece of vellum that lay upon it.

"Perhaps it is too ambitious, my lord," murmured Jenkins. "You have never before tied anything but a mail-coach and—"

"I have got these drawings straight from Eugenia's papa," the earl muttered. "And if Uncle Robert can tie an Orientale, so can I. I am thirty years younger at least."

"I dare say, my lord, that age has not much to do with it. Your uncle has a valet, you know, and most likely—"

"No. Markson does not tie Uncle Robert's neckcloths for him, Jenkins. Uncle Robert ties his own. These are diagrams of how he ties an Orientale. I am going to figure it out if it kills me."

"Do not say that, my lord."

"No, I ought not, eh? But I shall tie it, Jenkins, and before dinner, too. I do thank you for the information concerning Miss Bedford and I will deal with it promptly, I assure you. Now, be off. Dinner approaches and you are needed belowstairs, I have no doubt."

Wickenshire watched as his butler departed and then carried the vellum back with him to the looking glass, propped it upon a ladder-back chair, tossed the neckcloth he had already ruined over the open door of the clothes-press and fished out a new one.

It is not that I wish to impress anyone in particular with the intricacies of the knot in my neckcloth, he thought, staring intently into the looking glass. It is simply time that I learn to tie something besides a stupid mailcoach.

"Well, perhaps I do wish to impress someone," he grumbled then, twisting his hands about amongst the cloth in a most ungainly fashion. "But it is highly unlikely that Miss Bedford will take notice. Gads! It is not bad enough that I must appear before her in my work clothes and stutter and stammer to her about sheep and—and—horse manure—and teach her sister to ride astride, but now she thinks me poor as a church mouse, as well! Most likely she will not even come to dinner lest she eat my last crust of bread. No, no, she will come to dinner. She has not failed to come to dinner yet."

With a squint and a muddled curse, Wickenshire peered once again at the vellum and set about, with teeth clenched, to achieve the veriest utmost in fashionable knots.

Serendipity could not be easy. As soon as her own gown was securely fastened, she sent Bessie off to look to Delight, declining her abigail's further assistance. She ran a brush through her short, golden curls, placed the little pearl necklace that had once been her mama's around her neck, tugged on the loveliest pair of white lace gloves and then began to pace. She paced the length of the chamber and then the width of the chamber and then the length of it again. Her heart fluttered in her breast. She felt her cheeks redden and longed for her mama's chicken-skin fan to hide behind.

However will I explain such a hasty departure? she wondered. Though I may convince Lord Wickenshire that Lord Upton is not detestable, what excuse can I give for leaving on such short notice? I cannot say, "my lord, it has come to our attention that you have barely a feather to fly with, and so we can none of us impose upon you any longer." What explanation can I give?

I shall say that Lord Upton has—has—appointments

in Town, she decided. And I will tell him that I do not think that I am the person to teach Lord Nightingale to sing. Oh, he will think me most ungrateful and a featherbrain to boot. Well, but let him think that, then, because I dare not mention his finances. He would be so very embarrassed by that, he would sink, all red and stuttering, right through the floor.

A tiny smile fluttered across Serendipity's face. The poor dear, she thought. He is so very charming when the cat has got his tongue. "He is a dear," she whispered, coming to a standstill, "even when the cat has *not* got his tongue."

Eugenia. What will I tell Eugenia? If Lord Wickenshire has not mentioned his circumstances to her, it is because he does not wish her to know. Certainly it is not my place to— I will tell her that Lord Upton and I have come to an understanding, that I was mistaken about him. I will say that his actions and words of an earlier day are not to be held against him.

"Are they not?" Serendipity murmured then. "Why am I so eager to overlook his earlier callousness? Perhaps I was not mistaken about him. Perhaps *now* I am mistaken about him, and my first impression was the correct one."

Still, he would not propose to bring his aunt to Town to provide propriety if he were not intent upon having us with him, she mused. And he did propose to do just that. I must trust him. Delight and I have nowhere else to go except back to London.

Of course I will trust in him. It was my wicked imagination turned him into a villain and an ogre. My annoying imagination working at a feverish pace. Well, I shall just tell Eugenia that I was mistaken about Lord Upton, have decided to return home in his company and that it is he who wishes to depart by Monday next. Yes, I will tell Eugenia and Lord Wickenshire only that and no more.

Serendipity gave a tiny nod of her head just as the

dinner bell was struck. My goodness, has it grown so late already? she wondered, amazed. She peeked into Delight's room to discover her sister already gone down. With quick steps, Serendipity hurried to the staircase. "But what will I do about Lord Nightingale?" she whispered to herself as she began to descend. "How can I depart when I have not taught that rascal to sing one note?"

Deep in thought, she hurried down the steps and swirled around the newel post at the first floor, her slippers barely touching the worn carpeting. And then she slammed into something solid, something slippery and green and gold. Her slippers were definitely not touching the worn carpeting anymore at all, but flying upward as she gasped. Two arms reached out to save her, but could not, and she landed with a loud *kathump!* right upon her derriere in the middle of a faded rose on the carpet.

"Gads! I am so very sorry!" exclaimed Wickenshire, going down on one knee beside her. "Are you all right, Miss Bedford? When you did not join us in the drawing room, I thought to come and see what could be the matter and— I did attempt to avoid you, but you were rushing so— You were thinking of other things, were you not, because you did not even see me?"

"Y-yes," managed Serendipity with only the merest stutter. "I was th-thinking of something and r-rushing and I did not s-s-see you at-at-at-a-a-all!" To her horror, she burst into tears, right in the middle of the vestibule.

Wickenshire, flustered, scooped her up into his arms as if she were some wandering lamb and carried her into the morning room. He sat down on the window seat, set Serendipity upon his knees and allowed her to cry extensively against the shoulder of his green velvet jacket—the very one that made him look exactly like a frog. He patted her back awkwardly with one large, rough hand and muttered bits of nonsense in her ear. "You do not need to do this, you know," he said at last. "Mama will still give us dinner, even if we are late."

Serendipity gurgled in his arms.

"Truly, Miss Bedford," he continued, encouraged by the gurgle, "Mama rarely boxes anyone's ears for being late to table, nor does she send them to bed without their dinners. At least, she never has done in all my experience, and I have known the lady a goodly number of years."

Serendipity sniffed and gurgled again. "I am n-not crying be-because I am l-late to dinner," she managed, ceasing to lean upon his shoulder and sitting up to look down at him, knuckling the remaining tears from her eyes.

"You are not?" he offered, making his forest green eyes open very wide, pretending disbelief.

"No, and you know very well that I am not," she said with the tiniest grin.

"Yes, 'tis truth. I admit it. You are not hurt from your fall or from knocking into the likes of me? I expect my chest is quite as hard as the floor."

"N-no. I am not hurt at all. I am only—only—sad."

"Why so?"

"B-because Delight and I m-must leave W-Willowsweep."

"Yes, I have heard something about that."

"You have? Oh, Lord Upton must have spoken to you in the drawing room. I did not think—"

"Not Lord Upton in the drawing room. Jenkins in my chambers. He says that you believe me to be poor as a church mouse and that you have changed your opinion of Upton. You have decided to accompany that villain back to London, Jenkins says. But you will not, Miss Bedford."

"I w-will not?"

"Absolutely not. I forbid it."

"You *forbid?*"

"Yes, and if you are about to get your hackles up over that word as Eugenia does, I pray you will not until you hear me out. I am not poor, my dear, and you and Delight and Bessie are not in the least burdensome. And the new Lord Upton is to be trusted just as far as my Cousin Neil is to be trusted—which is about as far as a dog can spit."

NINE

Having dabbed inexpertly at the tracks of her tears with his handkerchief, Wickenshire set Miss Bedford upon her feet, took her hand and led her back out into the corridor and toward the dining room. "Do not fuss, Miss Bedford," he murmured as Serendipity's free hand went to her hair. "You look lovely."

"I do?"

"Like a bright blossom just opening to shimmer its color amidst the morning dew."

"S-sometimes," Serendipity breathed, "you say the most fanciful and perfectly enchanting things."

"Me?"

"Yes. 'A bright blossom just opening to shimmer its color amidst the morning dew.' A perfectly exquisite phrase designed to send a young woman's heart to fluttering."

Wickenshire halted abruptly and stared down at her.

"Do not look so amazed," she giggled. "It is true. There are things you do and say that are so dear and so charming. Well, telling Delight that she was kissed by Glorianna, for instance, and speaking of spring hesitating just beyond our reach, and the entire episode of the magic jonquil. Do you know that that jonquil is still alive and blooming in Delight's room?"

"Ah—yes."

"It *is* you!" Serendipity accused with a wide smile.

"I was not certain. I thought perhaps Mr. Jenkins, or Eugenia, but it is you who does it. I see it in your eyes."

Wickenshire nodded. "Little enough to do for a wee bit of a girl, replace a jonquil every few days."

"But when do you do so?"

"Most often very early in the morning, before she wakes, so that it will be opening to greet the sun just when her eyes are opening to do likewise. Most days I am out and about before the sun has risen. Did it, Miss Bedford?"

Serendipity studied the glorious green of his, oh, so serious eyes. "Did it? What it? I mean—"

"My perfectly exquisite phrase of but a moment ago. Did it set your heart to fluttering?"

Serendipity lowered her gaze. "Yes," she replied very softly, unwilling to deny the truth and yet fearing to acknowledge it aloud. "Yes, it did."

Wickenshire inhaled a bit raggedly, rubbed his hand against the back of his neck, then reached down and took both of Serendipity's hands into his own. "Miss Bedford," he declared, "I give you my word that you and Delight and even your little Bessie are wanted here—needed, in fact. You are none of you a burden to me. I will answer any questions that you wish for me to answer when we have time alone. But until then, I beg you, do not set your mind on leaving Willowsweep. Please, do not."

"Sera, are you not coming in to dinner at all?" asked Delight, skipping out through the dining room door to discover them in the corridor. "We are having lambling pie an' pork puddin' and there is apple tarts for dessert. Apple tarts with clotted cream atop! Oh, *do* come in to dinner. We have gone an' started without you and Nicky, 'cause everyone was terr'ble hungry, but Lady Wickenshire says we mayn't proceed to the apple tarts until the both of you have eaten. Please come," she urged, tugging mightily at her sister's arm and Wickenshire's as well.

* * *

"By George, I had forgotten all about her," Wickenshire said, staring up like the others as his mama tugged the muslin from off the portrait that hung above the mantel in the yet-to-be-so-much-as-dusted back parlor.

"Look, Sera," Delight cried as the portrait came into clear view amidst the several lamps that the group had carried with them. "That lady has been kissed by Glorianna, too!"

"Just so," agreed Wickenshire, gazing at the indication of the wine-red stain that blighted Elaina Maria Chastain's perfectly represented countenance.

"Kissed by whom?" queried Upton. "Whatever is the child talking about?"

"Nothing important, my lord," offered Eugenia directly. "Goodness, but she has the most intimidating eyes. I should dread to have her take me into dislike. What made you think to seek out her portrait, Neil?"

"Invisible ceilings falling."

"What?" Wickenshire's eyebrow cocked considerably. "Do not say the fourth-floor ceilings have come down, Neil. They have not, have they?"

"No, Nicky. Invisible ceilings—or something invisible, at any rate, for we did hear a number of things tumbling about, Upton and I, and went off in search of them. But we found nothing. And so I thought—"

"The work of the Witch of Willowsweep, he told me," finished Upton for him. "And then he invited me to view the lady."

"A witch?" squeaked Delight, her eyes widening and her mouth forming into a tiny O.

Lord Wickenshire was on one knee beside the child before the thought that had pierced Delight's mind even occurred to Serendipity.

"She was never a witch. Do not you believe it, Delight. No one beloved of Glorianna was ever so terrible a thing as a witch. No one Glorianna has kissed can ever be evil."

"What was she then, Nicky?" sneered Neil, knowing

full well that the child feared to be a witch herself because of the similar birthmark. "Tell us, if you please, for I have never heard her called anything but the Witch of Willowsweep."

"She was a well-educated lady forced to deal with heathens," Wickenshire responded, his eyes growing deathly cold. "Much as Delight and I are forced to do at this very moment."

"Boys, cease and desist," the dowager cautioned. "I will not have you squabbling as you were accustomed to do when you were children. Lady Elaina was Nicky's great-great-great—oh, I do forget how many greats, Delight, darling—but she was his auntie. She came all the way to Great Britain from Barcelona to be married to Nicky's very many times great Uncle Chase."

"Yes," nodded Neil, "and when she discovered that the villagers would not bow to her every whim, she burned down the entire village and three of the Willowsweep barns."

"Enough," growled Lord Upton, catching the angry glow in Serendipity's eyes and jabbing an elbow surreptitiously into Spelling's ribs. "Your tales are frightening the child, Neil."

"Oh? Oh!" Spelling remembered in that split second that he had been given the role of kind and generous gentleman and that Upton was depending upon him to perform it—at least until they had got Miss Bedford and her sister back to London. "I do apologize, Miss Delight. I did not intend to frighten you," he said hurriedly. "I was merely quizzing Nicky. He does get so very defensive about his antecedents. Lady Elaina Maria was not a witch at all, really. She was more of a—faery princess."

Delight's gaze wandered from Wickenshire to the portrait to Mr. Spelling and back to Wickenshire again. "I thought she is your Auntie Elaina," she whispered to the earl in a hushed voice.

"Yes."

"Then why does Mr. Spelling call her your Auntie Cedents?"

Eugenia could not contain herself. The Witch of Willowsweep! Why had she not remembered? Why had her papa not remembered either? She wished to seize Jenkins by the arm and whisper it in his ear as he set the tea things before Lady Wickenshire in the drawing room later that evening, but of course, she could not. She settled instead for gazing up at him with what she hoped he would recognize as a most desperate look.

Catching the gaze aimed in his direction, Jenkins cleared his throat and nodded. His cheeks blushed just the tiniest bit, but no one noticed his response at all, except the exultant Eugenia—and Serendipity, who had been watching the silent exchange with mounting apprehension from the very beginning.

Serendipity held her peace all through tea and did not once mention to Eugenia that Mr. Jenkins appeared rather flustered this evening, though she longed to do so. What could be going forward between the two of them? Certainly she now had more reason to suspect an illicit romance, but she could not accept that Eugenia would think to take part in such an unequal alliance. And most assuredly not with such an elderly—

"Miss Bedford?"

The very sound of Wickenshire's voice sent all thoughts of Eugenia and Jenkins flying from Sera's brain.

"Miss Bedford?"

"Yes, my lord?"

"I wondered if you would care to stroll with me through the garden? It is not at all chilly this evening, and the moon is three-quarters full."

"There is a garden?" Serendipity asked, amazed that in all the days she had been at Willowsweep, she had not once noticed it. "Where?"

"At the rear of the house, Miss Bedford, just beyond the terrace."

"There is a terrace?"

Wickenshire's face was crinkling, in the most charming manner, into laughter. Just observing it in progress proved enough to turn Serendipity's mind to mush. What is wrong with me? she wondered. I am asking the stupidest questions.

"Come, Miss Bedford, drink up your tea and I will prove to you that there is a terrace and a garden, though one has been crumbling for years and the other growing wild, without the least check upon it."

"And Eugenia and I shall accompany you, shall we not, Eugenia?" declared Lady Wickenshire promptly.

Eugenia nodded. As much as she wished to meet with Jenkins around one corner or another, she was well aware that her Aunt Diana's sense of propriety would not allow Nicky and Sera to wander off alone. At least if she strolled with her aunt, she could slow their steps enough so that Nicky and Sera might get far enough ahead to hold a private conversation if they desired to do so. And the more Eugenia saw of them together, the more she hoped that they desired to do so.

"Will you join us as well, Neil? Lord Upton?" Lady Wickenshire invited with a smile.

Lord Upton was about to agree to it when a glare from Spelling caused his opening mouth to snap shut.

"No, thank you, Aunt Diana," Mr. Spelling drawled. "Tired. Think I shall take myself off to bed."

"Yes, me too," agreed Upton, puzzled, but taking his lead from Spelling. "Country. Rise early. Not accustomed to it. Wears a fellow out."

"I was hoping to get you alone," said Wickenshire with a sigh as he strolled with Serendipity upon his arm. "But we are far enough ahead of Mama and Eugenia that they will not overhear us, I think."

"No, they are so far behind that they cannot possibly overhear us. How beautiful it is here. The air smells so very wonderful and we are surrounded—"

"—by thickets and thorns and weeds."

"No, truly—"

"Truly, by thickets and thorns and weeds. But it will be a proper garden soon, I promise you, just as Willowsweep will be a proper house. Who told you that I was poor as a church mouse?"

"Bessie. She said that you had not enough servants to do all that must be done about the place, and that she must take care not to use too much lamp oil or too many candles."

"Damnation! I told Jenkins to provide the girl everything she required."

"He did. I am certain that he did, but your servants are apparently very careful of you, my lord. They do not wish to put you to extra expenditures on their behalf. And so Bessie, you know, Bessie came to think that you were very poor, and she told me the same and—and—well, one need only open one's eyes to see that Willowsweep . . ."

Wickenshire nodded. "Willowsweep is in wretched condition. But I have come here, Miss Bedford, to restore it. I have other estates. Two, in fact. And they are quite acceptable. And I have other servants. Mama only brought with her the few she thought necessary to her comfort, because she would join me here, you know. I am not allowed to pass judgment upon the furniture and knickknacks and such. I have dreadful taste."

"But you work on this farm yourself, every day, my lord. With your own two hands and barely a soul to assist you."

"Yes, and my traveling coach is old and my face is brown from the sun and my hands are cut and callused. I will not deny it, Miss Bedford. I am far from rich as Croesus. But I am not poor either. I was once. Pockets entirely to let. But I was merely thirteen then, and had no idea what full pockets were like, so it did not have any great effect upon me."

"Thirteen, my lord?"

"Yes, thirteen when my papa died and the duns descended upon Mama and me. It was a fearful thing, Miss Bedford, the day I took the title Earl of Wickenshire. I thought never to be able to replace all that my papa had destroyed. But I have done a splendid job of it so far. I am good at farming, even better at building and repairing. And best, Miss Bedford, at budgeting. Not only can I afford to hire you to teach Lord Nightingale to sing, and provide you and Delight and Bessie chambers in my house and places at my table, I dare say that I could even afford to hire myself a valet if I thought I had need of one."

"You are not putting on a brave face, are you?"

"Not at all. But I will tell you something I ought to have told you when first you came. If you can teach Lord Nightingale to sing, if he sings a song for a small gathering on the first of June, I shall inherit near three hundred thousand pounds from my Aunt Winifred's will."

Serendipity's jaw dropped.

"Just so, Miss Bedford. That will pay off every remaining debt and see Willowsweep restored in less than six months. But I will not have a penny of it if Nightingale does not sing. And if you leave me—"

"I will not go," Serendipity declared emphatically. "I will not leave Willowsweep until Lord Nightingale sings like a diva, my lord. I give you my word."

"We cannot possibly do it now!" Upton exclaimed hoarsely. "It is practically the middle of the night, Spelling!"

"What better time to abduct the wretched bird?"

"Yes, but what are we to do with it? You have already

said that we cannot wring its nasty neck. It will raise a ruckus and the entire household will be upon us."

"Most of the household, Upton, happen to be strolling about the garden at the moment."

"The servants—"

"Are occupied in the kitchen, banging pots and pans about. And besides, they have grown accustomed to Nightingale screeching and squawking at this hour of the night. If they take note at all, they will think it is merely his usual ruckus."

"Still, we must have a place to stow the thing where it will not be found and—"

Spelling shot his cuffs in exasperation. "Why do you think I have spent most of my time here out riding about the place, eh, Upton?"

"Because you cannot abide to remain inside this wretched house and do not hesitate to let it be known."

"Well, there is that. But no, I have been searching for a place to stow the blasted bird. And I have discovered just the spot, too. You do wish to take Miss Bedford off to London by Monday next, do you not? Well, we cannot do that if the bird disappears on Sunday night. Everyone will suspect us then. But this way, we shall be present to offer our aid in the search for Nightingale. We will search high and low for a few days before we even propose to give up on the thing and take our leave."

"Yes, but, you do not wish for the bird to die, Spelling. You cannot simply stuff it into some cave or something and then drive off to London and abandon it. The thing is complicated. You ought to ponder it a bit more, I think."

"No, we must seize upon the opportunity provided us," Spelling declared. "Which I intend to do, and you had best help me to do it, too, Upton. I will spill my guts to Miss Bedford about your plans for her else."

"You would never!"

Spelling, his patience wearing thin, took Upton's arm

and propelled him from the drawing room, down the corridor, straight into the Gold Saloon.

"Rascally villain!" Lord Nightingale squawked in greeting from the very top of the chandelier.

"Yes, good evening to you, too, featherbrain," Spelling drawled in response. "Look what I have brought you, Nightingale. You cannot see it properly from up there. Come down and take a closer look. Go and sit over there, Upton. He will not come with you all poised to pounce upon him."

"I am *not* poised to pounce upon him."

"No, but he don't know that. Go. Sit. Look, Nightingale. Almonds. I brought you almonds all the time when I was a lad," Spelling continued in a voice that came close to a coo as he lowered himself into the chair that Wickenshire generally occupied. "Always hoped you would choke on them. Come on, you rascally villain, you know me. Come down and take one or two."

Lord Nightingale cocked his head. Lord Nightingale ruffled every one of his feathers. Lord Nightingale lifted one foot from the chandelier; then he lowered it and raised the other. He stretched his neck downward at an angle to gain a closer view of the nuts resting in Spelling's open palm; then he straightened to his greatest height and flapped his wings, sending the dangling crystals upon the chandelier to shaking and shimmering.

"Come on, sweet Nightingale. That's a good old boy. Come to Neil and have an almond or two, eh?"

Upton jumped straight up out of his chair as, with one flap of the great wings, the parrot soared low over his head and across the room to alight on Spelling's shoulder. With a nod and a shuffle, the macaw sidled down Spelling's arm to take a closer look at the intriguing Indian nuts.

"While you are up, Upton," droned Spelling quietly, "divest yourself of your coat, will you?"

"My—my—coat?"

"Yes, so that once I have got the fiend, we may wrap him up in it. That will keep him quiet."

It occurred to Upton once again that seizing upon this opportunity was an utterly stupid thing to do. Spelling may have discovered a place to keep the bird, but they had not once discussed how to get it out of the house or to that place. "I rather think we ought—" he began.

"Do not think, Upton," Spelling broke in, still in the same calm drone. "Just take off your coat and be ready to wrap it around him when I give you the word."

Lord Nightingale stretched quickly out and seized one of the almonds and scooted all the way up Spelling's arm, hopping onto the chair back, where he proceeded to study the nut carefully, twizzle it about in his beak and at last eat it. "Knollsmarmer," he muttered, fluffing his feathers and eyeing the remaining two almonds resting upon Spelling's open palm. "Sweet bird. Knollsmarmer."

"Yes, sweet bird indeed," drawled Spelling. "Have another. Nothing to fear, Nightingale. Come down and take another."

Upton began to struggle out of his coat, drawing the parrot's attention in his direction. Nightingale squawked and scuttled across the chair back until he was almost hidden behind Spelling's head.

"Do not make such an exhibition of yourself, Upton."

"I am not making an exhibition of myself. I am attempting to do as you asked me. There," he sighed as he slid the coat down one arm and then the other.

"Good. Now just stand still, will you, and cease to be such a great distraction. Come, Nightingale. I know you want another. You are the greediest bird ever born when it comes to almonds."

The parrot remained behind Spelling's head, however, for another three minutes before he thought it safe to make another foray upon the Indian nuts. Then he stepped carefully down Spelling's arm, seized the prize and scooted out of reach.

"Well, you are never going to catch him that way. He will not stay near your hand long enough to—"

"He will stay long enough. He will stay upon this last almond, Upton. He merely wishes to be certain that I intend him no harm."

Spelling proved correct. The third time that the parrot came down his arm, he perched upon Spelling's wrist and twizzled the almond about in his beak without taking one step backward. Spelling brought his other hand around slowly and began to stroke Nightingale's breast feathers. "Good old fellow," he murmured. "You are such a good old fellow." And then he clamped his fingers about Nightingale's legs, shook his wrist free of the parrot's claws and scooped the bird into his lap. "Now, Upton," he called, attempting to cover both of Nightingale's wings with one hand. "Now, damn it! Bring your jacket. Toss it over him."

Lord Nightingale screeched and squawked, flapping one great wing and then the other. His formidable beak poked at the hand clasping his legs until he found the tender skin between Spelling's thumb and forefinger. He grabbed hold of it, biting with considerable force as Upton rushed across the room.

"Ow! Damnation!" Spelling cried, tears mounting to his eyes.

Upton tossed his coat from three feet away. It tumbled down over Spelling's arm, slid from off Nightingale's sleek feathers and dropped to the floor. Spelling sprang to his feet. "Ow! Ouch! Let go, you featherbrain!" he cried, loosing his grip upon the parrot's legs. "Nightingale, do not bite!"

"Awwk! No bite!" squawked the parrot, flapping madly up into the air and soaring about the room in a panic. "No bite. No bite. Awwwk!" He flew upward, touching the ceiling, and downward, soaring like a demon just above the floor. He narrowly avoided a set of chair legs and angled upward again. He turned just short of hitting an old credenza, flapped barely in time to miss

Upton's ducking head. Spelling grabbed at him and he banked left and rose high into the air, turned and came plunging down directly at Spelling, who yelped and ran, taking cover on his knees behind a sopha and dragging Upton with him.

"Bite!" squawked Nightingale. "Bite villain! Bite villain!" And then he was soaring upward again, his right wing barely clipping one of the oil lamps, sending it smashing to the floor.

Oil splattered and hissed as the flame from the wick flickered over it. Flames bubbled across the ancient carpeting and rippled up the legs of Wickenshire's favorite chair. Nightingale continued his flight upward, circling and squawking and screeching. Upton left the cover of the sopha and dove across the room for his coat. Spelling stood, opened the door and then struggled madly to divest himself of his coat. In moments both of them were swatting madly at the flames, fanning them to even greater heights and shouting loudly, "Fire! Fire! Fire!"

TEN

Serendipity was so lost in the glimmering moonlight that caught itself up in Wickenshire's grateful eyes that the first clanging of the great brass bell outside the kitchen door seemed nothing more than an enchanted ringing in her ears. But when Wickenshire's gaze left her at the sound and he muttered, "What the deuce?" she rapidly regained her hold upon reality. Abruptly he placed a kiss upon her nose and then dashed away, not back along the broken cobbled path, but straight across the neglected garden, leaping over bushes and brambles, trampling wildflowers underfoot, his long legs carrying him quickly and surely toward the closest doors to the house—the French doors that opened off the terrace into the sun room.

"Fire!" a voice shouted as the bell clanged again and again. "Fire!" Shadows scurried through the moonlight from the kitchen door, down the hill toward the well house.

"Sera! Hurry! The house is afire!" cried Eugenia, waving frantically at her. The dowager Lady Wickenshire, having lifted her skirts, was already fleeing toward the line of fantastical phantoms forming beneath the glowing moon. "Hurry, Sera!"

"Delight!" Serendipity gasped, lifting her skirts and sprinting to Eugenia's side. "Delight is asleep in her chambers!"

"Nicky will get her," Eugenia declared confidently. "We must help with the water, Sera. It will take all of us—Neil and Upton and their coachman, too—to make a chain long enough to get the buckets from the well to the house! Even that will not be enough. Oh my gawd! There!" she cried as they ran, pointing up to the outline of flames licking at a window near the rear of the building on the first floor.

"We will never get water all the way up there!" Serendipity gasped, stumbling over a broken cobble, but regaining her balance before she fell. "There are not enough people to send the buckets all the way up to the first floor."

"It is the Gold Saloon!" the dowager exclaimed as they drew near. "Girls, quickly, get in the line." And then she did the most extraordinary thing. She lifted her gown as high as her waist and in one great tug, tore her petticoat free of its moorings. Letting her gown fall back, she dunked the undergarment in the bucket she held. She passed the bucket to Eugenia and set off at a run for the house, calling as she ran, "John, Jenkins, Bobby, wet your coats and give them to me!"

In a flash the coachman, the butler and the groom were struggling out of their jackets and soaking them in water and passing them to Her Ladyship as she dashed past them and into the burning building.

In the midst of nightmare, Serendipity imagined her movements sluggish and clumsy, and thought that no matter how she tried, she could not carry the full buckets the space of twenty yards fast enough, nor return the empty buckets at anything but a most lethargic pace. "Hurry, must hurry," she urged herself, gasping for breath as the weight of a full bucket slammed into her hands and then an empty bucket replaced it at the end of her short, frantic journey.

"Sera, there!" cried Eugenia, pausing a moment to point, the weight of the full bucket drawing one of her shoulders lower than the other, the rope handle cutting into her hand.

Serendipity looked up. Lord Wickenshire stood at the kitchen door, Delight in his arms. He set the child down and spoke in her ear and placed the bell rope into Delight's tiny hands. He disappeared and returned, depositing Bessie upon the doorstep from which she fled with alacrity into a position in the line. Then he snatched up one of the buckets and darted back inside.

The bell rang and rang, its steady, horrible clanging increasing the panic in Serendipity's breast. Why had the earl set Delight to such a task? What good to keep the clamor of the bell alive when all who could be awakened to fight the fire were already fighting it?

Stop, Delight, she thought, her hands smarting from the bucket handles and her legs heavy as lead and her shoulders aching. You only make it worse. You only make the fight appear more futile. The bell cries out that all is lost. All is lost. All is lost.

And then horses raced into Serendipity's view. Men leaped from the bare backs of bays and greys and blacks to fill the enormous gaps in the line. With shouts and slaps, they sent their horses darting out of the way, and of a sudden, the heavy buckets began to come faster, smoother, bouncing into her hands and through them. Going from one to the other in a line where no one was required to labor twenty or thirty or forty yards to deliver up the water to the next person.

"Thank God, Squire Hadley and his men have heard the bell!" Eugenia cried. "Oh, thank God! We shall save Willowsweep now, Sera. I am certain of it."

Hope blossomed inside Serendipity. Of course! His Lordship had set Delight to keep the bell ringing in order to call his closest neighbor to his assistance. Willowsweep was not going to burn to the ground! Squire Hadley and his men were not going to let it! No, they were not and neither was she. She fought her way out of panic, nightmare and despair, and renewed her own efforts, swinging heavy buckets forward, passing empty buckets back, all thought of her aching limbs gone from her.

At last, after what seemed both moments and eternity, flames no longer licked at the first-floor windows. A shout went up from inside the house, followed by cheers from those outside. Serendipity turned, and no bucket met her hand. The fire had been defeated! Willowsweep, smoky and charred in places, still stood. She swiped at the perspiration upon her brow and allowed herself to feel the pain in her shoulders and neck and back once again.

"I have never been so exhausted," sighed Eugenia, setting her empty bucket upside down upon the ground and sitting atop it. "Sera! Your hands are covered in blood!"

"Y-yes. It is from the bucket handles. Yours are bleeding as well, Eugenia. I expect everyone will be in need of soap and water and basilicum."

"Perhaps, but you have ground the lace of your gloves right into your palms, Sera. Did you not think to take them off? No, of course you did not. We did none of us think of such minor things. Come, let me help you remove them before the blood dries the lace right to your skin."

She found Wickenshire seated alone in his study, his coat and neckcloth and waistcoat missing, his shirt covered in soot, his eyes red from the smoke, and his dark hair curling madly about his head. He made to rise as she entered the room, but Serendipity waved him back down. "No, do not, my lord. You are exhausted."

"Your hands?" he asked, rising regardless and taking her bandaged hands into his own. "I cannot tell you how sorry I am that you should be forced to endure—"

"It is nothing," Serendipity assured him, allowing him to lead her to one of several chairs gathered about the table that served as his desk. "I am grateful that I could help, and most certainly, I am in your debt for rescuing Delight and Bessie."

"Balderdash. Likely they did not require a bit of rescuing. We managed to keep the fire confined to the Gold Saloon, the gallery beside it and the corridor just beyond. All the furniture is ruined, of course, including the pianoforte. But then, you cannot play with your hands injured at any rate, so it matters not. I did not know if Hadley and his men would come. We do not actually know each other, Hadley and I. Certainly, he has not heard that bell ring for any reason in twenty years and more."

"Neighbors must depend upon one another in the country. Surely you would have ridden to him had you deduced him to be in dire circumstances. It is what neighbors do, whether they are new to each other or not."

"Yes." Wickenshire sighed, leaning his head against the back of his chair. "Yes, had I heard a bell clamor so loud and long from Hadley Grange, my men and I would have gone to see what must be done, and hastily too. Why are you not up in your bed, Sera? It has been hours since the fire. Hadley and his men are long departed. Everyone else is fast asleep. The sun is near to rising, I should think, and you ought not be sitting here alone with me in my study."

As if the sight of him so subdued, so pensive, were not enough to engage her deepest emotions, the very tone of his voice wrenched at Serendipity's heart. "No one will care that I sit with you awhile, my lord. We are becoming friends, are we not? Friends are meant to comfort one another. What will you do about Lord Nightingale?"

"I cannot think. His cage can be saved with a bit of ingenuity, but it will take me a day or two. I expect I must give him another room to stay in and make him some new toys and a new swing and . . . He will not come down off the draperies, no matter what I do or say. He has fallen asleep up there, I think."

Serendipity's gaze followed the earl's own to the parrot perched, still as a statue, on one of the drapery rods with his head tucked beneath one wing.

"I have tried everything to make him come down, but he was badly frightened, I think, and will not abide anyone's approaching him. Even Mama could not get him to step down on her arm, though she made the attempt when I asked it of her. If Nightingale is harmed, if he is burned or his lungs have filled with smoke, I—"

"Where did you find him?" Serendipity interrupted. "He was not in the Gold Saloon all through the fire?"

"No, not there even by the time I reached it. Neil and Upton said that the door to the Gold Saloon was open and Nightingale nowhere about when they passed it and discovered it aflame. I assume the wretched bird has been in here through all the hubbub, for here is where I found him after I saw the squire and his men out. I do not think I can bear it, Sera, if Nightingale is harmed and will not allow me to help him," he added, his voice faltering just a bit.

"I knew you cared greatly for him."

"You did?"

"Yes. Lord Nightingale is not simply your means to a fortune, is he?"

"Well, he was at first, but that was before—before we came to know each other properly. Nightingale, do come down," he said then, with some exasperation. "How can I help you if you will not come near me?"

Lord Nightingale brought his head from beneath his wing and glared at Wickenshire with one amber eye.

"I cannot think why the door to the Gold Saloon should have been open," Wickenshire mumbled. "It has not been left open since Nightingale took up residence there, though I am grateful it was left open tonight. Still . . . it ought not to have been. One of the oil lamps was smashed across the carpeting, you know. It was that started the fire."

"An oil lamp?"

Wickenshire nodded. "It is all my fault. I ought to have paid attention."

"Attention to what, my lord?"

"To the notes, Sera. But then, you do not know. I have not said anything to you about them. Nor to Mama or Eugenia either."

"Tell me now. Please. Perhaps—"

"Someone has been leaving notes in the stables for me to find nearly every Tuesday since I arrived here in January. And the last note Jenkins discovered inside the house. Gawd, what a dunce I am to have ignored them. They have all been threatening; all urged me to leave Willowsweep."

"But why? Who?"

"I have not the least idea. But I ought to have done exactly as they said, because whoever wrote them . . . I think they must have started this fire as a way to convince me to depart."

"Did—did Mr. Spelling and Lord Upton see no one?"

"Only smelled smoke and went to look for it. In the library, they said they were. Neil wanted something to read. And they smelled the smoke and stepped out into the corridor and discovered the Gold Saloon open and flames licking at the carpeting. But they did not see a single soul about."

"Villain," muttered a long-silent voice from the drapery rod. "Bite. Villain." And then Lord Nightingale took wing, flew once around the room and came to land on Lord Wickenshire's shoulder. "Villain. Villain. Villain," he cried raucously in Wickenshire's ear, making the earl wince, and then the parrot began to tug at the wild curls which were already standing on end atop the earl's head.

"Ouch! Not so very hard, you scoundrel!" Wickenshire protested, a smile rising to his eyes.

"Knollsmarmer," Nightingale replied, ceasing to tug upon the curls and sidling down Wickenshire's arm, then hopping into his lap and turning on his back, his big, clawed feet sticking up into the air. "La-la-la-laaaaa!" he sang, in a voice exactly like Serendipity's.

"You old rascal!" Wickenshire cried. "You are not harmed at all, are you? You have merely been pouting all this time, and I afraid to take myself to bed, worrying that I might find you dead in the morning. And you can sing, by George! Did you hear him, Sera? He is not hurt and he can sing! It is not a real song, of course, but it is a remarkably good beginning!"

The joy that lit Wickenshire's face as he rippled the bird's breast feathers with one long finger set Serendipity's spirits to soaring. "Oh, you make a pair," she declared. "When you did not come up the stairs to your bed, Lord Wickenshire, I thought to discover you walking about, cradling a dead parrot in your arms and grieving. And now just look at the two of you."

"Yes, just look at the two of us," agreed Wickenshire. "Do you know that your eyes glisten like the noonday sky in summer, Sera, when you look at the two of us?"

Eugenia could not sleep a wink. Despite the quiet time in the drawing room when her Aunt Diana had served everyone a bit of brandy and some cakes to settle their nerves, Eugenia's heart still pounded and her thoughts flitted so rapidly through her mind that she could not catch on to one before it was replaced by a second and a third.

The notes, the fire, the parrot, Neil and Nicky and Jenkins. She must speak to Jenkins and as soon as possible, too. Her papa's face appeared before her, and then Lady Wickenshire's, and then, of all things, Lord Upton's.

"No, no, Lord Upton cannot be of any help," she murmured to herself, tossing about in her bed. "He knows nothing. Barely knows his own name, I should think."

But the vision of Lord Upton would not subside as quickly as had the others. He had looked an entirely different person all rumpled and streaked from the fire, his golden locks darkened at the edges by the soot and his extremely handsome countenance lined with grime.

Perhaps I am overlooking something, Eugenia mused in silence. Now that I come to think of it, there was apparent in his face a certain dissipation that I had not noticed before. Bah! He can know nothing of this whether he is ogre or angel or somewhere in between. He barely knows Nicky, and he was never privy to the tale of the Witch of Willowsweep before Neil told him of it and took him to view the portrait.

"Oh, if only Jenkins could . . ." she whispered into the darkness and then ceased to whisper abruptly at the sound of scratching upon her bedchamber door. Perhaps Sera cannot sleep and has come to see if I, too, am awake, she thought, fighting her way from twisted bed-clothes, slipping into her robe and slippers. "I am coming," she called softly, tugging on the second of her bedroom slippers. "Do not go away. I am coming," she called again as she turned the wick up upon her lamp and scuffed her way wearily to the door. "Is it you, Sera?" she asked, lifting the latch and pulling the door inward, and then she gasped the tiniest little gasp.

Lord Upton, finally scrubbed clean of soot and grime, slipped into his nightshirt, twitched his tasseled nightcap snugly down over his still-damp curls, wrapped himself in a warm flannel robe and stalked down the corridor with lamp in hand to bang upon Spelling's door.

"Yes, yes, come in, Upton. Clean, are you?" called Neil from the adjoining chamber. "I have just got clean myself. Gawd, what a thing! I thought Willowsweep would burn to the ground." He came strolling into the room dressed in a ruby red caftan and rubbing at his hair with a towel. "I have got some brandy. Nicky sent it up. Thought we might care for a bit more of the stuff. Not bad, actually," he added, tossing the towel onto the back of a chair and crossing to fill two glasses from a bottle upon one of the windowsills. "Tax-free, I expect, but still, not bad."

Upton accepted a glass, lowered himself into a chair and took a slow, thoughtful sip. "We could have been killed."

"No. Highly doubtful, old fellow."

"House as old as this, should have gone up in seconds."

"Piece of luck that it did not. But we should have got out safely if it had, I assure you. No one would have expected us to remain inside had it got so far out of control as to spread up the walls or into the ceiling. We should merely have dashed out into the corridor, down the servants' staircase and out the kitchen door."

"Stupid bird," grumbled Upton. "I have come to tell you here and now, Spelling, I am *not* going near that wretched bird again. If you must steal it away, I will drive the coach for you, or whatever, but I am not going back into the same room with it ever again! Come Monday, I am taking little Miss Bedford and her sister and going back to London, by post if I must."

"Henry," soothed Spelling. "You are overwrought. Of course you need not hire a postchaise to carry you to London. You shall leave in my coach, with me."

"Yes, but what about the bird? You cannot just walk in and grab the bird. You must realize that now."

"Nightingale was a close thing, Henry. We might have had him. If I had been wearing gloves, for instance."

"No, I am not attempting the thing again, not even if you wear gloves. I tell you, Spelling, that parrot attempted to kill us. I saw the intent to do murder in his eyes as he soared over my head."

Spelling could not help himself. He grinned. "Really, Upton, intent to do murder? A parrot? I think not. You have had a most violent shock to your sensibilities. You will not think the same after you have calmed down sufficiently and got some sleep."

"Tried to murder us, damnable bird."

"Balderdash! Sleep will alter your entire view of the situation, I promise you. And it may well be, dear fellow, that I shall not find it necessary to abduct Lord Nightingale after all. It may well be that the confounded beast has gone into shock from all the hubbub and will refuse to speak, much less sing, for a long time to come. If he ain't already dead or flown outside. You do not think he is dead or flown outside? That would be ghastly. Neither Nicky nor I will have the money then."

"No, no, he ain't dead or gone. Saw your cousin attempting to lure him down from a drapery rod in the study as I passed by."

"Ah, good! So much for the Sisters of the Resurrection. They will not see a penny of the inheritance. Luck is with us, Upton!"

Upton's eyebrows rose as high as his nightcap. "Luck? With us? When we nearly burned to death?"

"But we did not burn to death, and Nightingale is alive and within our reach. We are heroes, Henry! We were the first ones to spot the fire and cry out the alarm and attempt to put it out. Even Nicky gives us credit for our courage and quick thinking."

"Only because he was not present when the whole thing began," sighed Upton. "He would toss us out on our ears if he knew what really happened."

Serendipity, unable to persuade Lord Wickenshire to abandon Nightingale and go upstairs to his bed, left him in the study with the bird on his lap pecking at his shirt studs, and climbed the stairs to the second floor alone. Her lamp turned low, she was just turning from the staircase into the corridor when she heard a soft scratching sound and halted at once. Cautiously, she peered around a bit of molding into the corridor and drew in a great breath. There was someone standing far down the passageway, holding a lamp in one hand and scratching upon Eugenia's door with the other.

Serendipity nibbled at her lower lip and squinted through the semidarkness. Certainly it was a man. A rather tall, lanky man in what appeared to be robe and slippers. Well, it could not be Lord Wickenshire. Perhaps it was Eugenia's cousin, Mr. Spelling. But why would Mr. Spelling be scratching upon Eugenia's door at this hour of the night? Lord Upton? Oh, certainly not! And then, for a moment, the man raised the lamp nearer to his face and the flame showed Serendipity a longish nose and a splendid chin. Its low flame set well-trimmed, greying hair to glimmering for a moment.

Jenkins! And Eugenia's door was opening! Serendipity thought that her heart would stop right then, right there. What could it be to bring Lord Wickenshire's butler to scratch upon Eugenia's door in the wee hours before dawn? Could it be the same thing that had sent him there before? A note to be passed from one to the other of them? At this hour? Oh, it could not! Perhaps he had come in answer to the pleading look that Eugenia had bestowed upon him in the drawing room. Or perhaps the fire had caused some unfortunate occurrence and the servants required—but no, it would be Lord Wickenshire's door or Lady Wickenshire's door that Mr. Jenkins would scratch upon then. Eugenia was no more than a guest in this house and had no responsibility for the servants.

And then Serendipity's heart dropped all the way down to the toe of her left slipper. Eugenia had opened her door farther. Was she actually going to allow him entrance? Was she going to invite that—old rogue—into her chamber? Oh, great heavens!

What can I do? Serendipity almost nibbled right through her lower lip in agitation. Eugenia will be ruined. Ruined! She will be forced to marry a butler—if Lord Wickenshire does not shoot the man—and her papa will disown her and no one of any consequence will ever acknowledge her again! What can I do? Oh, Eugenia, do not let him in. Please, please, dearest, no matter if you think you love him, do not let him in!

ELEVEN

"Who are you spying upon, Miss Bedford?"

The unexpected whisper in her ear nearly sent Serendipity into a seizure. She jumped; the lamp flew from her hand; she squealed and dove after it.

"Damnation, not again!" growled Wickenshire under his breath, diving after it as well. "Ow! Sons of Siegrid!" he hissed, hot oil splashing his wrist as he captured the lamp with one hand and caught Serendipity around the waist with the other to keep her from hitting the floor. "Are you all right, Sera? None of the oil spilled upon you? What a dolt I am to surprise you so! You might have been badly burned."

"I am fine, my lord," Serendipity whispered. "But you—"

"Nothing. It is nothing. A brief unpleasant sensation is all. Deuce take it, I hope we have not waked anyone. It will be parson's mousetrap for us, m'dear, if Mama or Neil discover us alone together, and on the second floor, and me practically naked. Thank goodness you are not in your nightdress—What?" he asked, faltering to a stop because Serendipity, instead of paying him the least attention, had loosed herself from his grasp and was peeking around the molding. "Sera, who *are* you spying upon?"

"No one— It does not matter— There was a—man in the corridor, but he has vanished now." Thank goodness, Serendipity added silently. Jenkins must have heard us and scurried back out through the servants' entrance, and Eugenia has closed her door. Oh, thank goodness.

"A man?" asked Wickenshire. "Do you mean Neil or Upton?"

"No."

"Then who? By gawd, Sera, it might be the fellow who started the fire. What did he look like?"

"No, no, it was certainly not . . . It was . . . Mr. Jenkins," Serendipity replied. "I—I did not wish him to see me wandering about so late. He was merely on his way to his quarters, I am certain, but I did not wish him to see me . . . so very late." She knew perfectly well she sounded like a featherbrain, but she could not tell him the truth—that Jenkins and Eugenia—

But someone should be told, she thought. Someone who can wield considerable influence over Eugenia and bring these assignations to a halt. Well, I shall speak with Eugenia myself, first, she decided then. And I will tell His Lordship the truth only if Eugenia will not hear me out.

Wickenshire set the lamp upon a table behind them. He placed both arms gently around Serendipity, his hands clasping at her waist, and peered over her shoulder and around the molding for himself. "Well, Jenkins is gone now," he whispered in her ear. "Come, Sera, let me see you safely to your chambers. You did not see anyone else, eh? No stranger lingering near *your* chamber? I ought to have thought— I never set anyone to search the house for— Perhaps that is what Jenkins was about. Never mind, I shall go into your room first and make certain that no fiend has ducked in there, and we shall both go through the dressing room to check upon Delight."

The gentle intimacy of his arms about her waist and the warm tickle of his breath against her ear sent a warmth flaring through Serendipity. Her cheeks flamed; her hands perspired; her insides came alight as if an entire waterfall of brandy were tumbling about in there, warming her all over.

"Truly, you need not," she managed breathlessly.

"I must. M'duty to see that you and Delight are perfectly safe." His hands slithered from the waist of her gown with a quiet hissing, and one of them swallowed her right hand without a moment's pause, while the other retrieved the lamp. He led her to the door of her chamber, opened it, and turned to smile down at her.

"Stay right here, Sera, until I have checked behind the draperies and under the bed and in all the other places a fellow might hide. I shall come and tell you when I deem it to be safe." His lips were oh so close to her own. His breath, warm and smelling of brandy. Serendipity had the oddest urge to press her lips right against his. But she did not, coloring instead that the notion should so much as enter her head.

No, I shall never do such a thing. Attack the man? Force him to kiss me? I think not, she scolded herself in silence, gazing up into green eyes aglow in the lamplight. But if he were to kiss me of his own free will, I should not fight against him, I think.

Wickenshire's heart tumbled about in the sorriest manner. It bounced against the cage of his ribs like an India rubber ball, and the longer he gazed into Serendipity's perfectly sultry blue eyes, the more it tumbled. If only, he thought as his heart thudded for the sixteenth time against the highest of his ribs. If only I were not so very proper, I would kiss the girl here and now. But then, I am not the sort to be stealing kisses from innocent young women in the dead of night. Likely she would scream and wake the entire household if I did. Even more likely that I should tilt the lamp and douse us both with hot oil. Neil might do the thing with aplomb, but not me.

With a muffled sigh, Wickenshire stepped away from Serendipity and, lamp held high, entered her chamber and began to search in every place he thought it likely a man might hide.

* * *

Jenkins, try though he might, could not keep from sweating like a man in a high fever. Perspiration rolled down between his eyes to form droplets at the very tip of his nose. It dribbled down his chin and into the high-standing collar of his nightshirt. Every single hair on his head was wet with it, and even his toes in his slippers were growing soggy. "Miss Eugenia, please. I cannot," he whispered miserably, his hand shaking so badly that oil splashed up the sides of the lamp he held, though he was not so unlucky as Wickenshire and did not spill the stuff out upon himself.

"Hush, Jenkins. Whoever it is will hear you."

"Oh, dearest gawd," moaned Jenkins under his breath, his heart thumping rapidly and raggedly in his breast.

Eugenia could not help but smile. She attempted to take his arm and lead him across the room to the window where it was quite likely they would not be overheard by whomever had turned into the corridor and made such a dreadful noise doing it, too, but Jenkins would not budge one step beyond the threshold.

"I ought not have tugged you inside, Jenkins," she whispered as quietly as she could. "But I was not think-ing and I just did. I am so very sorry."

"Y-yes, Miss Eugenia," the butler nodded.

"Do not look so woebegone, Jenkins. You have done nothing wrong."

"N-no, Miss Eugenia, b-but I am in your ch-ch-chamber."

"Just barely, Jenkins."

Jenkins was, in fact, so close to the chamber door that Eugenia brushed right up against him when she went to open it the merest bit to see if all was clear at last. That subtle touch of robe against robe sent Jenkins hopping two whole steps out of her way without one word passing between them.

"Well, I thought I heard Nicky mutter something, but

he would have turned in the other direction at the top of the stairs, so likely it was Sera," Eugenia sighed, closing the door again. "She is gone now. No one at all in the corridor. We were quick enough, and she did not see us, I think."

"Thank heavens," Jenkins sighed, stepping hastily around Eugenia, opening the door and bolting out into the corridor.

"Jenkins!" Eugenia hissed as he poised upon the outer threshold, about to run off. "Why did you come?"

"B-because of the w-way you l-looked at me in the d-drawing room, miss. I thought it m-must be s-something important that you w-wished to convey to me." His stutter grew less as the cool air of the corridor swirled about him and he felt himself more or less returned to his proper station. His skin began to cool a bit, and though he continued to perspire, droplets were not leaping one by one off his nose. "I did not know if it was something could wait until the morning."

"I knew you had understood my gaze, Jenkins," Eugenia whispered happily. "You are always to be depended upon when a person is in need."

"Just so, miss," Jenkins nodded, gazing uneasily about him for any hint of another's presence, though his heartbeat had begun to slow and his hands had ceased to shake.

"It is Elaina Maria Chastain, Jenkins," Eugenia told him excitedly. "I wanted to tell you. The notes refer to the Witch of Willowsweep. They must. I cannot think why we should all have forgotten about her. If Neil had not sought out her portrait to show it to Lord Upton, I should not have given her one thought yet. All this time we have been attempting to link the witches with something that Nicky has done since he came to Willowsweep. But it is nothing that Nicky has done at all. Now we must deduce, Jenkins, who it is still thinks of the witch and why he uses her in an attempt to intimidate Nicky."

Jenkins nodded. "I had not thought, miss. Of course,

'tis the Witch of Willowsweep. I shall set about to consider who of the staff and the neighbors knows the tale and might make use of it to send His Lordship packing. That I will."

"Excellent, Jenkins. We shall both sleep on it and consult together in the morning."

"Yes, miss," Jenkins assured her and then scurried off to the servants' staircase, closing the baize door behind him so very softly that not even Eugenia heard the merest sound.

Well, that was frightening for a moment, she thought as she closed her chamber door behind her and divested herself of robe and slippers. How very sweet of Jenkins to come as soon as he could to discover what it was I required of him. And after the fire and everything. Truly, he is the kindest and most reliable gentleman. Nicky is so very lucky to have him. I do wish Mr. Taligore were more kindly and reliable, she thought, recalling her papa's stern old butler. But he has not lived with us forever as Jenkins has with Nicky. That is the difference, I expect.

With a smile of recall for Jenkins's nervousness at being in her chamber, Eugenia climbed up into bed, turned down the wick upon her lamp and closed her eyes. "If it was Sera in the corridor," she murmured, her eyes popping open again, "I wonder what she could have been doing there? She ought to have been asleep hours ago."

No sooner did Spelling arrive at breakfast the next morning than his cousin looked up and remarked upon the piece of sticking plaster between his thumb and forefinger. "What the deuce happened, Neil? I thought you said you had not got burned."

"No, but it seems I cut myself on something. Cannot think what," Spelling replied, silently cursing Lord Nightingale for having bitten him so soundly as to have drawn blood. "Nothing terrible, Nicky. I shall live. What are you doing here at this hour? No barns to mend? No cows to milk? No sheep to herd?"

"Sent Bobby Tripp into the village to hire some hands to tend to the animals for today. I have got a Gold Saloon to clean up. Be required to haul most of the furniture outside and make a bonfire of it, I expect. Thank you, Neil, for rising to the occasion last evening. If you and Upton had not—"

Spelling's eyebrows arched. Another word of thanks from Nicky? "Not to think of it. Do the same for anyone."

"I thank you regardless. You are positive that you did not see anyone lurking about, eh, Neil?"

"Not a soul." And then Spelling's eyebrows arched to an even more substantial height. "Am I to gather that you think someone set that fire, Nick? Deliberately?"

"Well, I might think that somehow Nightingale had set the lamp to tumbling, but he is generally very wary of lamps. You must know that to be the case, Neil. Stays far away from lamps and lighted candles. I expect your father taught him to do so. And the door was wide open, you said. Nightingale would not have been able to open the door."

By Jove, thought Spelling. I had forgotten all about Papa teaching the wretched bird to avoid flames. Upton was correct. That beastie did have murder in his heart. He knocked that lamp to the floor on purpose!

"My, but you are looking quite thoughtful this morning, Neil," observed the dowager as she joined them. "Whatever puts such a look upon your face? It is serious, I think."

The gentlemen rose until she was seated and then resumed their breakfasts, Wickenshire sipping at a cup of coffee and Spelling pushing a bit of beefsteak about on his plate.

"Nicky, I accepted an invitation from Squire Hadley last night. We are all to attend an entertainment there on Saturday evening. He said that you had sent your regrets, but he was so very kind as to come help us, and I thought—"

"Yes, Mama. Perfectly all right. We ought to attend if he still wants us."

"He does. Mrs. Hadley, he said, would be thrilled that we had changed our minds."

Wickenshire nodded. An entertainment at the squire's. Yes, and a most unexceptionable way in which to make the acquaintance of a goodly number of respectable families in the neighborhood. An opportunity, perhaps, to discover who wished him gone from Willowsweep so badly that they would risk burning the house to the ground to send him running.

An entertainment at the squire's, thought Neil. What an excellent idea! Hadley Grange does not lie all that far from Willowsweep. If there are enough people from the neighborhood present, well, my absence for a quarter hour or so in order to abduct Nightingale will not be noted. "A fine idea," he concurred, aloud, grinning. "Nicky needs a bit of fun, Aunt Diana, do not you think? From sunup to sundown he is always working. It will do him good to meet his neighbors and socialize a bit."

"Just so," nodded the dowager. "And you and Lord Upton will enjoy it as well, I am certain. And the girls, well, they will be overjoyed, because Squire Hadley did mention that there was like to be dancing. You know how young ladies love to dance."

"Indeed," Spelling grinned. "Do not look so forlorn, Nicky. Upton and I and my coachman will join in to help you and your people with the Gold Saloon. Have it smelling like a lavender pot before Saturday evening. You will not lose anything at all by attending the squire's little party."

Serendipity sat in Wickenshire's study, staring out the window and singing, "Wee Willie, Wee Willie, go 'way from m'door," over and over again, but her mind was not focused on it. Nor did she notice one bit of the breathtakingly blue sky visible through the window. Lord Nightingale might have flown down on her shoulder and begun picking out her curls one by one and she would not have taken note of that either. Her entire mind—except for the bit of it that repeated the silly phrase of the song—was focused upon the two dreadful secrets that she had learned last evening and the chilling events that might be anticipated at Willowsweep because of them.

"Wee Willie, Wee Willie," she sang as she thought: *It sounds worse than it is. Eugenia has conceived a passion for His Lordship's butler.* "go 'way" *But Eugenia is a sensible girl.* "from" *I shall just speak with her and explain that such things are not done.* "m'door." *Well, they are done, but at the peril of losing one's entire future.* "Wee Willie, Wee Willie" *Eugenia will come to her senses. And if she does not,* "go 'way" *I will explain that everyone will blame His Lordship for the liaison* "from m'door." *because it happened in his establishment and Jenkins is his butler.* "Wee Willie," *That will bring her around. She loves Nicholas dearly, I know.* "Wee Willie" *She has told me so any number of times.* "go 'way" *She will not wish to hurt him by some silly affaire with a butler.* "m'door."

No, the thing with Eugenia is not so very bad. It is this business of someone attempting to frighten Nicholas from Willowsweep by burning down the house. Great heavens, what a fool the person must be! We might all have been killed!

Nicholas? she thought then, her cheeks tinging with pink. *Oh, I ought not think of him as Nicholas. What is wrong with me that I should do such a thing? Papa must be turning about in his grave. I am not so young as Delight that I may dispense with propriety in favor of friendship. Though he did say that we were becoming friends.* "Oh my goodness!" she exclaimed then, right in the midst of a 'Wee' and a 'Willie.' "Oh, my goodness, he called me Sera. Right out loud. He called me Sera last night and I did not take note of it until this very moment!"

Her heart fluttered the merest bit and the most pleasant smile rose all the way up into her eyes. "He called me Sera."

"Villain!" exclaimed Nightingale, pigeon-toeing his way across the carpet, pushing a wooden bead that Wickenshire had given him to play with. "Bite! Villain!"

Serendipity laughed. "No, no, he is not a villain to have called me Sera, Nightingale. And I do not wish for you to bite him. What I wish you to do, sir, is to pay attention and to learn this song. We do not have a pianoforte any longer, so you cannot stomp about upon the keys while you are listening. But you must listen, dearest. And you must learn. You can make N-Nicholas's life so very much easier if only you will set your mind to it and sing this little song."

"Yo ho ho," muttered Lord Nightingale, pushing the big wooden bead along. "Yo ho ho. Knollsmarmer."

"Nicholas," Serendipity repeated, tasting his name upon her tongue and lips. "Nicholas."

"Knollsmarmer," insisted Nightingale, pausing to blink up at her through one amber eye. "Knollsmarmer ditcompon."

"What? Nightingale? What did you say?"

"Awwk! Knollsmarmer!" screeched the parrot at the very top of his lungs, and then he fluffed up his feathers, beat his wings and sailed to the back of one of the chairs, where he became thoroughly involved in pecking at his nails.

Knollsmarmer ditcompon, mused Serendipity. I have never heard that before. Ditcompon. What sort of word is that? And who in the world could have taught it to him? A man, most definitely. But the more I hear, the more I am certain that Nightingale does not speak in the same voice when he says Knollsmarmer and now this ditcompon as when he says his other words. "Oh, you are a smart bird, are you not?" she cooed, then, as the parrot came fluttering into her lap. "Such a very smart bird. Did you see who started the fire in your Gold Saloon, Nightingale? I will wager you did. I will just wager that you know precisely who started that fire. If only you could tell me, I would have some idea of how to begin protecting Nicholas."

"Protecting Nicky?" asked Eugenia, standing on the threshold with her hand upon the door latch. "Protect Nicky from what? Sera? Do cease staring at me with your mouth wide open and tell me what you were going on about just now."

"Wh-what are you doing here, Eugenia?"

"I have just come to lure you outside and away from that ball of feathers for a stroll in the garden. It is the most beautiful afternoon, and you have been locked away in here practically forever. And now you are definitely joining me, because I intend to discover precisely what you were speaking of a moment ago."

They strolled through the overgrown garden, across a narrow little bridge, past the paddock and off into the north field without so much as noticing that they had left the immediate vicinity of the house, two young women in dresses quite fit for the country and stout shoes fit for the country as well. The sunshine proved so warm that they unbuttoned their pelisses and doffed their bonnets as they wandered, and if they did pause in their wandering and conversation now and then to stare, surprised, into each other's faces, for the main part they continued on their way without one thought as to where they were bound or just how long it might take them to get there.

"I cannot believe," grinned Eugenia, "that you thought Jenkins and me to be . . . to be . . ."

"Well, but what was I to think? You were in the stables that night, and it might well have been Jenkins strolling out to meet you. And then, you know, I saw the note pass between you. And last night—well, it was very late, and he in his robe and slippers and you likewise. I thought I should faint when first I saw him there."

"But now you know the truth, and you will not betray me to Nicky, will you?"

"No, never. But you must allow me to be of help as well, because I know all about the notes."

"I cannot think why Nicky would tell you about them."

"I do not think that he planned to do so. He was just so very sad and tired, and he thought the fire to be all his fault, you know, for not abandoning Willowsweep as the notes demanded of him. And Lord Nightingale would not even look at him, much less come down from the drapery rod."

"Come down from—Sera, when did Nicky speak with you about the notes?"

"A-after the f-fire."

"Yes, but when after the fire?" Eugenia's eyes lit with the most intriguing glow. "It was not when we were all gathered in the drawing room, passing about basilicum and brandy, was it? No, it was not! Sera, you were coming upstairs from an assignation with my cousin!"

"No, it was not an assignation, Eugenia. I could not settle down and so I dressed and went downstairs—just to wander about a bit—the study was lighted and the door open, and he was there, exhausted, but refusing to leave that bird for one moment."

Eugenia giggled. "You are very lucky, you know, that no one discovered the two of you alone together at such an unreasonable hour. Why, men and women have been married for less than that."

"Oh, pooh, they have not. And even if they have, we did nothing at all improper. It is not as though Lord Wickenshire came sneaking up the backstairs to my chamber in robe and slippers."

Both girls laughed at that, and, arms entwined, with

Eugenia rolling only a little bit, they continued their stroll.

"I think, you know, that this entertainment at the squire's will be most convenient for someone," Eugenia ventured at last. "Jenkins and I had our own little meeting at last."

"Where? However did you manage with no one noticing?"

"Oh, absolutely everyone noticed. We were helping to clean up the Gold Saloon, you see, along with everyone else, and we just happened to work side by side. We discussed it for the longest time and no one paid us any attention."

Serendipity laughed. "What better place for a private meeting than right in the midst of chaos."

"Exactly. And Jenkins agrees with Nicky that the person who wrote the notes also started the fire. We both suspect he will use our trip to the squire's to do something else terrible. Jenkins must be on his guard Saturday evening."

"But I thought that your father suspected one of the staff and he had charged you to spy upon them for just that reason."

"Yes, but now I think that Papa is wrong. None of the staff could possibly have set that fire. They were all of them together having their dinner. Jenkins vows that not one of them left their little dining room belowstairs even for a moment. Jenkins brought our tea and then returned to dine with them, and they were in full view of each other until the fire was discovered."

"Unless the person who set the fire was not the same person who has been writing the notes," mused Serendipity. "You do not think there are two villains, Eugenia?"

"Two villains? Jenkins and I did not consider that. Well, there is Neil, of course. He has always been a villain. But he has been surprisingly circumspect this visit."

TWELVE

Wickenshire reined Grace in and peered about him with some agitation. He had been out for an hour, the short spring twilight was threatening and still he could find no sign of Eugenia and Serendipity. "What can the two of you have been thinking to stray so very far?" he muttered to himself. "I cannot so much as *see* the house from here. Eugenia!" he called then. "Serendipity! Answer me, do!"

He listened in silence for a reply, but hearing none, urged Grace forward. The north field, he thought. Cook said that she had seen them leave the garden and stroll off into the north field. But I have crossed near all of it and there is not a sign of them. "Eugenia!" he called again. "Serendipity!" And then he searched his memory for any place they might have gone to take cover if some sort of accident had occurred. "The barn," he murmured and turned Grace to the right, following along the woods that bordered the stream. He kept the mare to a trot, hoping to hear one or another of the young women call for help, or at the least to hear them speak to one another as he passed by, but only the noises of the field and stream reached his ears.

The barn had been built of stone and timber years before the construction of Willowsweep had begun, which made it at least four centuries old and possibly older. Why it had been built and by whom, no one ever said.

Tales of faeries and knights and witches are apparently much more interesting than tales of barnraisers, Wickenshire thought with a smile. Still, I should like to know who— "Ah, there it is, Grace. Not so soggy as it was a few weeks ago, eh? We shall not need to wade through flood waters to reach it tonight. Eugenia!" he called again. "Serendipity!"

"Here! We are here, Nicky!" came an answering call, and in a moment a white handkerchief was waving at him from the entrance to the barn.

Wickenshire urged Grace forward at a gallop and, reaching the barn, leaped to the ground before the horse had so much as come to a halt. "What the devil has happened, Eugenia? Do you have the least idea what time it is?"

"No, what time is it, Nicky?"

"More than time that you and Serendipity were home and dressing for dinner. Where is she? She is not injured?"

"No, no, we are neither of us injured," Eugenia assured him with a smile. "But we did neither of us know precisely what to do, because we had strayed so very far, you know, and the one is so large and the other so tiny. Well, that is not precisely true. We might have carried the one home quite easily, but we did not like to make the other walk all that way—especially when I might get us lost, for I did not take note of how we got here, and the house is completely out of sight."

"The one what? The other what? Have you completely lost your mind, Eugenia?" Wickenshire grumbled, stalking past her into the barn. "This is not a place to linger. One strong wind could bring it down about your ears. Miss Bedford? What is that?"

Serendipity giggled. She could not help herself. In the dim light, the expression upon His Lordship's face was priceless.

I shall remember this particular look upon his precious face until the day I die, Serendipity thought. "It is a puppy, my lord. And just in case you should wonder, this beside it is a kitten. Eugenia and I have been sitting here on the straw attempting to conjure a way of taking them back with us to Willowsweep, but though Eugenia can well carry the kitten, I cannot do the same with the puppy—not so very far as Willowsweep, at least."

"Not so far as three steps outside the barn," observed Wickenshire, crossing to her and being immediately set upon by a puppy of indeterminate lineage but sufficiently intimidating size. "Must weigh near a stone."

"Oh, more, I think," Eugenia offered, coming up beside him.

"And he is the wiggliest thing," sighed Serendipity.

Wickenshire bent to gather the puppy up into his arms and laughed as a pink tongue wet his cheek. "By George, more than a stone. You are right, Eugenia. But to whom does it belong?"

"We thought it might belong to one of the shepherds," Serendipity said. "But it does not."

"It does not?"

"No, it does not. Do you know that you have only two shepherds in your employ, my lord? Well, most likely you do."

"The elder McIntire and the younger McIntire, Nicky," Eugenia said. "And the elder McIntire was just going out to move his flock when this puppy came bounding to us out of the woods. It is a bit mucky, is it not? Likely it has been in the woods for days and days."

"Weeks and weeks," observed Wickenshire, gazing at the puppy he held, its fur covered in mud and grime and burrs.

"Yes, and McIntire the elder would not own him," Serendipity continued the tale. "He said his son would not either. Most likely one of the villagers went to drown a litter, he said, and this one escaped. So he said we might keep it."

"Who said you might keep it?"

"The elder McIntire, Nicky," Eugenia declared. "Were you not listening at all?"

"Nice of McIntire to be so free of my hospitality."

"Do you mean to say that we may not keep it, my lord?" asked Serendipity, gazing up at him forlornly, a tiny ball of black and white fur nuzzling at her chin. "I mean—them. We found the kitten as well. At least, the puppy carried it to us in his mouth. I think they have been fellow wanderers amidst the thorns. It would be unkind to rescue one without rescuing the other."

"And I expect it would be the unkindest thrust of all to rescue you and Eugenia without rescuing either one of them, eh, Miss Bedford?"

"He is going to laugh," giggled Eugenia. "No, do not glare at me, Nicky. You *are* going to laugh. I can see your lips twitching. That means we may keep the both of them, does it not?"

Wickenshire carried them home in two shifts, taking Eugenia and the kitten up before him first and then returning for Serendipity and the puppy.

"Do hold him tightly, will you not, Miss Bedford? I could not bear to have him wiggle free and fall and you, in all kindness, go leaping after him."

"No, no, I will see that he does not wiggle free, my lord," Serendipity assured him as he stepped into the stirrup and swung up behind her, his arms going around her waist to handle Grace's reins. The very closeness of him sent a warm glow pulsing through Serendipity's tired limbs and produced an exhausted but satisfied smile upon her face. "You are truly the most wonderful gentleman," she said. "I imagined you to be all sorts of different people, you know, when Eugenia wrote to me about your offer of a position, but I could never have imagined you to be the very special gentleman you are."

"Who? Me?" asked Wickenshire.

"Yes."

"A very special gentleman?"

"Indeed."

"You mistake, Sera. I am barely a gentleman at all. Only my title makes me so. I am nothing but a poor, uneducated farmer."

"Never."

"Yes, and so Neil and his friends and all of the *ton* will tell you one day, too, when you go to London for your Season. I smell of the stables and cattle and sheep. My hands are rough and callused from the shears and the flail and the plow and the scythe—not to mention hammers and saws and any number of other instruments of torture."

He chuckled, embarrassed, and Serendipity turned the slightest bit to look up at him. Maneuvering the puppy into a one-handed grip, her other hand reached up to touch his cheek, caressing it with the gentlest downward stroke. "You are so much more than a farmer," she said softly. "So very much more. You are everything a true gentleman could ever hope to be."

Wickenshire's pulse pounded erratically in his wrists and at his neck and in his ears, and he grew so very red that even in the last of the twilight, Serendipity could see the blush on his neck and cheeks.

She had pity upon him and turned to face the front again, regaining her double-handed grip on the puppy. "I shall never have a Season in London," she said after a full three minutes of silence. "Mr. Wiggins—I mean to say—Lord Upton will not give me one if he is as villainous as you think."

"No, but I will give you a Season once Nightingale sings his little ditty for Trent and Neil. Mama has already proposed that it be so in—in partial payment, you know, for your teaching Nightingale in the first place."

"Oh!" gasped Serendipity in surprise.

"Yes, and when Delight has reached the proper age— if the gentleman you choose to marry cannot properly afford to do so—I shall see that Delight has a Season in London as well."

He was thinking to give Delight a Season in London? Serendipity could not believe it! No man, not even her own papa—as much as he had loved Delight—would have thought to expend the sums it would cost to give Delight a Season. "But her face," she whispered in awe. "Do not you think it would be a great waste to present to Society a young woman with such a blemish?"

"No. Why? Delight is a—delight! It would be unforgivable to keep such a splendid and special person out of reach of the very gentlemen who stand most in need of her."

"Well, but do you not think that Delight would be ignored and, worse, made the object of any number of jests? It would be cruel to place her in such a situation."

"Balderdash! Teach her to be proud of who she is, not ashamed of how she looks. There are people—ladies and gentlemen both—more severely disfigured than Delight. Only—only—you cannot see their disfigurements because they are on the inside. Deep inside. In their hearts and souls. Like my papa," he added in a much quieter voice. "Like my papa and—and—me."

Wickenshire, Upton and Spelling all strolled, laughing, into the drawing room that evening after dinner.

"Never seen anything like it," Spelling snickered. "Extraordinary."

"Ought to write a poem upon it," agreed Upton, grinning. "Immortalize the occasion."

"An Ode to Suds and Fur," Wickenshire proposed, his eyes alight with glee. "Oh, fairest of butlers, What is it you wear?" he intoned.

"A waistcoat of soap suds, A shirtfront of hair," Upton joined in.

Lady Wickenshire gazed up from her crocheting and cocked an inquisitive eyebrow. "You have all stayed too long with the wine, have you not?"

"No, we have not, Mama," Wickenshire chuckled. "We have all of us gone down to check on the fate of Eugenia's and Miss Bedford's newly acquired pets."

"Yes, Aunt Diana," continued Mr. Spelling, "and strolled into the midst of chaos."

"Wet, furry chaos," laughed Lord Upton. "Jenkins attempting to clean the scoundrels in a tub of sudsy water."

"In went the puppy, out jumped the kitten. Off ran Jenkins, chasing the kitten around the room. Out jumped the puppy to join the fun and chase Jenkins around the room," Wickenshire grinned. "Oh, Mama, it was a sight to see! In the tub, out of the tub, around and around the kitchen, and then the wet little beasties scuttled under Cook's skirts to hide from Jenkins, and Jenkins grew beet red wondering whether or not to go after them. And Cook laughed and laughed."

The dowager could envision it and began to chuckle, herself.

"Have Eugenia and Miss Bedford gone off somewhere?" the earl queried. "They truly ought to see this amazing circus before it is totally over. We came to fetch the lot of you so you should not miss all."

"Off to bed," replied the dowager. "Both of them. Weary from their long walk. And though it sounds most wonderful, I do not think I wish to add to Jenkins's humiliation by going belowstairs to peer at him as though he were some freak at a fair."

"No, perhaps not," Spelling admitted. "Though it truly is something to be seen, Aunt Diana."

"I am certain it is, Neil. But I am quite content to remain here and work upon my doilies. You gentlemen must entertain yourselves this evening."

"Well, I am all for going back downstairs and watching the show," declared Upton.

"Do go then, Henry," urged Spelling. "Enjoy! Jenkins will most likely convince you to help him, though. I warn you of that. My cousin's butler can be most persuasive when he is desperate."

"You are not coming?"

"No, no. There is something I wish to discuss with Nicky." Spelling waited until Upton had gone off down the stairs and then took his cousin's arm. "Join me in your study a moment, eh, Nicky? I assure you, it is quite important."

Wickenshire looked Spelling up and down with some suspicion, but consented to stroll with him down the corridor and into the study. "What, Neil?" he asked once he had stepped inside and closed the door.

"Villain!" Nightingale cried from the top of a bookshelf. "Awwk! Villain!"

"Stow it, you wretched bird," Spelling grumbled. "Go perch on a pipe. This has nothing to do with you, feather merchant."

"It does not, Neil?" asked Wickenshire in some amazement. "I thought, perhaps, that you wished to speak with me about Nightingale learning to sing."

"It matters not to me whether Nightingale learns to sing, Nick. In fact, I rather hope he does. I am in possession of a fortune as it is. Why should I wish to deny you yours and keep it for myself, eh?"

"Possibly because you were born greedy and have grown steadily more so for all the years I have known you."

"Nicky, I am astounded to hear you say such a thing! Is this the Cousin Nicky I have always known? Speaking so freely, without one thought for my sensitivities?"

"Yes, well, I am rather astounded to have heard me say it, too, Neil. I ought not have done, though it is the truth."

"I know it is truth, Nick. But I am attempting to curb my greed. A man cannot devote his entire life to the acquisition of money, or he will miss out on—things."

"Oh."

"Do not look such a sobersides," Neil exclaimed into the growing silence between them. "I cannot possibly keep Nightingale from learning to sing, and I have no intention of harming the old fellow. Why should I wish my stepmama's money to go to the Sisters of the Resurrection? Which is what will happen, you know, should the rascal die or disappear and not be found again. I am not at all charitable. The Sisters of the Resurrection be damned, I say. Now, enough conversation about that fool of a bird. I brought you in here because I mean to do you a favor."

"Another one? But you have already saved Willowsweep from burning to the ground, Neil. Anything more and I shall be in your debt forever."

"Bah! I cried 'fire' two or three times. Nothing. This favor will be the making of you."

Wickenshire's left eyebrow tilted the slightest bit. "Ought we not sit down then and discuss it?" he asked, motioning toward the table and chairs.

"No. It is not a thing can be done sitting down. I have decided to teach you to dance, Nick."

"You have what?"

"Decided to teach you to dance. We go to Squire Hadley's on the morrow and there will be dancing. Young people in the country do almost always dance at such things. It will not be at all formal, but still . . . You do not know how to dance? I am not mistaken in that, am I, Nicky?"

Wickenshire felt the back of his neck begin to flush. He prayed with all his might that the pink tinge would not come to stain his cheeks as well and humiliate him completely before his cousin. "I have never . . ." he began and then stuttered to a halt. "What puts such a notion in your brain? Why should I wish to dance at Hadley's or anywhere else?"

"Just as I thought. Too much work, Nick, and not enough play. You never took the time to learn. But every gentleman ought to know how to dance. You do wish to impress Miss Bedford, do you not? I have seen the way you look at her when she is not aware, Nicky. You have fallen in love with the chit."

"I do not look at her in any sort of particular fashion," Wickenshire protested. "I merely find her—pretty—which is not at all exceptional, because she is. That does not mean that I have—have—developed—feelings—for her. Your head is stuffed with beans, Neil."

"No, my head is stuffed with romantic notions," sighed Spelling, beginning to move chairs to the side of the room. "And I know how a man looks when he wishes to impress a young lady and cannot think how to go about it. Do not go on protesting, Nicky. Allow me to do this one good deed for you, eh? And even if you must persist in the denial of any feelings for Miss Bedford, you cannot deny that you should like to know how to dance. Grab an end of this table, Nick, and we will set it to the side or there will not be enough room."

Thoroughly puzzled by what could have put such a notion as teaching him to dance into his cousin's head, but longing, now that the subject had been broached, to know just a bit of what went into the exercise, Wickenshire grabbed an end of the table and they moved it as far from the center of the room as possible.

"Knollsmarmer," muttered Lord Nightingale, having flown from the bookshelf to the chandelier the moment Spelling had begun to rearrange the furniture. "Villain. Knollsmarmer."

"Someday," Spelling grumbled in return, "I am going to discover what knollsmarmer means, Nightingale, and if it is as insulting as I think, I am going to wring your neck."

Wickenshire could not help but chuckle. "You do not know what knollsmarmer means either, eh?"

"Not a clue. Come out in the center here, Nicky, and stand opposite me. I shall be Miss Bedford and you shall be—"

"Myself."

"Just so. Of course, there ought to be music, but we shall do just as well without it. I shall hum, eh? First, the Skip and Dip, because that is the very newest of the lot."

"The Skip and Dip? That is what they call a dance? Really?"

"Yes, really. It is actually a variation on one of the country dances."

"Oh. Neil, why are you doing this?"

"I have already told you, Nicky. Because I have noted the way you stare at Miss Bedford when she is not staring at you—and vice versa, I might add."

"But even if you are correct—I am sorry, Neil," Wickenshire sighed, stuffing his hands into his breeches pockets and shaking his head in disbelief, "but even if you are correct, why should you care? You have never liked me since we were both in short coats. Why should I believe that all of a sudden you have developed considerable goodwill toward me?"

"True enough. We have not been close, you and I. So I will confess, Nick. I do not care whether you and Miss Bedford are attracted to each other or not. But I let my tongue run wild this afternoon, after you set out to bring Eugenia and Miss Bedford home. I said that it would not surprise me if you had developed a *tendre* for the chit. Upton, of course, called it impossible. He said that he would be surprised beyond measure if such a stuffed shirt as you even knew what a *tendre* was. And our discussion got a bit heated, Nicky, and . . . I wagered Upton that you would prove my point for me by singling out Miss Bedford at the Hadley's . . . by dancing with her—twice—one set after another, which is a most exceptional thing to do, you know. I wagered Satan's Son on it, Nick."

"Satan's Son?" Wickenshire's eyes grew wide. Satan's Son was the finest hunter in all of England and Ireland both and provided Neil with a veritable fortune in stud fees once the hunting season ended. "You are impossible, Neil. Your papa spent forty years mixing and matching bloodlines to produce that horse. There ain't another like him anywhere."

"Just so. Which is why I cannot afford to lose him to Upton, Nicky. You can understand that, can you not? I shall be devastated if I lose him."

"Yes, and it will serve you right."

"No, it will not serve me right. No more than it served your papa right to lose everything he had. It is a sickness, Nick. A man opens his mouth and a wager falls out."

Wickenshire opened his mouth and closed it again without one word falling out.

"You could not help your papa, Nick," Spelling pleaded, "but you can help me. I will never wager anything again as long as I live if only you will do this for me. Besides, Upton called you a farmer, a country bumpkin who would be lucky if he recognized a dance floor when he fell face down on one. Truly, Nick, I cannot bear to lose Satan's Son. I helped Papa to birth him. And you do have a *tendre* for Miss Bedford, so it would not be cheating, so to speak. I ought to win the wager just because I am right."

"You did what?" Upton asked in amazement.

"Taught him to dance, and convinced him to distinguish Miss Bedford by dancing with her twice in a row at the Hadleys' Saturday evening. Well, I taught him the best I could in so short a time. I mean to say, Upton, he is not near as clumsy as I imagined he would be."

"But why, Spelling?" Lord Upton sat down on the window seat in Spelling's bedchamber and positively glared at him. "Have you turned against me? Do you mean to squash my hopes concerning that spoiled Bedford witch and her sister by marrying her off to your bumpkin of a cousin?"

"No. Do settle down, Upton. My intention is merely to be certain that Nicky will be fully occupied that evening and not sitting about bored, with time laying heavy upon him. Once he sets foot on the dance floor, he will be occupied watching his feet for a good half hour or more, and that is precisely the time I shall depart the Hadleys' and set off cross-country to Willowsweep and steal the parrot. Yes, and the numbskull will not so much as notice that I have gone. He will be certain, like all the rest of the company, that I was right there all the time."

"By gawd, Spelling, you have imagination, I will give you that. But even though you have taught him enough of the steps, how do you know he will dance with her twice in a row? I mean to say, even if he *has* developed a *tendre* for the chit, you cannot depend upon his wishing to announce it to the world."

"Oh, Nicky don't care about that. Not now. Not when he thinks me near to falling into the same pit as his papa and sees an opportunity to help me out of it."

"Falling into the same pit as his papa? An opportunity to help you out of it? By Jove, Spelling, what else, exactly, *did* you tell the poor half-wit?"

THIRTEEN

Serendipity made her way unsteadily to one of the chairs gathered around the study table and sat, laughing so very hard that tears streamed from her eyes. She took a series of deep breaths in an attempt to stop, but the puppy came bouncing across the floor and stood with front paws on her lap, cocking his head from side to side and then stretching upward and wiggling his bottom in an attempt to pull himself up high enough to lick at her tears. "N-no. Down, s-sweetest," Serendipity managed through her laughter.

Across the room, Delight turned to gaze innocently at her sister. "What is funny, Sera?" she asked innocently.

Serendipity, unable to reply at that precise moment, shook her head helplessly. Oh, if only she could paint well, she would paint the picture that had met her eyes as she had entered the room and she would keep it forever within her sight. Delight and the puppy and the kitten, all with their backs to her, had been looking up at Lord Nightingale who stood regally upon the very top of his cage wearing a tiny little cape tied about his feathery neck, the cape's hood fitted properly over his head.

"Yo ho ho," Nightingale declared and sent her into another spasm of laughter.

"You ain't laughin' at Lord Nightingale, are you?" asked Delight, coming to stand beside her puzzling sister.

"Oh—oh—n-no!" Serendipity assured her.

"Good, 'cause that would be 'stremely rude, Sera, when he has got all dressed up jus' for you this morning. Nicky fixed his cage, see. An' he is so very happy to have it back. An' he wanted to look perfeckly splendid when you came to teach him."

"Oh, he d-does. He looks perfectly splendid." Serendipity gave up pushing the puppy down and lifted him into her lap. "Wherever did he get such a marvelous cape? I did never know he possessed anything like it."

"Isn't it wonderful? I thought it might be too big, but it fits perfeck."

"You made it, Delight?"

"Uh-huh. Lady Wickenshire is teachin' me to crochet, an' I have practiced on this cape for Lord Nightingale. I am goin' to make one for Stanley Blithe and Sweetpea, too."

"For—S-Stanley Blithe and Sw-Sweetpea?"

"Uh-huh. I promised them. They seed Lord Nightingale's an' wanted their own."

"Which of them is S-Stanley Blithe and which is Sw-Sweetpea?" Serendipity asked, gazing at the puppy on her lap and the kitten that Delight now held in her arms.

"That is Stanley Blithe," said Delight, pointing to the puppy, "an' this is Sweetpea. An' they are both of them very smart, Sera, an' already know their names."

"No, do they? Already?"

"Yes, jus' watch," said Delight, placing the kitten on the worn carpeting and dashing across the room. "Come, Stanley Blithe," she called just as the puppy was wiggling out of Serendipity's lap in an attempt to follow the running child. "Come, Sweetpea," Delight called again. The kitten, not to be left behind by the puppy, dashed off directly after him. "See, Sera? They know precisely who they are."

"Y-yes, dearest. S-so they do."

"Yo ho ho," repeated Lord Nightingale, sidling to the edge of the cage and peering across at Serendipity in a most piratical manner while nibbling experimentally at the edges of his hood. "Morning, Nightingale."

"Oh!" Serendipity stared at the bird.

"Sera, he sounded jus' like Nicky, did you hear?"

"Indeed. Exactly like. His Lordship has taught him a new phrase. I wonder if he even knows that he has done so. Well, we shall have to tell him, shall we not?"

"Oh, yes!" Delight replied, hugging herself with both arms. "We mus' tell him right away. He will be so happy!" And before Serendipity could say another word, Delight was tugging at the study door and dashing out into the corridor with the puppy and the kitten both at her heels.

"They will not find him, I think, my Lord Nightingale," Serendipity smiled, rising to shut the door after them. "He is likely out in one of the fields or pastures. Come, let me untie your cape, sir. You cannot be at all comfortable in the thing. There, much better," she cooed as she swept the cape from off him, folded it neatly and placed it upon the study table. "Now, my lord, back to our lessons. Are you listening? You must pay strict attention, you know. You cannot simply sing notes, you must sing a verse. 'Wee Willie, Wee Willie, go 'way from m'door,' " she sang then in her sweet contralto, wandering off to gaze out the study windows. " 'I tell thee for true that I love thee no more. Oh, hear what I tell thee. B'lieve what I say. And please, Sweetest William, I pray thee go 'way.' "

Jenkins heard her song, vaguely, as he sat upon a stool in the butler's pantry with the door closed and locked, one lamp his only light. He thought, for a moment, what a fine young woman Miss Bedford had proved to be and hoped with all his heart that she would, indeed, get the parrot to sing. He fiddled with a piece of vellum on the counter before him and sighed the saddest of sighs. Truly, his heart was not in this. He detested the idea, but it must be done. If only His Lordship would heed the warnings before anything frightful happened.

Not that the fire in the Gold Saloon had not been frightful, but it had had nothing to do with the notes. Certainly no one involved in *The Undertaking* would set the house afire. By heaven, if Willowsweep burned to the ground, it would ruin everything. They had been searching for another, equally accessible, property since first Master Nicholas had announced his intention to reside at Willowsweep, but so far their search had proved fruitless.

"If they cannot discover another property, then Willowsweep it must remain," Jenkins muttered under his breath, tickling at his chin with the quill. "Dear Lord, Master Nicky can certainly not remain here! It would be the very death of Mr. Ezra if something should go wrong and Master Nicky be thought to be involved." Damnation, he thought then, why must His Lordship be so mule-headed? If it were Mr. Neil, one glance at one note would have sent him darting for safety.

Not one thing has gone as expected since I penned the very first note, Jenkins thought, frowning. Who would have thought that His Lordship would send the wretched thing off to Mr. Robert? Master Nicky generally despises to depend upon anyone but himself. And yet, off he sent it in the next day's mail. Thank gawd Miss Eugenia's papa did not give Mr. Ezra a thought. But why should he send Miss Eugenia to snoop about? Little Miss Eugenia, of all people. By Jove, if I had not been on my toes that night, if I had not noticed Miss Eugenia going to the stables and Miss Serendipity following me, I should have been discovered directly. It was a near thing. But Miss Eugenia trusts me now and thinks me to be helping her. Thank goodness for that.

Jenkins sighed again and studied his reflection in one of the ancient silver pitchers, and then he began to write.

*Take heed, my lord, and depart this cursed place
before the roiling evil of it bring thee to despair.
The Witch of Willowsweep be not dead. She merely
slumbers.*

Now that Miss Eugenia had finally remembered Lady
Elaina—it yet boggled Jenkins's mind that neither Master
Nicky nor Mr. Robert had—it was time to make it even
clearer that the threat came from that very mystical direction. Though whether Lady Elaina must rise up from
the dead in order to drive His Lordship from Willowsweep, Jenkins had not yet decided. It was looking
quite decidedly as though she must.

At least I need not concern myself with being caught
out delivering this missive, Jenkins thought with some
relief. Miss Eugenia will be at the squire's the entire
evening. Why, I may stroll straight down to the stables
and pin the thing to Master Nicky's saddle if I wish.

"Stanley Blithe and Sweetpea?" asked Wickenshire,
sending Grace off in Bobby Tripp's care and kneeling to
pat both of the furry heads flanking the child before him.
"Whyever should we call the puppy Stanley Blithe, Delight? I thought perhaps Wellington or Hercules. He is
going to grow into a very large dog, you know."

"Yes, and he will be braver an' stronger than any dog
that ever lived," Delight nodded, her fists planted upon
her hips like a tiny washerwoman. "Jus' like Lieutenan'
Stanley who was used to be in love with Sera. An' he
will always be the most happiest dog in all the world, so
he will be blithe, will he not? I asked Lady Wickenshire
if he would be blithe and she said indeed he would an'
that he is blithe now, too."

Wickenshire grinned. "Just so. He is perfectly blithe,
and since he will always belong to you, I suspect he
always will be blithe. And Sweetpea? It is because she

is sweet, yes? And has eyes as green as spring garden peas?"

" 'Zactly! I knew you would guess that one."

"But I should never have guessed Stanley Blithe," the earl said, standing and taking Delight's hand into his own. "How pleasant to discover the three of you waiting for me after a hard day of work. I have men in the fields now, so my work is not so very hard, but still, it is exceeding wonderful to have you meet me. Your sister did never tell me about Lieutenant Stanley who used to love her. Is he handsome as well as brave?"

"Oh, yes. An' he wears a red coat, which is just the thing to set a young lady's heart to goin' pitty-pat. That is what Sera said, that his coat set her heart to goin' pitty-pat."

"I see. Come along, you two," he called over his shoulder to the animals as he led Delight up the hill toward the house. "Keep up, rascals, or you will miss your dinners. Does Lieutenant Stanley not love your sister anymore?" he asked.

"I don' know," Delight replied most seriously. "He has not come to call since forever. Not even when we stayed in London. I waited and waited for 'im, but Sera said he would likely not come, and he didn't, neither. Maybe he don' love her anymore. Or maybe he is dead," she added with the unconcern of the young.

They entered the house by the kitchen door, shooing the kitten and puppy in before them. "Food for the beasts, Mrs. Daniel," Wickenshire ordered high-handedly and then spoiled the authoritarian effect with a chuckle. "We do have food for these beasts, do we not?"

"We do, my lord," smiled the cook, surveying the lot of them. "We have mutton and meal for Stanley Blithe and carp and cream for Sweetpea."

"Ah, so you have been introduced by name, have you? Not that you did not have a name or two for them last night when Jenkins was chasing them all around your kitchen."

"I made their highnesses' acquaintances very properly the moment that Miss Delight came down the stairs this morning, my lord. Will rule the house one day, these two, right along with Lord Nightingale, I think."

Wickenshire smiled at her but said nothing. Her words and Delight's earlier ones had combined to set his mind awhirl. "Come, Delight, onward and upward," he said distractedly, tucking a handful of sliced carrots into his coat pocket and leading her out of the kitchen. "We must check on Nightingale, eh? See what trouble he has gotten into this day."

No sooner did he open the door to the study than Nightingale came sailing at him from across the room and landed gracefully on his shoulder. "Morning, Nightingale," the macaw said in Wickenshire's own voice.

"Surprise! Me an' Sera were goin' to tell you!" cried Delight gleefully, jumping up and down. "But Sera is not here an' now Lord Nightingale has gone and telled you hisself!"

"Well, I'll be jangled!" Wickenshire exclaimed, strolling farther into the room with the parrot on his shoulder. "He sounded just like me! And I did never think to be able to teach the old—buzzard—anything. Well, we ought to have a celebration, Delight. Of course, all I have is a pocketful of carrots, but—here, take one, and I shall make a toast."

"A carrot toast," concurred Delight, holding one round slice in her hand.

"Exactly. A carrot toast. Nightingale, you will join us, will you not?" he added as he offered a slice of carrot to the parrot. "And now my piece. And . . ."

He knelt down upon the floor so that the three of them would be more of a height and held his slice of carrot up in the air. Delight held her carrot high as well. "To Nicky and Nightingale and Delight," he declared. "May we always go on as nicely as we do! Now we must tap our carrots together, Delight, like glasses, you know. And do not forget to tap Nightingale's as well. Excellent! And now we crunch!"

Serendipity came to a halt upon the threshold and watched as the toast was made and the carrots were tapped and crunched and swallowed by at least two of the participants—Nightingale preferring to fly with his, once it had been tapped, to the top of the bookshelf and to peck it into submission. Sera nibbled upon her lower lip and studied them through a haze of rising tears. How precious they were, Nicholas and Delight together. How careful he was to involve her in the most charming little moments—moments that the child would remember with joy for the rest of her life. Moments to be treasured in the best of times and the very worst of times, in youth and in age.

He gives her gifts more precious than gold, Serendipity thought as the gentleman and the child laughed together, unaware of her presence. Such a heart as Nicholas Chastain's is a rare and priceless gift. How fortunate are Delight and I to share in the sweetness of it, if only for a time.

"Miss Bedford? We did not hear you come." Wickenshire looked up at her, his eyes more welcoming than any Serendipity had ever before found focused upon her. "We are being quite silly, but you will not hold silliness against us, will you?"

"Never," she smiled, brushing away a tear with one quick swipe of her hand.

"Is something wrong?" The smile left his face at once. He rose and crossed to her. "You are crying, Sera."

"No, I am not. It is merely something in my eye." You, she thought. It is you in my eye—the vision of you and all that you are and have been and most certainly will come to be. But she did not say anything at all like that. She merely placed her hands into his and smiled up at him. "You have heard Lord Nightingale's new phrase, I think?"

"Just so. And I was that surprised to hear it, too."

"He was overcomed, Sera," Delight added, coming to join them as their hands parted. "His jaw just dropped right open, just like this!"

Delight's imitation of a jaw dropping set the both of them to laughing.

"Did I really look like that?" Wickenshire asked teasingly. "By Jove, I am surprised you did not run screaming from the room. I certainly should have done."

Wickenshire had the devil of a time to get himself ready for the evening at Squire Hadley's. Stanley Blithe sneaked into his dressing room and persisted in tugging at the legs of the earl's breeches while His Lordship was attempting to don them. Then the puppy dashed off to fight a violent battle with one of Wickenshire's dress shoes, swinging it about and letting it fly, rushing after it and stomping it into submission. Wickenshire was forced to wipe puppy spittle from the highly polished leather with what he discovered—too late—to be his last clean handkerchief. And, try as he might, the earl could not locate the studs for his best dress shirt or the buttons for his collar and was obliged to ring for Jenkins, who discovered them, in two twitches of a cat's tail, right in his jewelry box where they ought to be, embarrassing Wickenshire no end.

For some reason, His Lordship's hands began to tremble just as he was about to attempt the new Orientale and he destroyed five neckcloths in a row. His patience nearing an end, he let himself be convinced by a constant barrage of advice from Jenkins and a constant barrage of barking from Stanley Blithe, to settle for a Mailcoach, but found that he could not tie that knot either. He hurled three more neckcloths to the floor, stomped upon them for good measure and announced in a great bellow that Squire Hadley and his entertainment might go to Hades for all he cared, he had every intention of spending the evening at home.

"My lord, you do not mean that," Jenkins reproached him, a stern look in his eyes. "Her Ladyship and the young ladies are so looking forward to it. And they will not go, my lord, if you decline to attend. Take a deep breath or two while I take the puppy back to Miss Delight where he ought to be, and then we shall try the Mailcoach again. You *can* tie a Mailcoach, my lord. You have been tying one for years."

Wickenshire knew that to be so. He took a deep breath, found one remaining neckcloth in his dresser drawer and set about the process while Jenkins and the puppy were both absent. Oddly enough, he had not the least trouble tying it this time. He studied himself in the mirror and sighed. He took his brush and comb and attempted to coax his dark curls into something that resembled a fashionable style. He stared at his face and noted—not for the first time—how strange was the color of his eyes and how positively common was his nose and how brown were his neck and his face from years of working in the sun.

"It does not matter at all, my lord," said Jenkins quietly, returning to find the earl glaring at himself.

"What does not matter, Jenkins?"

"Whatever about yourself makes you frown so. It does not make a bit of difference."

"No, I expect you are correct. I cannot change my face. Still, I ought to have gone to the village, to the barber. That might have done some good."

"Balderdash, my lord. I hear that Lord Byron wears his hair in just such a way and any number of London's fashionable young gentlemen attempt to copy it."

"Does he? Byron?"

"Indeed. Shall I have the coaches brought 'round, my lord?"

"Are the ladies ready?"

"Yes, my lord."

"By all means, have the coaches brought up then." Wickenshire watched Jenkins leave the chamber, took one last look in the mirror and then lifted his chin and strolled from the dressing room. He paused for a moment in his bedchamber and glanced out through the parted draperies into the sky beyond the windows. A full moon was rising, pale and watery-looking in the descending twilight. It will not shine like gold tonight, he thought. Not for me. It will remain a ghost of a moon, for a ghost of a gentleman.

"Bah! What a coward I am. What a puling infant to be so concerned with my own self. What does it matter? I shall go to the squire's, and if Sera will consent to dance with me, I will do my best to prove capable—and if I find I cannot remember one step that Neil taught me, I will apologize and laugh at myself and beg her pardon."

But he did not wish to beg her pardon. He wished her to think him an excellent partner and a regular wonder of a conversationalist and a proper dandy. And he wished, as well, to lead her out into golden moonlight for just a moment or two. To see the perfect circle of the moon shining full and bright upon her guinea gold hair.

I will not have them in my life forever, he thought, remembering Mrs. Daniel's words in the kitchen. Serendipity and Delight, Stanley Blithe and Sweetpea will not rule this household. They will be gone from here after the first of June, unless I can think of some way to make them stay. Unless they wish to stay—a bit longer. Just a bit longer. But I expect they will not wish to stay. Even if this Lieutenant Stanley fellow does not love Sera any longer—though most likely he does—there will be some other gentleman soon enough. Perhaps even a marquis. She deserves a marquis, a woman as fine as Sera.

He left his chamber and, knowing he was late, hurried to the staircase and descended it with one hand upon the bannister, two steps at a time. He did not truly look about him until he reached the second from the last step, when he glanced to see Serendipity gazing up at him from the vestibule in an undergown of forest green silk covered by an overdress of Banbury lace. A cloak of matching green velvet with fur trim lay across her shoulders, falling in soft folds to the floor. Immediately behind her, Neil and Upton were helping Eugenia and Lady Wickenshire to don their cloaks, and Jenkins awaited Wickenshire with greatcoat over one arm and hat and gloves in hand.

"I am—I am s-sorry to have kept you standing about," he managed, his gaze never leaving Serendipity. "I h-had a spot of trouble. You are perfectly lovely, Miss Bedford."

"Yes, and so am I and so is Eugenia," declared the earl's mama with a most peculiar look upon her face. "Do come and don your coat and hat and gloves so that we may be off, Nicky. We do not wish to be late on our first evening at the squire's or Mrs. Hadley may never invite us again."

"Of course she will invite you again," laughed Neil. "You are the dowager Countess of Wickenshire, Aunt Diana. It is a blessing to Mrs. Hadley if you merely wave in her direction from your carriage, much less set foot on her parlor carpet."

"Just so," agreed Upton. "Shall we go, Miss Eugenia?" he queried, placing his hat at a most rakish angle upon his curls, and offering Eugenia his arm.

"Indeed," the dowager replied, taking Neil's arm and allowing him to open the door and escort her from the house. "Come, Eugenia, Lord Upton. Do hurry, Nicky," she called over her shoulder. "And do not forget to bring Serendipity with you. We ladies shall take the first coach and the gentlemen, the second."

"I do not think that I have ever seen you look lovelier," Wickenshire managed as he descended the remaining two steps and Jenkins stepped forward to help him into his coat.

"You have never seen me dressed for a social evening, my lord. This is now a most unfashionable dress, I am sure. But it does not matter in the country."

"No, not in the country," the earl agreed, hastily tugging on his gloves.

"No. And it does make a regular pair of us, does it not?"

"A pair of us?" Wickenshire asked, offering his arm and leading her out and down the front steps.

"Yes. You are wearing your green velvet tail coat. I asked Jenkins if he thought you might, and he thought it certain that you would because—"

"—it is my very best one," he finished for her.

"Exactly. And so I wore this gown, and now we are both green," she said, giving his arm a squeeze. "Do you not remember what you told Delight about that coat? Well, sir, now we are both enchanted frogs. You and I together."

FOURTEEN

Mrs. Hadley pranced about her house in ecstasy, from the drawing room to the parlor to the sun room to the winter parlor and back again. Her round little cheeks glowed red with excitement, her dark eyes twinkled and her hands waved this way and that as she spoke to one group of guests after another. Even Wickenshire, who was not an especially good judge of such things, recognized that for the squire's wife, this evening was a triumph. "I expect I am happy we came, Mama," he admitted, sipping at the glass of burgundy he held and looking around the winter parlor. "Mrs. Hadley seems a very nice sort."

"Oh, dearest," Lady Wickenshire replied, tugging him down beside her on a chintz settee, "the woman simply bubbles with excitement. Not only is she the very first hostess in the neighborhood to have you, and therefore may present the Earl of Wickenshire to all her neighbors, but she has caught herself a viscount and a gentleman worth a King's ransom in her net as well. Every woman here envies her, let me tell you."

"No, really? You too, Mama?"

"Well, no. But I have not been concerned with Society for a goodly long time, Nicky. I cannot think the last time I hosted a dinner or a ball or so much as an alfresco luncheon."

"You will be able to do all of it again soon."

"If Lord Nightingale sings."

"He will sing, Mama. I am sure of it. Sera, I mean to say, Miss Bedford, has got him to sing a scale. It will not be long now before he learns a verse of song as he must."

Lady Wickenshire studied her son's face intently. "I think you may call her Sera, dear one, when we speak privately. And I wish you to understand, Nicky, that it does not matter to me."

"What does not matter to you?"

"Whether Lord Nightingale sings or not. It would be marvelous if he did, of course. I want him to sing for your sake, my darling. But if he does not, you must not feel as though you have disappointed me in any way. You have never disappointed me in all your life, Nicholas. Do you understand what I am attempting—and quite badly, too—to say?"

"Yes, Mama," grinned the earl, "but you need not fret about it. Nightingale is going to sing, and by the first of June, too. Oh, there is the squire waving at me. Another of the neighborhood gentlemen I must be introduced to, no doubt."

Lady Wickenshire's gaze followed him as he crossed the room to be gathered into a group of older gentlemen standing near the hearth. Her eyes lit with pride and her smile widened. Sera, she thought. He called her Sera without even stuttering. I do hope that bodes well for the future because she is the most delightful young woman.

Having lost sight of their escorts, Eugenia and Serendipity had wandered into the sun room to find themselves surrounded by a bevy of eager young ladies, all wishing to know about the gentlemen who stayed at Willowsweep.

"What is he like, your cousin the earl?" asked Squire Hadley's youngest daughter, Fiona. "Papa said he never saw such a man in all his life for fighting a fire. Oh, we are so very sorry, you know, about the fire. I ought to have said that the first thing, I expect."

"Nicky is the most extraordinary gentleman in all of England," Eugenia replied quietly. "And he is most courageous."

"Oh, but you would say that," grinned Miss Plymouth, the eldest of the vicar's daughters. "He is your cousin, after all."

"Yes, but Mr. Spelling is her cousin, as well," Serendipity grinned, "and Eugenia does never refer to him as extraordinary."

"Mr. Spelling is well known in London," observed Lady Melody Jolynes who was a guest of the Hadleys'. "Mama says that he is sought after by all of the very best hostesses. He is rich as Croesus, she says. Is he?"

"Yes," laughed Eugenia.

"And Lord Upton is the most handsome gentleman I have ever seen," added Miss Emily Plymouth. "I do hope we are going to get up some dancing tonight, Fiona. Perhaps Lord Upton will wish to dance with me. I have never danced with a lord before."

"And there are two of them here tonight," declared Fiona Hadley triumphantly. "Papa has got us two lords with one blow. I expect we had best get up some dancing. It would be a shame to waste them."

"All you need do, Upton, is to keep an eye on Wickenshire once I have left the establishment. Keep him occupied, you know. Though you will not need to do much, because he will be dancing for a good part of the time."

"I know. I know," murmured Upton as the two wandered, nodding to this one and that, from the back parlor into the front parlor. "It is not your cousin worries me, Spelling. The ladies are bound to notice your absence. They will be counting on you to dance right along with the rest of us."

"Not to worry, Upton. I am just about to provide myself with an adequate excuse for not dancing."

"You are?"

"Yes," replied Spelling as they reached the threshold to the front parlor. One step and Spelling caught the toe of his shoe beneath the edge of the carpeting. He stumbled, his arms windmilling, into the group of guests gathered there. Upton grabbed for him, but Spelling knocked the sustaining hand away and fell, one knee thwacking loudly and ominously against the floor. Everyone gathered around him, ladies and gentlemen alike.

"No, no, I am fine, ma'am," Spelling declared as Mrs. Hadley herself bent over him, her eyes filled with concern. "Terribly embarrassed is all. All my fault. Here, Upton, give me a hand up, eh? Ow! Deuce!" he added as he regained his feet. "I have twisted my confounded knee again, Henry."

"Ice!" gasped Mrs. Hadley, her hands flapping ineffectually in mounting horror. "You must put some ice upon it, Mr. Spelling. I shall send Montrose for ice at once."

"No, my dear Mrs. Hadley," Neil protested, an arm about Upton's shoulder, making a great show of bending and unbending his knee without putting the least weight upon it. "Just took a whack is all. I shall settle down into a chair and keep off of it for the rest of the evening, and it will be fine in the morning, I assure you. Help me to that chair, Upton, if you will."

"Are you certain that I may not—"

"My dear madam," interrupted Spelling, "I will not allow my clumsiness to inconvenience you. Such a marvelous gathering! Such a wonderful hostess! You must enjoy your triumph to the very fullest and not worry about me for one moment. My only regret is that the young ladies will likely wish to dance and, regrettably, I do not think that I—"

"Oh! Oh, of course not, Mr. Spelling. Of course you

must not dance. I shall tell Fiona not to depend upon you."

"Blasted faker," whispered Upton into Spelling's ear as Mrs. Hadley departed.

"Just so," grinned Spelling. "But a marvelously good one."

As the clocks struck ten, an entire flock of pretty ladies seized on gentlemen's arms, dragging them laughing and protesting into the Hadleys' drawing room, where the brothers and fathers, husbands and uncles made short work of moving all the furniture to one side of the room and rolling up the carpet. Mrs. Elvina Hadley, Miss Fiona's sister-in-law, then searched through sheaves and sheaves of music until she had collected all she thought suitable. Whereupon she sat down at the pianoforte and played an acciaccatura to get everyone's attention. "We will begin," she announced, smiling, "with a country dance and then go on to a splendid new piece by Robert Constable called, 'Oh, Sir John, Do Not.' "

A veritable cheer went up from all of the young people.

"Constable," observed Upton as he stood beside Eugenia. "The Skip and Dip has reached the country just as Spelling thought it might. I must go and tell him so."

"Is he all right, my lord, all by himself in the front parlor? Ought he not come sit in here where he may at least be part of the company?"

"No, no, he is not alone, Miss Chastain," Upton protested at once. "Any number of the more elderly gentlemen are with him. Discussing Wellesley, last I heard. But he will be pleased to know the Skip and Dip has reached the hinterlands. I wagered him it had not, you see, and now I owe your wretched cousin five quid."

"Go, then, if you must, my lord," Eugenia said, "but

do not forget to return, will you? There are any number of young ladies praying that you will ask them to dance."

"And are you one of them, Miss Chastain?"

"Oh, heavens, no! I should look like a one-legged chicken hopping about upon the dance floor. I would not think to subject any gentleman to the embarrassment of partnering me."

Eugenia watched Lord Upton make his way across the room and out into the corridor, and then she followed him. Nodding to this new acquaintance and that, grinning at Serendipity, giving her Aunt Diana an enormous smile, she moved through the makeshift ballroom and into the corridor. I do not believe for a moment that you must rush off to Neil to make good upon a wager, Lord Upton, she thought as she saw him turn into the Hadleys' front parlor. I do not believe that any more than I believe that Neil was clumsy enough to trip over the edge of a carpet. Something is afoot with the two of you.

With her rolling gait causing her slippers to whisper an oddly staccato song along the carpeting, Eugenia made her way into the library which stood one door down from the front parlor. Through a floor-to-ceiling casement window, she stepped out onto a tiny balcony and, pressing herself close against the brick of the house, she moved cautiously to the parlor windows, one of which had been left open to cool the crowd that had gathered within. She reached the window just in time to hear Neil announce to the other gentlemen that the dancing had begun and that he would make use of Upton's arm to get him into the drawing room to watch the fun.

Eugenia could not believe it. Into the drawing room to watch the fun? But had not Lord Upton said . . . ? With a silent sigh, she made her cautious way back toward the library, a gentle breeze playing with the long hem of her skirt. She was just beside the casement when she heard the two of them speaking. They had not gone to the drawing room at all, but directly into the library!

"I am off to Willowsweep then, Upton, to attend to

that wretched parrot. Best return to the drawing room quickly, or Eugenia will wonder what keeps you."

"And if anyone should come searching for you?"

"Say that I hobbled off to the privy. That will do. I shall be back before the dancing ends."

"I hope," muttered Upton.

Eugenia huddled against the outside wall. Off to Willowsweep to attend to that wretched parrot? she thought. What has Neil in mind to do? I just knew that he came to Willowsweep to ruin Nicky's chances. I knew he did!

Wickenshire screwed his courage to the sticking point and, as Serendipity came laughing from the country dance, he stepped out before her and petitioned her to join him in the Skip and Dip. Serendipity looked up at him, her eyes wide.

"The Skip and Dip, my lord? It is the very newest dance."

"Yes, so I have discovered. Everyone in London is wild about the thing, Neil says. What? Do you think I will embarrass you, Miss Bedford, if I attempt it? I promise you I will not."

"But your mama confided in me that you had never learned to dance, my lord."

"Well, my mama does not know everything about me. I have, in fact, learned to dance very recently, and I do know the steps to this Skip and Dip thing, I promise you."

Serendipity giggled. She could not help herself, he looked so very determined and serious. "I should be delighted to dance with you, Lord Wickenshire," she replied, "but I have not been out in Society since Papa died well over a year ago, and so I have never encountered the Skip and Dip before tonight."

"No?" Quite abruptly Wickenshire's somber countenance dissolved into a most enchanting grin. "How fortunate for me."

"How so, fortunate?"

"Why, because if I make some great mistake, you will not even know it! Come, Sera. Let us give it a try. I did not think it at all complicated. And you are such a wonderful dancer. It is likely your feet will know precisely what to do after the first time through."

"But the first time through, my feet will perform outrageously," Serendipity laughed.

"Well, I cannot say what my feet will do at all. They have never actually been called upon to dance to *music.*"

The dowager Lady Wickenshire was most amazed to see her son lead Miss Bedford out to join the set. Whatever makes Nicky think he can dance? she wondered. But he is grinning his most charming grin, and Serendipity is smiling so widely. Well, perhaps she intends to teach him the steps right here and now. Oh, I do hope that Nicky takes to dancing a great deal better than he ever took to singing or there will be utter chaos upon the floor.

There was indeed chaos upon the floor, but only a bit of it was Wickenshire's fault. Truth to tell, Mrs. Elvina Hadley enjoyed the lively music so much that she played it with ear-shattering enthusiasm, which made the earl's plan to call out the steps to Serendipity most difficult. Lady Melody, who danced beside them with Lord Upton as partner, did not know the steps either, so Upton had to shout above the music as well. And any number of brothers, whose sisters had dragged them into the dance, had never heard of the Skip and Dip in their lives, thus causing their sisters to resort to a similar technique.

Serendipity found herself whirling right when Wickenshire cried "Twirl right," and whirling left when Upton cried "Twirl left," and joining hands and releasing them and skipping forward and back and forward again depending upon whatever voice rose above Mrs. Hadley's music. Lady Melody did the same. And the brothers could not hear their sisters at all and began to swing the girls about with shouts and laughter, mucking up the steps, but inventing new steps on the spot.

A jolly muddle of a dance it turned out to be. Those who did not know the patterns were laughing so very hard and attempting such odd things that those who did know the dance began to grin and ignore the correct steps and join in the fun. Dancers hopped and skipped and jumped about, dancing first this way and then that, changing partners at the most unexpected moments and then seizing their partners back again when they thought they ought. If one pair of them formed an arch anywhere upon the floor, everyone else rushed to the spot to dance under it. If one pair began to do a bit of a reel, four more couples were likely to reel right along with them for a measure or two while other couples skipped around them. Oh, it was a madhouse, to be certain, and not one of the spectators on the chairs in the far corner failed to watch in fascination and take a turn at attempting to guess what the young people would do next.

Jenkins was alone in the stables at Willowsweep, in the tack room, pinning his note to Wickenshire's saddle, when he heard the first of the whispers come from beneath his feet. His face grew pale in the lantern light. Now? They are coming now? he thought. But they cannot. They never unload but at the dark of the moon, and the moon is as full as it can get! And besides, Master Nicky is still in residence. How dare Captain Sebastian come when the master of the house—

With mind awhirl, Jenkins carried his lantern to the far corner of the room and set it carefully down. He tugged two heavy bags of oats out of his way and slipped his fingers into a hole in the floorboards. He jerked the boards upward. The trapdoor, its hinges well oiled, veritably flew open.

"Sebastian?" he called hoarsely downward.

"Aye. Is't you, Tommy?"

"Yes, of course it is me. What are you doing here?"

"Goin' about are business, Tommy, me lad. Me an' the lads be goin' about are business like we a'ways does."

"But you cannot be going about it now, Sebastian. It is a full moon and His Lordship is in residence and—"

"Hush, hush, Tommy. I be knowin' about His Lordship an' all, but 'tis of no consequence now. None whatsomeever. The *Silver Scupper* has run aground an' be aspillin' her guts all over the tide. By termorrow the sea will be aroilin' wif cutters and the shore aboilin' wif excisemen. Ride amongst the waves a minit longer wif the ballast we be carryin', we cannot."

"Damnation," mumbled Jenkins. "What was she carrying, the *Silver Scupper?*"

"Brandy, me lad. 'Tis what she a'ways does carry. An' them kegs be abobbin' about on the waves even as we speak. Jist abeggin' fer the tide to carry 'em in and the taxmen to discover 'em. Saints in heaven, Tommy, you could not expect us to bide are time awaitin' fer the dark o' the moon amidst sich a mass of cutters as there are like to be by termorrow?"

"No," sighed Jenkins. "How much have you got, Sebastian?"

"Buckets an' barrels an' boxes full. Ever'thing that would hold it, we did fill wif it. Do not be frettin', Tommy. We bean't takin' nothin' up no farther than the entrance to the house. Ain't at all likely as His Lordship will ever know."

"Not unless the excisemen come pounding upon the door."

"Not even then, me lad. They may search Willowsweep from bow to stern, but they willn't ever fine this passageway."

"No, perhaps not."

"Sartainly not, unless they do be snoopin' about amongst the rocks and fine how we come. That be the only way."

Jenkins took solace in this thought, though he knew it to be most untrue. Anyone might discover the passage in which Sebastian and his crew stood. All they need do was notice one of the doors to the old servants' staircase and follow it downward to the very end. But then, if Mr. Ezra had not reminded him exactly what to look for, Jenkins would never have rediscovered the doors himself.

The Skip and Dip ended and Wickenshire stood holding Serendipity's hand in his own upon the floor. "We were magnificent," he grinned. "I have never heard so much laughter from so many directions all at one time."

"Well, I cannot think why anyone should laugh," replied Serendipity, a teasing twinkle in her eyes. "I thought we all performed to perfection. Oh, we had best move, my lord. Mrs. Hadley is striking up a waltz."

"Yes, best move," nodded Wickenshire, taking her into his arms. "I can waltz, too, you know," and he swirled her into the dance with as much enthusiasm as he had displayed in the dance previous, making her suddenly breathless.

They circled the floor in quite an acceptable manner, until they neared the French doors that led to the balcony overlooking the Hadleys' garden. At that point Wickenshire's feet seemed suddenly to rebel, and in moments Serendipity found herself dancing beneath the light of the moon.

"I ought not to have done that," Wickenshire whispered, ceasing to waltz but keeping his arm around Serendipity's waist. "I ought not to have done that at all. Most improper of me."

"Indeed," whispered Serendipity. "What could you have been thinking, my lord? We must dance back inside at once."

"Not at once. Please, Sera. May I call you Sera?"

"You have been calling me Sera for days."

"Yes, but I did not think you had noticed."

"I have noticed."

The true golden ball of a moon Wickenshire had yearned for glinted down upon the guinea gold of Serendipity's hair, sending the earl's heart to thrumming. He took a long, steadying breath, not believing his good fortune. His eyes glowed with such devastating longing that Serendipity could not speak a word or move a muscle or think one clear thought of her own as she gazed up at him.

"You are so beautiful in moonlight," Wickenshire whispered, like a man lost in dreams. "A maiden woven of glories and triumphs, dreams and desires, sparkling with the golden dust of Glorianna's faeries. Even your eyes twinkle tonight with golden lights. I never thought to see you so. I could not believe that I should ever have the privilege."

Serendipity, her limbs frozen, felt her heart melt right down into her slippers—both of them.

"How could any man who once loved you ever let you go, Sera? Lieutenant Stanley must be a Bedlamite, or is he dead, or is it that the war has separated you and you long for his return?"

"L-Lieutenant S-Stanley?" As the look in his eyes and the loveliness of his words had melted her heart, so the wonderful warmth of Wickenshire's arm securely around her seemed to be melting her brain as well. "Lieutenant Stanley?" she said again.

"Indeed. The brave gentleman after whom Stanley Blithe has been named."

"S-Stanley Blithe was named after—Lieutenant S-Stanley?"

Wickenshire nodded. "The gentleman who loved you and whose red coat—how did Delight say it?—whose red coat set your heart to going pitty-pat."

"I have not thought of Lieutenant Stanley in over a year!"

"You have not? But Delight said that he loved you,

and I . . . assumed that you loved him. How could you not think of him?"

Serendipity, Wickenshire's spell upon her broken by the outrageous way in which his eyebrows were arranging themselves into a puzzled frown, began to giggle and quickly covered her mouth with one hand. But it did no good. Tiny snorts escaped, and tears of glee started to her eyes.

"By Jove, the man loved you and he has gone off to war, Sera. You ought not be giggling about him."

Serendipity shook her head. "N-no," she managed from behind her hand, and then was besieged by another fit of giggles.

Wickenshire let go her waist and took a step back. His hands went to rest upon his hips, pushing back his coat to reveal the green and gold waistcoat he wore beneath. "May I ask what is so very humorous, Miss Bedford, about a gentleman going off to war?"

"N-nothing. Oh, n-nothing," cried Serendipity in a choking whisper, tears running freely down her cheeks. "I am— I have— L-Lieutenant Stanley has not gone off to w-war, simply to B-Bath. He serves in the militia. He spends his d-days upon the parade ground and then goes sh-shooting pheasants."

"Oh. My mistake."

"No, no. Certainly Delight could not have known and . . ." Serendipity paused to swipe at her tears and sniffed. Wickenshire reached immediately for his handkerchief. Serendipity, seeing him do so, held out her hand to accept it.

"I, ah," Wickenshire brought his hand, empty, from his pocket and stared down at her open palm.

Serendipity's palm wilted at once. "I beg your pardon, my lord. I thought you to be about to offer me your handkerchief."

"Yes, I was but I, ah, do not have one with me at the moment. You did not love Lieutenant Stanley? Truly you did not?"

"He was a charming rascal who teased me mercilessly for the time his regiment was quartered near our home, but he did never love me, nor I him. I merely made some foolish comment within Delight's hearing, I expect. I do not so much as remember the incident. Why do you not have a handkerchief, my lord? Have you lost it?"

"No, I, ah, made use of my last clean one to wipe puppy spittle from my shoe while I was dressing," murmured Wickenshire.

"P-puppy spittle?" Serendipity felt the giggles bubbling up inside of her again.

"Stanley Blithe was doing battle with it—my shoe— and I— Do not, Sera. Do not go off again," Wickenshire protested as Serendipity began to search hastily through the little reticule that hung from her wrist for her own handkerchief.

"I c-cannot h-help myself! P-puppy spittle! S-Stanley B-Blithe! D-Delight named him after Lieutenant S-Stanley!"

Wickenshire nodded. "B-because he w-would grow to b-be strong and b-brave," he said, his own eyes crinkling with glee and his breath coming in short gasps. "B-brave as the lieutenant and h-happy as well."

Serendipity nodded gleefully. "Lieutenant S-Stanley was always h-happy. H-happy that he w-would never actually be c-called upon to f-fight."

Wickenshire could control himself no longer. His strong arms reached out for her and pulled her close. His head bowed over hers and he burst into riotous laughter. Her head resting against his chest, Serendipity laughed just as heartily.

"Well, I cannot think what has you both in such whoops," interrupted a familiar voice, "but you must stop and at once."

"Eu-genia?" Wickenshire lifted his head to stare at his cousin and freed Serendipity from his arms at once. "Eugenia, my gawd, what is it?"

"Eugenia, what is wrong?" asked Serendipity, turning

about and becoming instantly aware of a subtle disorder to that young woman's clothing and hair, and a look of anxiety upon her face.

"It is Neil," Eugenia said, taking one of Serendipity's hands into her own and giving it a subtle squeeze though she spoke directly to her cousin. "Neil has sneaked out of this house, Nicky, taken a horse from the stables and ridden off to Willowsweep. I watched him go and I heard what he said. He said that he plans to attend to that wretched parrot!"

FIFTEEN

Serendipity held to the strap with both hands as the coach rumbled over the road toward Willowsweep. "I never thought this old thing could go so fast," she said and then blushed in the shadows, thankful that Lord Wickenshire could not see the color that washed up into her cheeks. "That is to say—" she began.

"Never attempt to restate it, Sera," Eugenia offered, clinging to the strap upon her side of the seat as well. "Nicky is perfectly aware of the age of his coach."

"Indeed," sighed Wickenshire, seated across from them. "It was my father's and not new then. But the team is good, and John excellent. He will have us at Willowsweep almost as quickly as Neil will get there by riding cross-country. We will be in time, I think, to stop him from seizing Nightingale. Nightingale will not fly upon his shoulder and beg to be taken off, you know. He is not fond of Neil."

"Are you certain Neil only means to abduct Lord Nightingale?" Serendipity asked anxiously. "It would take him only moments, you know, to—to—"

"No, Neil will not wring Nightingale's neck," Wickenshire replied confidently. "He will not even abduct the bird for long. Nightingale must reappear June the first in Trent's presence to prove that nothing dire has happened to him, because if he does not appear, the Sisters of the Resurrection will have Aunt Winifred's money. Neil would never allow that to happen."

"Thank goodness," breathed Serendipity.

"I do hope that Aunt Diana will be able to convince Lord Upton that we are all somewhere about the Hadleys' still," Eugenia thought aloud. "We do not need Lord Upton thinking to hurry to Neil's aid."

"Lord Upton is underhanded and dishonest and likely a cowardly worm to boot," Serendipity declared. "I doubt he would ride to anyone's aid. To think that he knew what Mr. Spelling intended and said not one word—actually helped him to slip away! Well, so much for his declarations of good intentions toward Delight and myself. I will not trust the man again. I was right in my first impression of him, Nicholas, and everything you said to me about him was correct. For shame that such a man should inherit my papa's title!"

Nicholas? Wickenshire's collar clamped itself around his throat, strangling him, making him choke. The night grew inordinately warm, forcing beads of perspiration to his brow and making the dark curls at the back of his neck grow seriously damp. All thought of Neil and his nefarious plot, whatever it might be, slipped from his mind. She had called him Nicholas. Did it mean that she intended their relationship to proceed upon a more intimate basis? Was he being offered the unimaginable opportunity to court this most remarkable young woman, despite all of his vile shortcomings?

Dreamer, he told himself. You have called her Sera any number of times. She merely intends to convey to you that it is acceptable. You and she are to be friends and upon a first-name basis. Pull yourself together, Nick, and cease this nonsense. You were never used to be such a mooncalf!

Neil reached the stables at Willowsweep and led the horse inside. He had not the least idea whose horse it might be. One of the neighbors who had ridden to the Hadleys', of course, but which of them, he did not know or care. The bit of blood had been standing docilely in the stable yard, saddled, as he knew any number of them would be, and none of the stablehands had been anywhere about, so he had stolen it.

No, I have not stolen it, he corrected himself silently. Only borrowed it for a time. I shall return it to the Hadleys' as soon as I have finished with Nightingale.

What the devil? he thought then, as he led the animal toward one of the stalls and noticed a lantern burning in the tack room. There ought not be anyone here at this hour. No one will be required until the coaches return. It is not as if there are any lodgings in this place. The building is too near collapse to house men in it.

Spelling closed the horse in a stall, wandered back to the tack room and peered around the door frame. By George, he thought. What the devil is that? A trapdoor? I shall have to look into *that* before I leave. No telling what Nicky's papa might have hidden away down there. Someone from the household knows about it, that is certain. But why go down in the dark and leave the lantern burning behind him? Well, because he has another light below, he thought then, nodding.

His curiosity tweaked to a high degree, he nevertheless moved on past the tack room and climbed the hill to the house. "Deal with that wretched bird first," he mumbled to himself. "Discover what lies beneath the stables another day. No telling but Nicky's papa stored his wine down there and Nicky knows nothing at all about it. Most likely the butler knows and is helping himself to a bottle or two."

Spelling slipped into the kitchen without being noticed. No servants lingered belowstairs. All had gone up to their own quarters and would likely remain there until they heard the coaches return. A minimum number of lamps and candles had been left lighted—one here, one there—in anticipation of the master's return, just as

Spelling had hoped. With quick steps, he made his way up the rear staircase to the first floor and then down the long corridor. Seizing the lamp left burning beside the Gold Saloon, he stepped into the ruined chamber for a moment, then set the lamp back and proceeded to the study.

"What a very thoughtful cousin you are, Nicky," he whispered, finding his way through that darkened room by the moonlight shining through the open draperies. "Put Nightingale to bed, by gawd, to make the whole thing easier for me."

Beneath the shawl thrown over his cage, Nightingale stirred, fluttered, and muttered "Knollsmarmer" quietly to himself.

I will knollsmarmer you, you blasted bird, Spelling thought, shaking open the burlap bag he had hidden in the abandoned Gold Saloon. See if I will not.

Jenkins poked his head up through the trapdoor and listened intently.

"See anyone?" called Captain Sebastian.

"No one. But I could swear that I heard—"

"Aw, you be jist a wee jumpy, me lad, on accounta we come early-like," growled Sebastian at the bottom of the ladder. "You said yourself that His Lordship be off at them Hadleys an' ain't like to be home before two at the soonest."

"Just so," muttered Jenkins, descending back into the passageway below the stables, "but it would be just like Master Nicky to discover some reason to come home early, and then where will we be?"

"I ain't got the foggiest where you will be, Tommy, me lad, but the lot of us will be ahidin' and aprayin' he don't fine us," chuckled the captain. "More o' me lads be acomin'. Git yourself back down 'ere, me fine fellow, an' lend us a hand. Quickest stowed, quickest yc be rid o' the likes o' us."

Jenkins scurried back down the ladder with amazing agility for a man nearing his fifty-eighth year. He had long before doffed his coat, and now, in his shirtsleeves, he helped to stack crate after wooden crate along the sides of the passage. "How many are there?" he asked as he and Sebastian accepted one crate after another from the line of sailors.

"I reckon as there be enough to supply the entire army for a year," grinned Sebastian, rubbing at his whiskery jaw. "Wellesley's army and Napoleon's both. Never thought to see m'darlin' *Peggy* ridin' so low in the water. Filled to the line and then some, she were, when we left Eire. Did we go down durin' the crossin', why the entire ocean would have been awash wif it. What a sight that would have been, eh, Tommy?"

"A sight I never wish to see," sighed Jenkins. "I cannot tell you how pleased I am that you did not go down."

"How do it be goin'? Does His Lordship be likely to leave this place anytime soon?"

"Not that I can tell," Jenkins muttered, wiping his brow with the back of his sleeve. "I told Mr. Ezra that threatening notes would not do the thing. More likely to make him stay, just to discover who the deuce wants him gone."

"Aye, told his nibs the same, I did."

"You did?"

"Sartainly. Ain't no coward, His Lordship."

"How do you know?"

"Well, 'tis only sensical, Tommy. Lookit what all he has done in 'is life, an' all what he hasn't. He ain't afeared o' hard work, nor what others might be athinkin' of 'im. No, an' he ain't afeared of the gov'ment neither, eh? I know how he boarded over them winnows when he were jist a wee lad an' dared them blighters to try an' colleck upon 'em af'erwords. Mr. Ezra be atellin' me 'bout it, proud as a peacock. Ain't no gentleman like His Lordship goin' to run from lines upon a piece of paper."

"Yes, but if he remains," sighed Jenkins, "and the excisemen should discover . . . well, they will lay it at his doorstep. You know they will. That cannot be allowed to happen."

"No, but I kinnot see why we do not tell the lad what's ahappenin', Tommy. I will lay odds that Mr. Ezra ain't ventured to ask would he be interested in joinin' in the fun, has 'e now?"

"His Lordship? Join in the fun?" Jenkins' eyebrows soared up into his hairline. "His Lordship involve himself with smugglers? Oh, I dare say not, Sebastian. Not a chance in the world."

Wickenshire leaped from the coach before it came to a halt, dashed up the step and in through the front door, leaving Serendipity and Eugenia to manage as best they could in his wake. He seized the candelabra that had been left burning in the foyer and mounted the staircase to the first floor two steps at a time.

"Well, for goodness' sake," declared Eugenia, hands upon her hips as she and Serendipity crossed the threshold. "How does Nicky expect us to follow when he has taken the only light? John," she called over her shoulder. "Come in for a moment."

The coachman nodded, climbed from his perch and tied the reins about an ancient hitching post, then hurried to the house. "What is it ye need, Miss Eugenia?"

"A light, John. Can you find one for us, do you think? His Lordship has taken the candelabra."

"I shall have a go at it, miss," the coachman replied, fiddling about in his pocket for his flints and walking carefully off into the shadows of the nearest antechamber. It proved to be a good three minutes before he emerged again with a lamp aglow in his huge hand.

"Thank you, John," Eugenia smiled, accepting the lamp from him. "You may go n——"

An unearthly shriek pierced the stillness of the house and cut Eugenia off short.

"What the devil!" exclaimed the coachman and reddened immediately. "I beg pardon, miss."

"It is Nightingale. I am certain it is Nightingale! I have never heard such a scream from him!" Serendipity cried, seizing the lamp from Eugenia's hands, hiking her gown up nearly to her knees and running up the staircase.

"Well, John," sighed Eugenia. "We are in the dark again. I most certainly cannot get up that staircase in the dark."

"I will fetch another lamp, Miss Eugenia."

"Cease and desist, you moldy old bag of feathers," Spelling growled, removing the perches and tossing them to the cage floor as Nightingale screeched. The parrot clung to the very back of the cage with both feet, and the moment Spelling's hands came near him, he struck out with his beak.

"You cannot bite me this time, you beetlebrain. I am wearing leather gloves," muttered Spelling. "Ow! Damnation! You can a bit! I am running out of all patience with you, Nightingale!"

"Villain!" Nightingale squawked. "Villain!" He ruffled his feathers defiantly, but Spelling was not to be denied. He caught the bird in both hands, loosing Nightingale's grip upon the cage, smoothing down his wings, supporting his breast as he had seen his father do countless times.

Lord Nightingale ceased to struggle as Spelling cradled the parrot against his chest a moment and then stuffed him into the burlap sack. He tied the sack closed with a piece of hemp, swung it over his shoulder and turned toward the corridor just as a cloud covered the moon. The room went black. Spelling knocked his shin against a table, groaned, spun about, tripped over a foot stool and crashed into a wall—and the wall seemed to move behind him.

"What the deuce?" Spelling muttered, feeling for the wall with his hand. "By Jove, I cannot be wondering about moving walls now," he told himself. "Every servant in the household will have heard that crash." He made his way a bit more carefully out into the corridor and heard Wickenshire pounding up the front staircase and numerous other feet stomping down the back staircase. Spelling cursed, grabbed the lamp from the corridor table and turned back into the study. Out the window, he thought, and then remembered that he was on the first floor and not the ground floor.

Holding the lamp high and looking about him for a place to hide, he saw the open door. "The damnable wall did move," he murmured in amazement. He had not the least idea what lay behind the door, but people were rushing in his direction, and it was going to be rather difficult to explain to Jenkins and the rest of his cousin's servants why he had Nicky's parrot in a burlap bag. He stepped through the doorway, shoved the door closed with his shoulder, discovered himself upon a set of ancient stone steps and set off in the only direction that seemed reasonable to take at that precise moment—down.

Wickenshire dashed into the study, three of the candles on the candelabra already out from the breeze of his charge up the staircase and down the corridor. Thinking only of Nightingale, he crossed directly to the parrot's cage to find the door hanging open, the perches laying upon the floor, and Lord Nightingale gone. He took a deep breath, crossed to the study table and used one of the still-lighted candles to light the lamp that stood there.

"Nicholas!" Serendipity spun around the door frame into the room. "Nicholas, did you—Where is he? Oh, my heavens, we are too late!"

"We cannot be too late," grumbled Wickenshire. "Nightingale was screeching only moments ago, and there was the most tremendous crash just before I reached the head of the stairs."

"Your L-Lordship, it is you," panted Bobby Tripp, crossing the threshold into the study followed by Mrs. Daniel and Bessie. "We th-thought you was a burglar."

"There was a burglar, Bobby. Moments ago. You came down the back stairs?"

"Yes, m'lord."

"You did not hear anyone upon the stairs below you? You did not see Mr. Spelling open the first-floor door or hear him descend ahead of you toward the ground floor?"

"No, m'lord. N-not Mr. Spelling nor no one."

Wickenshire's glance moved to the cook and Bessie, who shook their heads slowly from side to side in agreement with Tripp.

"No one upon the stairs below us, Your Lordship," offered Mrs. Daniel. "Certainly would have heard him if not seen him."

"What is happenin'?" asked a sleepy voice, and Delight, in robe and slippers, rubbing at her eyes with one fist, pushed her way from behind Bessie's skirts. Stanley Blithe bounded into the room as well, dancing joyfully around Wickenshire's legs, and Sweetpea toddled behind him, sat down upon the carpeting before Wickenshire and mrrrrowed up at him with wise green eyes.

"Nicky, Sera, did you stop him?" called Eugenia as the servants parted to allow her entrance and John Coachman with her. "Is Lord Nightingale safe?"

Wickenshire bent to pat Stanley Blithe's head and scoop Sweetpea up into his arms. He shook his head at Eugenia in answer, then shifted the kitten to one arm and offered his hand to Delight, who scurried over to him at once. "You did not see Neil as you came up the front staircase, Eugenia? He did not get behind me somehow?"

"No," answered Eugenia quickly. "He took the back stairs then. Has Jenkins gone after him? You had best go as well, Nicky. I do not think that Jenkins is quite up to tackling Neil."

Wickenshire's eyebrow cocked. "Jenkins? Bobby, where the deuce is Jenkins? Why did he not come down with you?"

"He were not upstairs," offered Bobby Tripp succinctly. "I did think he be belowstairs aworkin' on the silver, Lordship."

"Nicky, where is Lord Nightingale?" Delight queried softly. "He is not in his cage."

"No, dearest," Serendipity replied quickly, going to her knees beside her little sister. "Lord Nightingale has—has—"

"Gone for a stroll," Wickenshire provided, divining that Serendipity did not wish to worry Delight with the absolute truth. "Mr. Spelling has taken him out for an airing."

"In the middle of the night?" Delight asked, wide-eyed.

"Yes, well, Mr. Spelling is fond of walking at night. Stanley Blithe," he interrupted himself, "cease and desist. Come here at once, sir."

"Bessie, do take Delight back up to bed, and Stanley Blithe and Sweetpea with her," Serendipity ordered softly. "It is much too late for them to be roaming about."

"Stanley Blithe!" ordered Wickenshire in a most impatient and authoritative voice. "Cease scratching at that paneling and come here, sir. You are acting like a nodcock."

"Mrrrr-pft!" added Sweetpea.

"Rrrr-warf, errr-errr-mmm," whined the puppy, dancing undecidedly between the wall and Wickenshire.

"Mrrow?" asked the kitten.

"Rrrr-warf, errrr-oof!"

Wickenshire stared in wonder as Sweetpea jumped

nimbly to the carpeting and sauntered over to the portion of the wall which so intrigued Stanley Blithe. In a moment the kitten was sniffing and scratching at the exact same place.

"Well, I'll be deviled," said Wickenshire, walking in that direction himself. "What is it about the paneling that—Bessie, do not wait upon these silly creatures, take Delight up to her bed now," he interrupted himself in a voice that elicited startled looks from all present.

"Nicholas, what is it?" asked Serendipity as Bessie took Delight's hand and led her from the room.

"Ought we go back upstairs as well, Lordship?" Bobby Tripp queried hesitantly, Wickenshire's tone having given him a start.

"No, no, Bobby. Hurry belowstairs and fetch Jenkins. Tell him that I require his assistance and accompany him back up here. We may need to form a search party, the three of us and John."

"I will go with him and put the kettle on the boil," said Mrs. Daniel with a long look at Lord Nightingale's empty cage. "Like as not, someone will require tea before the night is out."

"Not easily hoodwinked, our Mrs. Daniel," observed Eugenia. "She knows that Mr. Spelling and Nightingale have not gone for a stroll. What are you and the creatures staring at, Nicky?"

Wickenshire's fingers wandered over the paneling for a moment; then his hand flattened over a portion of it just at waist height. He pushed.

"Rarf!" exclaimed Stanley Blithe with enthusiasm as the neatly concealed door sprang open.

Sweetpea said nothing at all but sauntered right through the thing and into the darkness beyond. In the twitch of a cat's tail, Stanley Blithe tumbled in after her.

Serendipity gasped; Eugenia caught her breath; John Coachman let out a long, low whistle.

Wickenshire went to get the lamp from the study table and shone it into the darkness beyond the door. "Steps," he informed those behind him succinctly. "Going up and down both, but Stanley Blithe and Sweetpea are going down." He drew back into the study. "John, do you know anything of this passage?"

"N-no, Lordship."

"Well, this is likely the means by which Neil escaped us, though how the deuce he should know . . . John, go stand guard by the front door and do not let Mr. Spelling pass regardless of whether he carries the parrot with him or not. Likely these are the earliest set of servants' stairs and lead only to other rooms in the house. If so, Neil will be hiding in one of them, waiting for an opportunity to escape the premises."

"I will go down to the kitchen and watch that door," Eugenia offered. "Mrs. Daniel will be caught by surprise else, should Neil appear there," and she was off behind John Coachman before anyone could protest.

"You are not actually going in there?" Serendipity queried, moving across the room to stare into the passageway.

"Indeed I am. Wait here and send Jenkins and Bobby after me, eh? No, no, send Jenkins up these stairs and Bobby down, just in case the animals are not following Neil and Nightingale at all but going down only because it is far easier for them on such short legs."

"Nicholas." Serendipity did not at all intend to whisper his name in such a passionate tone, but she could not help herself. There he stood with his hair all tousled, his prized green velvet jacket askew, his neckcloth awry from his mad dash up the staircase, and he was the most exciting, most handsome, most alluring gentleman she had ever seen. Her heart, already pounding from her own mad dash, beat faster than ever and in a new rhythm. "Be careful, Nicholas," she whispered, her elegantly gloved hand caressing his strong jaw for just an instant. "Be very careful, my darling. Mr. Spelling intends no harm to come to Nightingale, remember. And I should perish if any harm came to you."

Wickenshire blinked down at her in the oddest way—a long, slow blink, as if he were arising from some deep sleep. With one long, softly gloved finger placed strategically beneath her chin, he tilted her head upward a smidgeon and then bowed his head and brushed his cool, delicious lips against her own. "I can feel it happening," he murmured in an awe-filled voice as he straightened. "I never thought I should, not ever."

"What?" Serendipity whispered.

He blinked the odd blink again, and his lips twitched upward. "I can feel the frog in me becoming an earl at last. Do not fear, Sera. I will come to no harm, I promise you." And then, lamp in hand, he started cautiously down the worn stone steps with a puppy yapping and a kitten murring in front of him.

Serendipity began to pace the floor, stopping each time she passed the door in the paneling to peer into the darkened staircase. Twice she saw the light of Wickenshire's lamp flicker vaguely back at her, but the third time she saw nothing at all.

"Oh, do keep him safe," she prayed. "Please do. Let Mr. Spelling escape with Lord Nightingale if it must be so. We shall do without the fortune. I shall do all in my power to help Nicholas to do without the fortune. Only please, do not let this gentleman I have grown to love come to any harm."

"Miss Bedford," gasped Bobby Tripp running into the room, attempting to speak and catch his breath at the same time. "Miss Bedford, where has his l-lordship gone? We must find him and t-tell him. Mr. Jenkins bean't belowstairs like I expected at all. I c-cannot find him nowhere. Mr. Jenkins is f-flat out gone!"

SIXTEEN

"Knollsmarmer. Nodcock. Villain." The muffled mumble inside the burlap bag he carried made Neil grin the slightest bit.

"You do never give up, do you, Nightingale? If you could see where we are now, old boy, you would hesitate to say a word." He paused upon the steps and raised his lamp higher, hoping to see more of the passageway that surrounded him. Behind him were the stairs he had descended, of course, and ahead of him an enormous door of brass and beams. To either side, nothing but cold, dank walls of uneven rock. "We cannot be on the ground floor," Spelling muttered to himself. "There is certainly no such door as this leads to the outside. And no one could hide this door behind paneling. Where the devil are we? It feels as though we are in a cellar."

And then Spelling heard feet shuffling and voices whispering on the other side of the door and his heart leaped into his throat. Had they discovered him already? Were his cousin's servants, not knowing who had stolen the parrot, waiting with long guns for him to step out into wherever the door led? Would they blow his head clean off before they so much as noticed who he was, before he had the opportunity to spin them a Canterbury tale about how he had chased the robber himself down these stairs and saved Lord Nightingale, though the rob-

ber had run off before he could get a good hold upon
him?

"Yo ho ho," Nightingale stated as clearly as he could
from inside a bag, and Spelling felt him stepping about
in there—a sidle this way, a sidle that, pecking at the
weave with his beak.

"Be quiet, you wretched bird. You will betray our
whereabouts. Who knows but that they will miss me and
shoot you instead, dunderhead."

"Knollsmarmer," replied Nightingale. "Bite. Villain.
No."

"Shhhh," hissed Spelling, pressing his ear against the
door to see if he could make out who might be upon the
other side. Apparently, there were a number of people,
but he could not actually distinguish what anyone was
saying or recognize the voices. Spelling turned about and
started back up the steps.

There must be doors along the way, he thought, holding his lamp higher than he had when descending and
studying the walls on either side of him. If these are
indeed the old servants' stairs, then there are most definitely doors leading into other rooms of the house. I have
merely passed them without noticing, that is all.

He had climbed but ten steps and discovered not one
door when he heard the oddest noises from above him.
Snuffling and mewling and shuffling footsteps. What the
devil! he thought in wonderment. Someone else knows
about this passageway and is coming down, and he
sounds like a drooling madman! Damnation! Does Nicky
truly have some lunatic locked up in this place? Is that
the true reason he boarded over the windows upon the
fourth floor and not because of taxes at all?

There is a room up there locked tight! Spelling remembered then. Oh, m'gawd. Aunt Diana gasped when
she heard we stayed upon the fourth floor. Is this why?
Has Nicky actually locked some madman into that room
to provide us with chambers, and now the madman has
found his way into the passages! Spelling switched the

bag with Nightingale in it to his other hand, switched it back again. Took a step down. Took a step up. What the devil was he to do? A mewling, snuffling, shuffling madman was descending toward him out of the darkness, and armed servants awaited him beyond the door at the bottom of the stairs.

"Bobby, go back and look everywhere again," Serendipity ordered in a fear-filled voice. "Jenkins must be here somewhere. It is likely he lies injured and unable to summon us."

"It is?" asked Bobby Tripp in awe. "Mr. Jenkins?"

"Yes, yes, it is. You must search most carefully for him. You must find him, Bobby. He would not leave his post and the house without notifying His Lordship of his need to do so."

"No, he wouldn't never do that," agreed Tripp, "not Mr. Jenkins. Dedicated to His Lordship, he be."

"Just so. Off with you. Hurry. There is no telling but Jenkins is in sore need of assistance." Serendipity's heart fluttered with terror. She had been pacing the floor in nervousness, grappling with an undefined fear, but now her imagination soared. Mr. Spelling was so very desperate to keep Nightingale from singing that he would stop at nothing, not even at murdering such a fine old gentleman as Mr. Jenkins. Mr. Spelling was no longer rich as Croesus. He had lost all upon a turn of the cards and would rather die himself than live without the amenities to which he had grown accustomed. Abducting Nightingale was his only means to another fortune, and he meant to do the thing, no matter what. And now Jenkins was missing!

"Nicholas is in that passageway with a desperate murderer!" Serendipity exclaimed. "And there is no one to help him. I must warn him! I must!"

Her mind reeling with visions of a fight to the death between the two gentlemen, Serendipity seized the candelabra that Wickenshire had abandoned upon the table. She lit the snuffed candles from one of the three which remained lit, hiked her skirt up high enough to make descending the stairs as safe as possible and, entering the passageway, began a descent into darkness.

Nicholas is such a kind and noble man, she thought. He will not for one moment suspect how truly desperate Mr. Spelling must be. It will never occur to him to attack his cousin before he, himself, is attacked. Heavens, he will not expect to be attacked at all. No, he will not. Not Nicholas. He thinks only of getting Lord Nightingale safely back. He suspects Mr. Spelling mercly of a bit of envy and greed. He does not at all realize that Mr. Spelling has lost everything and would rather die than provide him the opportunity to teach Lord Nightingale to sing.

"I reckon as that's it," acknowledged Captain Sebastian cheerfully. "Do not be lookin' so woebegone, Tommy, me lad. His Lordship ain't at all likely to be discoverin' this passageway. Not any time soon, he ain't. Why, he ain't even set to work on the inside of the stables as yet, has he? No. An' Mr. Ezra's men will be acomin' to colleck these crates an' carry 'em off to Lunnon sooner than ye think. Ye need only warn his nibs as how his nephew ain't goin' to be scared off, an' he will warn his crew to be on their toes when they come for the stuff."

"Yes, but what about the excisemen, Sebastian? What if they should happen upon the entrance among the rocks and make their way up here? His Lordship will be deep in the briars then, and all of it a nasty surprise to him."

"Ye worry a sight too much, Tommy. They ain't discovered are hidin' place in all the years we been ausin' of it. Why should they be discoverin' of it now?"

"Even so, what if they do, and Master Nicholas gets up in arms over the excisemen coming onto his property without so much as a by-your-leave? Adamantly opposed to taxes, he is. Despises those who go about collecting them. Cannot be trusted to be reasonable in the face of excisemen."

"Aye, and who can blame 'im? He has felt their bite more than most of us, 'e has."

"He will likely rant and rave himself into a devil of a temper and land one or two of them a facer. It will end with the Horse Guards riding down here to take him into custody, it will. They will think him a smuggler, and what will happen then?"

"Then I expect Mr. Ezra must step in an' spin 'em all a tale what will make His Lordship appear innocent as a lamb."

"He is as innocent as a lamb, and it is my job to keep him that way."

"Aye, but if ye kinnot frighten him off like Mr. Ezra suggested, ye kinnot, Tommy. An' I for sure kinnot take these crates back aboard my *Peggy*. It all be in Mr. Ezra's hands now. He be responsible. Shhhh. What was that?"

Jenkins, his eyes widening, listened apprehensively. "What?" he whispered after a moment. "I do not hear anything."

"Not behind us, Tommy, in front of us. By gawd, the door be openin'!"

Spelling, having decided to take his chances with armed servants rather than a madman, peered out from a crack in the door that led into the well-lighted passageway that ran beneath the stables. When the barrel of a long gun did not immediately come into contact with his nose, he sighed in relief and pushed the door more fully open. "It is not at all what you think," he cried, stepping out into the open, his arms raised above his head, the burlap bag dangling from his right fist. "It is some huge mistake, I assure you."

"No. Bite. Birdie." Nightingale muttered from within

the bag, attempting to keep his balance as it swung in midair. "Morning, Nightingale. Morning, Nightingale."

"Mr. Spelling?" Jenkins gasped.

"Mister who?" Sebastian queried.

"Jenkins? Is it you? Oh, thank gawd! You have always been a reasonable fellow. You will not believe what has happened—" And then the mewling and the snuffling and the shuffling feet were coming down the steps directly behind him, and Spelling leaped across the space between himself and Jenkins and Captain Sebastian. And then he leaped back again and slammed the door shut, and remained there, leaning all his weight against it. "Jenkins, and you, whoever you are, come help me. The madman Nicky keeps locked up on the fourth floor has escaped and found his way into this staircase. He is chasing me and he will put an end to all of us if we do not hold this door against him!"

"His Lordship keeps a madman locked up on the fourth floor, an' ye be worritin' about 'im being compermised by a bit of smugglin', Tommy?" Sebastian asked, astounded.

"Madman? What madman?" Jenkins queried, staring at Spelling, then at the muttering bag, then at Spelling again. "Have you lost your mind, Mr. Spelling? His Lordship does not—"

"Mrrrrr." "Yip-yarf-arf." "Mrrrr," came from behind the door, and then the door began to push outward despite Mr. Spelling's efforts. Sebastian dashed forward and added his weight to the door as well.

"Be it a man soun's li' that? What be wrong wif the fellow?" Captain Sebastian managed, leaning against the door with all his might as it was pushed outward again, this time with such force that it nearly sent both him and Spelling flying. "Tommy, me lad, git yerself over 'ere an' lend a hand."

His lamp set upon the bottom step, Stanley Blithe and Sweetpea scrabbling around his feet, Wickenshire set his shoulder to the door a third time. Thing ain't barred, he thought. Saw it open. Bounces a bit even now. Someone is attempting to hold it against me. Where the devil am I? What is this a door to? Who the deuce is leaning upon the other side? It is not Neil. Neil could never have held against that last push.

He set his shoulder to the door again, much harder this time. "By Jove, whoever you are on the other side of this door, I will have your heart on my plate for dinner!" Wickenshire bellowed, and then he accidentally stepped on the puppy's paw and Stanley Blithe squealed and howled, which frightened Sweetpea into leaping upon Wickenshire's leg and scrambling up him to his shoulders, her claws digging in at every step.

"Ow!" Wickenshire roared. "Ow! Ouch! Stop! No! Stop!"

Serendipity gasped and tears started to her eyes at the anguished sound of Lord Wickenshire's cries. It is happening, she thought, attempting to descend the steps even more quickly. Nicholas has caught Mr. Spelling and Mr. Spelling is attempting to murder him! "No!" she shouted as loudly as she could. "You let him alone. Do not you touch him! Do not! I am witness to your hideous crime. You shall be hanged for it!" And in a moment, she came around a tiny turning in the staircase and saw Wickenshire's lamp glowing on the bottom step. The last of her candles snuffed out by the breeze she made, her slipper slipped upon the stone and she tumbled forward.

"Sera!" Wickenshire turned, and saw, and dove toward the staircase, kitten on his shoulder, puppy scrabbling at his ankles and all. He caught her, the sheer force of her fall causing him to spin around and stumble backward. When he knew he held her securely, he lowered her feet to the stone floor, but did not free her from his grasp. "Sera," he whispered, one hand going to smooth back her hair as the other held her tightly against him. "Sera, are you all right?" he asked softly as he kissed her brow and nose and chin and cheek. "You are not harmed? You did not twist an ankle? You have not scraped yourself against the stone?"

For a moment Serendipity quite forgot everything but the nearness of him, the softness of his touch and the heavenly sensation of his lips fluttering over her face. And then Sweetpea stretched her way from Wickenshire's shoulder to Serendipity's, and Stanley Blithe yapped happily, and Serendipity reached up to touch Wickenshire's closely shaved cheeks and gazed with relief into his remarkable forest green eyes. "Thank goodness he has not beaten you to within an inch of your life. He has not stabbed you or shot you dead."

"N-no. Who?" asked Wickenshire.

"Mr. Spelling. Oh, Nicky, I thought certainly he would take your life. He is mad with grief. He has lost everything, and he cannot bear for you to have his stepmama's money when he requires it so desperately. I thought certainly he would murder you the moment you caught up with him!"

"Mad with grief? Lost everything? Neil?"

"I heard you cry out, and I thought—I thought he had fallen upon you with some vile weapon.

"Neil?"

"Yes, yes, Mr. Spelling! Where is he? He is not here. He is gone, Nicholas. Oh, my clumsiness has allowed him to escape."

"No, no, he was never— It was the cat— I—"

On the opposite side of the door, his shoulder now pressed against the wood and thereby his ear in close proximity to the door as well, Jenkins, though unable to make out the substance of the conversation occurring on the opposite side, had recognized quite unmistakably the voice that had threatened to eat his heart for dinner. He groaned and sagged a bit.

"What a hue and cry the monster kin make," Sebastian observed, astonished. "But he be cammer now, eh? Thinkin' ta turn back ta his abode, do ye think? Tommy? What be the matter, Tommy? We 'ave held."

"Yo ho ho!" cried Nightingale in piercing tones from within the burlap bag still in Spelling's grasp.

Captain Sebastian came near to leaping out of his skin. He did, in fact, leap away from Mr. Spelling and his bag and the door. "It talks. This bloke has got a sack what talks, Tommy!"

Jenkins eyed Mr. Spelling and the bag and groaned again.

"It is not what you think, Jenkins," Spelling declared. "I learned that the man who set the fire in the Gold Saloon was coming back to kill the parrot and I—"

Jenkins shook his head.

"No, but it is truth, Jenkins!"

"It is His Lordship beyond the door," Jenkins whispered. "I should think of a better excuse than that if I were you, Mr. Neil. That one will not hold. Sebastian, it is His Lordship beyond the door."

"His Lordship? Makin' all them animal sounds an' howlin' like a rabid 'ound? He be a madman? An' this one, with the sack what talks, what be he?"

"The sack does not talk, Sebastian. Lord Nightingale is in the sack."

Captain Sebastian's eyebrows rose clear out of sight. "Lord Nightingale? There be a lord in there? A itty-bitty lord? Ye expeck me ta believe that, Tommy?"

"No, it is a parrot. Lord Nightingale is its name, but it is a parrot, and that bird is the very least of our problems. How the devil are we to explain you, Sebastian, and these crates, to His Lordship? He is here. He has not only discovered the passage, he has discovered us and your cargo as well. Once we cease to lean upon this door, he will come straight through it, and then our heads will all roll."

Spelling could not quite grasp what was going on between Jenkins and the odd-looking fellow who had first come to his aid, but he did deduce from their conversation that he was not the only person on this side of the door who was deep in the briars. "We will not cease to lean upon the door, then, Jenkins. That'll be the answer. We shall hold the door against him until Nicky gives up and goes away. You are certain it is Nicky?"

"Did you not recognize his voice when he called out about eating our hearts?" hissed Jenkins.

"Well, I thought it sounded like Nicky, but it did not sound like him snuffling and mewling and shuffling down the stairwell, let me tell you. Perhaps the madman simply imitates Nicky."

At that very moment, when none of them were the least prepared for it, Wickenshire gave a mighty shove upon the door and sent Spelling and Jenkins spilling to the floor. He burst into the passage, Stanley Blithe charging from behind him to bounce, with great enthusiasm, up and down upon Jenkins's shoulders and lick happily at his hair.

Spelling, his nose having hit the floor with a tremendous whack, groaned.

Wickenshire looked at him and then at Captain Sebastian, who was the only man still standing. "Who the deuce are *you?*" he growled at the captain. "And why did you think to keep me from opening that door?"

"Morning, Nightingale!" replied Wickenshire's own voice, and the earl turned abruptly to take note of the burlap bag which now lay on the stone floor, Sweetpea investigating it curiously, attempting to open the top with her paws while a great lump near the middle wobbled from side to side. "Awwk! Villain!" the great lump cried, sending the kitten scampering backward.

"Devil it, grab the bag, Nicky, or that wretched bird will find his way out and fly off somewhere and we will neither of us ever see him again," gasped Spelling, pushing himself into a kneeling position and swiping with his sleeve at the blood that gushed from his nose.

"I will get the bag," Serendipity declared and stepped out from behind Wickenshire to do so. "Do you stay right where you are, Mr. Spelling," she ordered, her eyes flashing. "If you move one inch, Nicholas will shoot you on the spot."

I will what? thought Wickenshire. Now, why would she say that? It must be obvious to everyone that I do not have a pistol.

"Sera, peek in and be certain that Nightingale is not harmed, will you? He had best not be harmed," Wickenshire added with a glare at a groaning Spelling, "or you will suffer for it, Neil."

"No, of course he ain't harmed, Nicky. Why would I harm the old blighter? My only intent was to . . . save him from that fiend."

"What fiend? That fiend?" Wickenshire asked, pointing at the captain.

"The fiend who set the fire. Had word he intended to strike again tonight, and this time at Nightingale."

"Oh, what a bouncer!" declared Serendipity. "Eugenia heard you plotting with that nasty Henry Wiggins to come and steal this poor parrot!"

"Stay right where you are," Wickenshire ordered the captain, and, his eyes never leaving Sebastian, he went to where Jenkins lay, scooted the puppy aside and helped his butler to his feet. "You are not badly injured, are you, Jenkins?" he asked, brushing at the butler's clothing. "Neither this man nor Spelling have harmed you in any way?"

For the briefest moment a glimmer of hope sparked in Jenkins's eyes. His Lordship thought him to be a victim of Mr. Spelling or Sebastian or both! But it could not last. The truth would shortly be apparent. He shook his head slowly. "I am merely bruised a bit, my lord."

"Lord Nightingale is fine as well, Nicholas," Serendipity added. "I do not think he is even upset about being in a bag. He appears quite interested in pulling out the weaving."

"Knollsmarmer," agreed Lord Nightingale, muffled.

"Good," Wickenshire nodded, stripping off his neck-

cloth, kneeling to put an arm around Spelling's shoulders
and placing the strip of muslin into his cousin's hand.

"No handkerchief, Neil. Use this. Why did you not
tell me you had lost everything? Did you think I would
not help you?"

Spelling, the neckcloth bunched into a ball and
pressed against his nose, stared up at his cousin in surprise. "M-me?" he managed. "L-lost everything? Wh-
when did th-that happen?"

"Never mind. I understand that you do not like to discuss it in front of everyone. We will discuss it when we
are alone."

Mr. Spelling stared up at his cousin, bewildered.

"Jenkins, do you feel well enough to carry Nightingale? Can you give Miss Bedford your support out of
this place?" asked the earl, rising to his feet and crossing
to the butler.

"Yes, my lord."

"By the way, Jenkins," Wickenshire added just as
Jenkins took his first step toward Miss Bedford and the
bird, "do you have the least idea where we are or who
this fellow might be? And what the devil are all those
crates?" he said, actually taking note of the long line of
wooden boxes for the first time. "I guessed myself to
be plodding down the servants' staircase from the time
of Lady Elaina. Someone of the earls built on around it,
eh? But I assumed it would end at the kitchen."

"Ye be unner the stables, Lordship," offered Captain
Sebastian, thoroughly enthralled with the goings-on.
"An' I be Cap'n Sebastian o' the sailing ship *Peggy
O'Shay,* out of Eire."

"Ireland? You come from Ireland?" asked Serendipity.

"Indeed, ma'am. Me an' m'crew."

"In the dead of night?" queried Wickenshire. "Jenkins,
take Miss Bedford to the house at once."

"No, I cannot," sighed Jenkins. "You have guessed
the captain a smuggler already. And tempting as it is to
walk off in innocence, I cannot. I have known Captain

Sebastian a considerable number of years, my lord. I have even given him a hand from time to time. And—I am the one who has been writing those notes and leaving them about for you, in the hope that they might frighten you back to Wicken Hall and thus keep you from discovering all this—muddle."

"You, Jenkins?" gasped Wickenshire and Serendipity together.

SEVENTEEN

Lord Upton and Lady Wickenshire returned to Willowsweep to discover the drawing room awash in light and Wickenshire, Serendipity, Mr. Spelling, Eugenia, Jenkins and a man dressed in the oddest fashion in the drawing room sipping tea.

"You have missed all the fun, Mama," Wickenshire drawled, balancing his teacup in one hand as he stood before the fireplace. "We have been chasing around Willowsweep like hounds after a fox."

"Have you? And did you enjoy yourselves immensely?" the dowager queried crossly, accepting a cup of tea from Eugenia.

"Aunt Diana, whatever is wrong?" Eugenia asked.

"Oh, nothing of great significance," sniffed the dowager. "Really, Nicky, could you not at least have taken proper leave of your host and hostess? Need you and the girls have raced away like beings possessed without one word to the squire?"

"But Mama, I did explain that—"

"Yes, yes, you explained to me, dearest, but you said not one word to Squire and Mrs. Hadley. There I sat, watching the dancing, attempting to convince Lord Upton that you were all still present when you were not and, at the very same time, forced to think of some excuse to give the Squire and Mrs. Hadley for your most unorthodox exit."

"What excuse did you give them, Mama?"

"I said that the lot of you were mad as hatters."

"Well, I expect that was better than telling the truth."

"It is the truth, dearest. And who is this—person?" the dowager asked, glaring at Captain Sebastian. "And why is Jenkins sitting here with teacup in hand as though he is a member of the family? Not that we do not treasure you, Jenkins," she added with a bare flicker of a smile. "You have always been the best of butlers. But it is quite extraordinary for you—"

"That gentleman is Captain Sebastian of the sailing ship *Peggy O'Shay,* Mama," interrupted Wickenshire. "Captain Sebastian is from Eire and a smuggler."

Lady Wickenshire's left eyebrow tilted the merest bit.

"And Jenkins is having tea with us because he knows all about Captain Sebastian and the smuggling. I have been prodding him for information."

Lady Wickenshire's left eyebrow tilted even more. "Nicky, I thought you came home to keep Neil from abducting Lord Nightingale. And now you expect me to believe that our Jenkins is a smuggler? No, wait! I have it! Neil has bribed Jenkins to hire this person to smuggle Lord Nightingale out of the country."

"No, no, that not be it atall, Ladyship," drawled the captain with the most bemused smile upon his face. "Tommy an' me din't know nothin' about this bloke atakin' the bird. Not ta begin wif, we did not. I be merely abringin' in of Mr. Ezra's cargo—a bit ahead o' time to be sure, but—"

"Mr. Ezra's cargo? Ezra's?" cried the dowager. "What has my brother to do with smugglers?"

"Yo ho ho!" interrupted a raucous voice and, with a great flapping of wings, Lord Nightingale soared into the drawing room, immediately followed by a yelping puppy and a kitten skidding around the door frame. The parrot zoomed in a circle just beneath the ceiling, then landed with admirable precision upon the earl's shoulder. "Morning!" he cried. "Morning, Nightingale!"

Lady Wickenshire stared at the macaw on her son's shoulder and at the puppy and the kitten scrabbling at his feet, and despite all her attempts to remain stern, she laughed.

"It is no laughing matter, Mama," Wickenshire declared.

"No, dear one."

"Apparently Uncle Ezra and Uncle Albert, Mama, did not make their fortunes by investing with the East India Company, as we supposed. Apparently they made them by investing in Captain Sebastian's East Ireland company."

"Aye," nodded the captain. "I bring it across from Eire an' they sell it—dezcreetly, ye unnerstand. Been doin' it fer years. *The Undertaking,* Mr. Ezra does always be acallin' it. An' it were a dangerous undertaking, too, early on. 'Course it still be dangerous. But early on we was offloadin' near Liverpool an' havin' to carry ever'thing overland down to Lunnon. Oncet ye married His Lordship, ma'am, why then I begin sailin' down here an' offloadin' in Little Wicken Bay, which makes the overland route a deal shorter an' safer."

"Am I to understand that—my husband—became a part of this?" asked Lady Wickenshire, her eyes widening.

"Aye, joined right in, he did. Gived 'im a share o' the flimsies, Ladyship, in return fer the use o' Willowsweep, though what he done wif the monies, I kinnot say."

"Gambled it all away," sighed the dowager. "Most assuredly."

"At any rate, Mama, there is nothing to be done about it now. We must only hope that no excisemen turn up on our doorstep until Uncle Ezra's men have gotten the goods out from under the stables."

"From under the stables, Nicky?"

"There is a passage leads under the stables, my lady," Serendipity offered quietly. "Captain Sebastian says that it goes all the way down to the shore."

"And one may reach it by going down the original servants' staircase," Eugenia added excitedly. "I did never suspect that the original servants' staircase still existed, but Jenkins says that is exactly what it is. If one goes all the way to the very bottom, a door opens directly into a passage under the stables. I expect it is that final set of stairs that you spoke of, Sera, that takes one down the hill."

"Yes, that is what I think, because I could not tell at all that I had left the house. I will lay you odds, Eugenia," Serendipity said, her eyes bright with excitement, "that the staircase and the passageway were built for Lady Elaina should the villagers rise up and wish to burn her as a witch. That is why all the entrances to it are hidden."

"Enough, Sera," declared Wickenshire, his eyes glowing with unholy humor. "We have had enough of your imagination for one evening, my dear. If you will remember, less than an hour ago you had Mr. Jenkins laying somewhere steeped in his own blood and Neil without a penny to his name. I thought Neil would die when he heard that his pockets were to let."

"It is not my fault," Serendipity replied primly, "if Mr. Spelling cares so little for his money that he does not know from one day to the next whether or not he possesses it."

"You lost everything, Spelling?" gasped Upton, who until now had remained strategically silent. "How? What the devil did you invest in? No wonder you were so intent upon stealing that bird."

Spelling groaned.

"So now Upton's words convict you, too. Proves Eugenia heard aright," Wickenshire sighed. "Save Nightingale from the fiend who set the fire, indeed." Lord Wickenshire stared down at his cousin who sat with a corner of blood-soaked neckcloth still pressed to his nose. "I would not put it past you to have set that fire yourself, Neil."

"It was Nightingale set the fire," protested Neil glumly. "All I did was attempt to pet him, and he began darting 'round the room like a thing gone mad. Knocked over a lamp, set the carpet afire. Upton and I had nothing at all to do with it."

"It matters not," Wickenshire declared. "You will depart Willowsweep first thing in the morning, Neil. And when you return to hear Nightingale sing, plan to spend the night elsewhere, eh?"

"You are tossing me out, Nicky?"

"No, I am requesting that you leave. I will be pleased to actually toss you out the door if you wish it, though."

Serendipity looked up from her tea to see the most gleeful light playing about in Wickenshire's eyes. Oh, but he is enjoying every moment of this, she thought. Just see how his eyes shine.

"Never mind, Spelling," offered Lord Upton with a definite sneer. "We have no reason to remain. Miss Bedford, we will be leaving tomorrow rather than Monday as we planned."

"Oh! No, I have decided that—" Serendipity began.

"Sera and Delight do not accompany you," Wickenshire interrupted her, his gaze falling upon Upton.

"Indeed they do. I had intended to inform you of it, but then I thought it better to just take them away with me. There is nothing to be got by arguing about it, Wickenshire."

"Not a thing," agreed the earl. "You and Neil will depart. Sera and Delight will remain. Simple, really."

"Remain? In a house where smuggled goods are stowed in the cellar? While there are excisemen swarming like bees about the countryside? Oh, I think not, Wickenshire. Someone is like to let the cat out of the bag, you know. A word here, a whisper there. The excisemen will be upon you before you know it. And my dearest cousin Serendipity will be ruined, right along with all the rest of you."

Eugenia gasped, and Sera gasped with her. Mr. Jenkins

coughed, and Captain Sebastian inhaled a loud, raggedy breath.

"You would never be so cruel!" exclaimed Serendipity. "Nicholas knew nothing. He did not so much as guess that—"

"Perhaps," drawled Upton, "the King's men will believe him when he tells them so. But I should not depend upon it, dearest coz. Really, I should not. An earl he may be, but an earl with a cellar full of smuggled goods. You know how to get to this cellar, eh, Spelling?"

Mr. Spelling looked from Lord Upton to his cousin to his aunt and then back to Lord Upton. He nodded.

Serendipity sat with her lips parted, but not the least idea of what to say. Her heart slowed to a dull pounding, and her eyes began to tear. She understood perfectly Lord Upton's threat. She and Delight must leave Willowsweep with him on the morrow or he and Mr. Spelling would lay information against Nicholas and all in this house, including Eugenia and Lady Wickenshire.

"I am so very sorry, sir," murmured Jenkins in the privacy of Wickenshire's dressing room. "Sebastian was not to arrive until a week from now at the soonest, but word came to him of certain people being most interested in the boats which came and went from Shamrock Cove. And, his cargo being loaded, he set out before they should become interested in the *Peggy O'Shay* in particular. He made outstanding time, too, my lord, and . . ."

"Yes, Jenkins, do go on," drawled the earl, unfastening his shirt studs and scooting Sweetpea out of the armoire with one stockinged toe.

"Well, then the *Silver Scupper* ran aground on the shoals and spilled kegs of brandy all over the tide."

"But they were not our kegs of brandy, Jenkins?"

"Oh, no, my lord!"

"Thank goodness for that. Not to change the subject exactly, but how could you, Jenkins, write cryptic notes in hope of frightening me away and then pretend to be interested in helping me to discover who wrote the blasted things?"

Mr. Jenkins, his fingers shaking as they applied themselves to the lacings of Wickenshire's breeches, stuttered and stammered a moment and then took a very deep breath.

"I have trusted in you forever, Jenkins," murmured Wickenshire. "Since I was toddling about in leading strings. I discovered soon enough that I could not depend upon my father, but you were always to be depended upon. And now you betray me just as Papa always did?"

"No! Never! The notes were only meant to make you depart until Mr. Ezra could discover some other place in which to land the merchandise and store it. He and Mr. Albert—God rest his soul—both held you in the highest esteem, my lord. And Mr. Ezra would not have you involved in such a havey-cavey thing as *The Undertaking* for all the money in the world. And . . . and . . ."

"And what, Jenkins?" asked Wickenshire, slipping his nightshirt over his head while Stanley Blithe leaped around him, attempting to seize the hem.

"And now you are involved in much worse," sighed the butler. "Now Mr. Neil and Lord Upton intend to blackmail you over something that is not at all your fault."

"Oh, I should not worry about them, Jenkins. I am perfectly capable of taking care of them. But that you should think I would be frightened away by notes about witches! It is most lowering."

"I told Mr. Ezra that you would not."

"And that you should keep such a secret as this from me for how many years, Jenkins?"

"More years than you have been alive, my lord. I was liaison between your papa and Mr. Ezra is all. I carried messages between them. I did never help with the—the cargo—but a few times, when your papa made me accompany him here."

"Well, that is nothing so terrible. I— The money! Jenkins, could it be my papa's share of the smuggling money that Aunt Winifred bequeathed to me?"

"It might well be, my lord. I cannot say for certain. Your Uncle Albert would never involve your mama, you know. And your Aunt Winifred did attempt to give you a large sum of money after your papa died. But you would not accept charity, you said, all uppity-nosed. Perhaps it was money owed your papa, and so she left it to you in her will so that at last you must accept it."

"Unless Lord Nightingale refuses to sing. In which case, I shall not have a bit of it."

"For goodness' sake, my lord, the parrot will sing. Your aunt would not leave you money with no possible way to claim it. Come to think of it, I did hear him sing once, while your Uncle Albert was alive. Your papa had sent me to . . . Well, that is beside the point. But he did actually sing."

"What did he sing, Jenkins? Perhaps if we start him upon it, he will remember and sing the entire thing."

"I—I cannot remember, my lord."

"Not so much as one word of it, Jenkins?"

"Well, one was a ditty about kissing and the other had to do with that word he always says. Knollsmarmer."

"He knows two songs? But there are thousands of ditties about kissing, Jenkins. And I cannot recall even one song with knollsmarmer in it." Wickenshire placed his nightcap upon his curls and padded in his slippers toward his bedchamber, Stanley Blithe and Sweetpea racing ahead of him. "You had best get some sleep, Jenkins. The dawn is not too far away."

"Yes, my lord," Jenkins replied, stuffing one shaking hand into his pocket while searching for the doorlatch behind his back with the other.

"Oh, and Jenkins—" Wickenshire called as he disappeared into his bedchamber.

"Yes, my lord?"

"Is the brandy we smuggle on the *Peggy O'Shay* as

good as the brandy they smuggle upon the *Silver Scupper?*"

"W-we do not sm-smuggle brandy, my lord," Jenkins replied.

"We do not? What do we smuggle, Jenkins?"

"S-s-soap, my lord."

Wickenshire poked his head around the bedchamber door frame and stared back into the dressing room at the butler. "Soap?" And before Jenkins could utter one word of explanation, Wickenshire roared into laughter.

Serendipity tossed and turned and muttered to herself for what seemed like hours. "I cannot bear the thought of returning to London with—that man! I was not mistaken about him. He is an ogre, a cruel, heartless ogre!" she whispered into the night.

Visions plagued her. The infamous Henry Wiggins stood over her with a riding whip as she, dressed in rags, fell to her knees upon the kitchen floor of the London town house, scrub brush in hand and bucket beside her, while from the corner of the kitchen, tied to a big copper kettle by a golden chain, a tearful Delight begged Lord Upton to have mercy upon her sister.

Then again, Lord Upton marched her up and down the streets of London, crying her for sale as would any fishmonger cry his wares while Delight clung to his sleeve, begging him to set her sister free.

And there were more ghastly visions—visions of degradation and humiliation and pure cruelty. But the vision that caused her to sit up abruptly in her bed and cry out was one of Nicholas climbing the thirteen steps to the gibbet outside Newgate. Nicholas, pale and drawn, standing very still upon the platform as the thickly braided rope was placed just so about his neck while in the crowd below, a laughing Lord Upton and Mr. Spelling forced her and Delight to watch the spectacle.

"Never!" she cried into the darkness of her chamber.

"Never! I shall see the both of you dead first!" And then she blinked and blinked again. "A dream," she murmured in relief as the door to her chamber absolutely flew open and a most disheveled Lord Wickenshire, nightcap askew, robe barely closed around him, dashed into the room.

"Sera? What is it? I heard you call out. Are you all right?" he asked, gazing about the chamber in bewilderment. "I thought . . . I thought . . . never mind. It was a dream, eh?"

"Yes," nodded Serendipity sheepishly, rubbing at her eyes with a fist. And then she took a good look at the earl and could not help but smile. I want always to remember him looking precisely like this, she thought. Such a strong, proud gentleman and yet he looks like the most endearing child. "You are— I woke you from a sound sleep, did I not? I am so very sorry, but—"

"There is no reason to be sorry. I expect we have all had bad dreams from time to time. We cannot do anything about them," he said in a hushed voice, and then he did the oddest thing. He stepped back to the chamber door, peered out into the corridor and then closed the door softly. He padded a bit awkwardly over to her bed and hoisted himself up upon the side of the mattress. "You are frightened of going back to London with that dastard, Upton. Do not be, Sera," he whispered, taking her hands into his, "because it is not going to happen."

"But, Nicholas, I must. They will report you to the excisemen else, and you will be arrested for a common smuggler."

"It will never happen," he replied.

"It will. I heard Lord Upton with my own ears. And the evidence is right beneath the stables, and Mr. Spelling knows very well how to lead them directly to it. Delight and I *must* accompany Henry Wiggins back to London and do whatever he says or you will be hanged, my darling."

"Am I? Are you certain?"

"Wh-what?"

"Your darling. Am I your darling?"

"Oh, yes," Serendipity said. "Oh, yes, Nicholas. You have come to mean everything to me."

"And do you trust me, Sera?"

"Implicitly. What on earth is all that noise?"

"Stanley Blithe and Sweetpea. They have discovered that I am no longer in my bed, have followed me here and wish to come in, but I have locked them out. Sera, I know that I am not the sort of gentleman a young lady wishes to— I mean, not the sort that a young lady finds— I am far from a young lady's ideal, I expect is what I mean to say."

"You are not far from *my* ideal, Nicholas. You are *my* ideal."

"No, I am positive that you had a very different ideal husband in mind before you ever came here, but you do not abhor me, I think."

"I love you," Serendipity murmured huskily.

"Do you? Are you certain? Because I love you, Sera. I have loved you from the moment I woke to discover you cavorting about upon the lawn in the moonlight with Eugenia, the two of you like faeries gone mad. But I did never think that—until we danced and—then when you came running down the stairwell after me— Are you certain that you love me?"

"Yes," whispered Serendipity, freeing one hand to lay it lightly upon his cheek.

"And will you marry me?"

"M-marry you?"

"Yes, Sera. I wish you to be my wife, but you must answer quickly, because any minute now, Stanley Blithe is going to grow impatient with scratching and whimpering and will begin howling. He will wake the entire household."

"Of course I will marry you," Serendipity declared, leaning forward, throwing her arms around Wickenshire's neck and covering his rapidly reddening cheeks with kisses. "I should be honored to marry you. You are the kindest, sweetest—"

"Arrrrooooooooow!" interrupted Stanley Blithe. He sat down upon his haunches outside the door and tilted his snout into the air. "Arrrrooooooow!" he cried again, plaintively.

"Mrrrrrrrrrow!" echoed Sweetpea in the best imitation she could muster, sitting down beside the puppy. "Mrrrrrrrrow!"

"Sera? Sera, is you all right?" cried Delight, pounding on the chamber door. "Sera? Stanley Blithe and Sweetpea is out here an' wants to come in, an' me too."

"What in heavens's name," exclaimed the dowager Lady Wickenshire as she shuffled down the corridor, tying her robe around her.

"What is going on?" asked Eugenia, stepping out into the hallway and scurrying after her aunt.

"Arrrrooooooow!" Stanley Blithe bellowed.

"Mrrrrrrrrow!" echoed Sweetpea.

"How the devil is anyone expected to sleep around here?" complained Mr. Spelling, stamping down the stairs from the fourth floor, Lord Upton in his wake. "What the deuce is going on now, Aunt Diana? Be quiet, you great peagoose of a puppy. By Jove, all we need now is that wretched bird to begin squawking."

"I cannot think why they should both be sitting outside Sera's door," murmured Eugenia.

"Sera," cried Delight, pounding upon the door with her little fist. "Sera, is you all right? I want to come in."

The chamber door opened, and the little group gathered in the corridor all inhaled at one and the same time.

"Nicky, what on earth!" declared his mama.

"Nicky!" Eugenia gasped, looking him up and down.

"Nicky?" asked Mr. Spelling, astonished. "Is this not Miss Bedford's chamber? What the devil are you . . . ?"

"Oh!" cried Sera, appearing from behind Wickenshire in nightgown and robe. "Oh, Nicholas, we are discovered!" she wailed, pressing the back of her hand to her brow in the time-honored dramatic gesture of despair. "I am compromised! You will be forced to marry me!"

"No, do you think so?" asked Wickenshire with a wicked grin as he slipped his arm about her shoulders.

"Most certainly. Our fates are sealed!"

"Well, I expect, if our fates are sealed—" Wickenshire said with a shrug.

"Nicholas Willoughby Chastain!" roared his mama. "Of course you must marry the girl! You cannot possibly think to compromise her and *not* marry her!"

"Nicky?" Spelling could still not quite seem to comprehend. "You . . . she . . . You, Nicky?"

"She cannot possibly go traipsing off to London with Upton if I marry her, either, Mama," Lord Wickenshire said, gazing down at the young lady trembling with suppressed laughter in his arms. "It would be most inappropriate."

Upton stood glaring at the both of them, his mind awhirl but unable to think of one thing to say as Delight jumped up and down happily beside him.

EIGHTEEN

"You need not worry about me, Nicky," declared Mr. Spelling the next morning as Wickenshire entered the morning room where Upton and Spelling were breaking their fast before taking leave. "I am not about to lay evidence against you. No, and I am not about to support Upton's claim or lead any excisemen to the booty, either."

"What?" Lord Upton's eyebrows both arched dramatically. "You cannot mean, Spelling, that you intend to let him get away with this—abomination! We have discussed it, you and I."

"No. You ranted and raved about it all night, Upton. I do not recall inserting so much as a single word sideways."

"Well, but—"

"Enough, Upton," Wickenshire interrupted, pouring himself a cup of coffee and taking the seat at the head of the table. "You are certain, Neil?"

"Of course I am certain. I have thought it all through, Nicky, and—"

"—you value your skin," Wickenshire finished for him.

"Exactly so. I know I have a tendency to get out of hand from time to time, Nick. But I have never gotten so very far out of hand as to threaten my own life. I believe in self-preservation. More than anything. And it is Uncle Ezra."

"What the devil are you whining about?" Upton exclaimed.

"He is not whining, Upton. You are not whining at all, Neil," Wickenshire assured him. "I understand you perfectly."

"Well, I do not understand a bloody thing!" cried Upton, gaining his feet so angrily that his chair crashed back against the wall. "Are you going to let this— farmer—intimidate you, Spelling? Is he to have everything? Your money? Miss Bedford? When we have the perfect means to stop him? Miss Bedford cannot be expected to marry a proved smuggler. No, she must come to me for protection from such a fellow. I am all she has, after all. And your money, Neil—she cannot possibly teach that wretched parrot to sing once we have taken her off to London. The money will be yours! What the devil are you afraid of?"

"Death," sighed Spelling.

"Uncle Ezra," Wickenshire drawled.

"One and the same," nodded Spelling.

Upton glared at them both. "Who the devil is this Uncle Ezra?" he shouted. "Some doddering old fool? And what the deuce has he to do with anything? He ain't here, is he, Spelling? And he ain't likely to say a word in Wickenshire's defense or he will be prosecuted for smuggling himself. My gawd, you are an out-and-out poltroon!"

"Just so," Spelling agreed quietly. "An out-and-out poltroon. A coward to the core."

"You are not, Neil," drawled Wickenshire. "Even my mama is afraid of Uncle Ezra, and he is her brother. Mad, you know," he added, glancing at Upton. "Strung a man up by his thumbs once because the color of the gentleman's waistcoat offended him."

"Balderdash," growled Upton, stuffing his hands into his breeches pockets.

"No, it ain't balderdash!" Spelling cried. "It is truth! Uncle Ezra has served up grass for breakfast to any number of gentlemen with sword and pistol both! And once, when my papa told him that he had the temper of a rabid hound, he lifted Papa straight up over his head and threw him down the staircase!"

"No, did he?" Wickenshire asked. "I never heard about that."

"You remember when Papa broke his arm, Nicky?"

"Um-hmmm."

"Well, that is how he broke it."

"Devil, you say. I wonder if my papa offended Uncle Ezra in some way?" Wickenshire said with the cock of an eyebrow.

"What has that to do with anything?" shouted Upton.

"My gawd, I never thought of that!" Spelling exclaimed.

"No, neither did I, until now."

"What are you two beetlebrains talking about?" roared Upton.

"My papa took an unfortunate trip down a staircase as well," Wickenshire explained, sipping at his coffee. "He broke his neck, not his arm. Uncle Ezra was with him at the time, as I recall."

Upton's eyes grew round; he sputtered; he blinked; he sputtered again.

"Just so," nodded Wickenshire. "Uncle Ezra. Ah, my dearest cousin, Eugenia, and my beloved betrothed," he added as the young ladies entered the room. "Come and sit with us for a moment, eh? You have brought good news, I think."

"Very good news," smiled Eugenia as Spelling and the earl rose to welcome them. "John Coachman and Bobby Tripp are safely off to London, Nicky. They left at sunrise, but you were fast asleep and so no one wished to disturb you."

"They are a good three hours ahead, then," Wickenshire said, pouring both the young ladies a cup of tea from the pot upon the table. "If thoughts of our Uncle Ezra are not enough to stop this nonsense, then certainly your news will do so."

"Do so what?" growled Upton, glaring at Serendipity and Eugenia in turn. "I am not afraid of a doddering old man, Wickenshire. Nor I ain't afraid of anything two chits can do."

"Do not be so very certain, my lord," Eugenia said quietly. "We have sent Nicky's coach off filled with Captain Sebastian's cargo. Not all of it, of course, but a considerable amount."

"So?" Upton sneered.

"They are taking it to Upton House," offered Serendipity, accepting a plate of toast and eggs from Wickenshire and smiling fondly up at him. "I have told them where they may store it there, in a secret place—one that it will take you years to discover, my lord. The servants at Upton House, having been loyal to Papa and myself for all these years, will not question what goes forward. I have sent a note along which explains that John Coachman and Mr. Tripp are to be left alone in the establishment until they have completed their errand. The servants at Upton House will do that for me, you know, even though you are their new master. It is such a little thing. So the cargo will be hidden, and only John Coachman, Mr. Tripp and myself will know where to find it."

"I do not see . . ." Upton began, and then his eyes widened.

"Just so," grinned Wickenshire, setting a plate of kippers and eggs and fruit before Eugenia. "Empty your duffle—pardon me, my dears—betray me to the excisemen, Upton, and Miss Bedford will do you an equally good turn. Whatever of the cargo is discovered here at Willowsweep, a goodly portion of it will also be discovered at Upton House. You, too, will be assumed a part of this cozy little undertaking, and we shall suffer a like fate, you and I."

"Well, of all the . . ." Upton fumed. "You are as nefarious as Spelling! All of you! Spelling, we must be off at once!"

"Willn't do a bit of good," mumbled Spelling around a bite of bacon. "Three hours ahead. Never overtake 'em. Finish your breakfast like a good fellow."

"Yes, do finish breaking your fast like a good fellow, Upton," Wickenshire urged with a wicked gleam in his eye, "and then you and I shall go off and discuss the dowries you are going to bestow upon each of your cousins—Serendipity and Delight both. You have inherited everything from their father. I expect he depended on you to do right by the girls."

"Well, I never!"

"No, I assumed you never—thought to bestow dowries upon them, I mean. Miss Bedford has intimated as much. But you will do so in writing before you leave this house, Upton, or the excisemen will be at Upton House before you can shake a cat."

The days that followed, Serendipity thought to be the happiest of all her life. She spent her mornings teaching Lord Nightingale to sing and her afternoons with Eugenia and Lady Wickenshire and Delight, strolling about in the increasingly fine weather, noting with awe the changes that Lady Wickenshire brought to the garden with the help of Mr. Jenkins and Bobby Tripp, and reveling in the newly greening grass beneath her feet and the blazingly blue sky above her head.

"He loves me," she thought as she watched Delight and Stanley Blithe and Sweetpea tumble about on the lawn.

"He is my fiancé; he truly wishes to marry me," she murmured each time Eugenia accused her of having stars in her eyes.

And each evening when Wickenshire came, at last, to sit beside her, to read to her or listen to her sing, to trifle with Delight and the creatures and speak gruffly to

Nightingale as the macaw rubbed a bright red head against his cheek, she thanked God that she had written to Eugenia and that the letter had brought her to this place. Her life and Delight's had grown and blossomed and bloomed into happiness, and all because she had given herself into the coarse but caring hands of an enchanted frog who wished to become an earl.

"Nicholas is everything wonderful and he wishes to marry *me*," she said in the drawing room one evening before dinner, in a voice so filled with awe that Eugenia laughed.

"Yes. I never thought to see the day that Nicky would ignore his lack of fortune and plunge ahead into matrimony in spite of himself. You have swept him off his feet, Sera."

"Ignore his lack of fortune?" Serendipity's eyes met Eugenia's on the instant. "But he will have a fortune, Eugenia, in less than a week. You will see. Lord Nightingale will sing, and very properly, too."

"So we all hope, but will Nicky accept the money?" Lady Wickenshire asked, staring up at a portrait of her husband.

"Accept the money? Of course he will accept the money. It is left to him by his Aunt Winifred." Serendipity could not think why there should be the least question of His Lordship turning down the bequest.

"It is ill-gotten gain, Sera," Eugenia enlightened her. "Nicky believes it to be his papa's share of the smuggling funds. Has he not said a word to you about that? Odds are that he will not accept it even if Nightingale does sing. Nicky is, above all, an honorable man, and the money was not gotten honorably."

"But—but—he needs the money!" exclaimed Serendipity. "It will take him years to have enough to marry and raise a family, else. He said so himself. And Nicholas has done nothing illegal."

"Except to allow Ezra to store his ill-gotten goods on Wickenshire lands. At least this one time he knows of it, and is allowing it." Lady Wickenshire shook her head sadly at her husband's portrait. "If only you had not been such a worthless ninnyhammer," she sighed. "You were forever wishing Nicky at the devil, and now you have placed him directly at the devil's doorstep. I vow, if you had not fallen down those stairs on your own so long ago, I should think nothing of pushing you down them myself, right this minute."

"Well, but there is my dowry," Serendipity proposed as they waited for Wickenshire to make an appearance so that they might proceed to dinner.

"I have gots a dow'y, too," offered Delight. "Nicky can have my dow'y if he needs it. Is Nicky poor, Sera?"

"No, no, he is not poor," declared Lady Wickenshire. "And he does not require anyone's dowry. That is for you when you are old enough to marry, little one. You will be glad of it then, believe me."

"Glad of what?" asked the earl, strolling into the room for all the world as if he had not worked the entire day with the shepherds, running the flock through the stream and washing the fleece clean of dirt and raddle so that it could be sheared once it had dried. "All done at last, Mama. We will begin shearing on Wednesday, after all this business with Nightingale has been settled. I expect Neil will come, don't you?"

"Of course Neil will come, and with his fingers crossed, hoping that Lord Nightingale does not sing one note."

"But he will," smiled Serendipity confidently, though her heart had grown heavy with the knowledge just bestowed upon her.

No sooner had dinner ended than Lord Wickenshire excused himself from the table and, taking Serendipity's hand, helped her from her chair and escorted her from the room.

"Where are we going, Nicholas?"

"Out to the garden, and hopefully, this time, there will not be a fire."

"Ought we? Without a chaperon?"

"I have already compromised you, gudgeon. Have you forgotten?"

"No," Serendipity whispered.

"I thought not. I cannot compromise you again, sweetest."

He led her down the tiny stone paths from which the weeds had been cleared and, coming to the end of one, took her into his arms and pressed his lips softly against hers. "I do love you, Sera, with all my heart, but . . ."

"But what? Nicholas, but what?"

"You were not truly compromised, you know. There is no reason at all that you must marry me. It was a game we played to save you and Delight from Upton, nothing more. Mama and Eugenia know the truth of it and will never say a word about that night. I promise you. You may safely find yourself a much better husband than I, and no one will think a thing of it."

Serendipity's heart thudded to the flat bottom of her right slipper and lay there gasping. "Oh, Nicholas, it is true what Eugenia and your mama said!"

"What did they say?"

"That you will not take the money even if Lord Nightingale does sing."

"I cannot," he stated flatly, watching with regret the tears that mounted to Serendipity's eyes. "Nightingale must sing, Sera. I pray each night that he will. But only because I have grown so fond of him and have no wish to give him to Neil. I cannot take the money, though, if he sings, any more than I can turn my Uncle Ezra over to the excisemen or call Neil out for setting my house afire. They must deal with their consciences, Sera, but I must live with mine.

"We shall both live with yours. I do not mind to be poor, Nicholas. I do not mind to have only a few servants, or to work with my own hands upon a house that requires my attentions. I shall take joy in gardening and sweeping and dusting. Yes, and in doing laundry as well. And we can raise children without a great fortune. Look at you, Nicholas. Your mama had barely any money at all, and she raised you to be the noblest of gentlemen. It can be done. People can be married and struggle through, if only they love one another."

"Do not speak so desperately, my love."

"But I must! I must! It makes not the least difference how hard life is, Nicholas, if that life is one we spend together. Can you not see that? Love is not the promise of ease and pleasure and extravagance. It is the union of two souls whose only wish is to be with one another always, no matter the suffering. I shall work until my hands are as rough and callused as yours without one regret, if only I may do so at your side—if only you and I may raise our children together, grow old together and comfort one another until death comes to rattle at our door."

He stopped her next word with a kiss and held her close within his arms in the diminishing twilight. "You are the best of women," he whispered in her ear, and then kissed it. "I cannot think what I have done to deserve you."

They sat around the large table in Wickenshire's study that Tuesday afternoon of June the first—Mr. Trent and Mr. Spelling, Lady Wickenshire, Eugenia, Delight and Serendipity. Before them at the front of the room, Lord Nightingale perched upon the top of his cage and Lord Wickenshire stood beside him. Serendipity had taught Wickenshire her little song, so that he might start the parrot to singing it. " 'Wee Willie, Wee Willie, go 'way from m'door,' " sang the earl in a tremulous baritone and not quite tunefully.

"Awwk!" cried Lord Nightingale. "Stubble it! Morning, Nightingale. Morning, Nightingale."

"No, no, you must sing, you old pirate," urged Wickenshire. "I shan't have the money, but I will be damned if I am going to lose custody of you into the bargain, sir. Come now, pay attention. 'Wee Willie, Wee Willie, go 'way from m'door.' "

"What the devil does he mean, he shan't have the money?" boomed a voice from the corridor. "Jenkins, what does the boy mean? By Jove, we will see does he have the money or not."

"Oh, my gawd," gulped Neil as his glance, along with everyone else's, went to the doorway. "Nicky, it is Uncle Ezra."

"Damned right it is Uncle Ezra," bellowed the gentleman who strode into the room in high top boots, double-breasted morning coat and buff breeches. His silvery hair shone in the sunlight from the windows. His blue eyes blazed with passion. His very appearance took Serendipity's breath away, made Eugenia tremble and caused Lady Wickenshire to squeak the merest bit before she rose and went to him and welcomed him to Willowsweep.

"Yes, yes, of course I am welcome here, Diana. You would not dare say otherwise. No one would, sweet thing. You are looking a deal older, dear heart, but still pretty, still pretty. Now, get on with it, Nicholas," he added, tucking almost all of Lady Wickenshire under one arm. "Jenkins has explained all to me in a letter. Now make the blasted bird sing."

Wickenshire grinned. He had not at all expected his incorrigible uncle to make an appearance. He had not seen him in five years at the least. "What are you doing here, Uncle Ezra?" he asked, his eyes alight with laughter. "I thought you never wished to lay eyes on me again."

"When did I say that? Never mind. I was mistaken. I wished to lay eyes upon you this afternoon, and I am doing so. Get the bird to sing, Nicky."

" 'Wee Willie, Wee Willie,' " Wickenshire began again

as his uncle took a chair beside his mama, " 'go 'way from m'door.' "

"Wee Willie, Wee Willie" muttered Nightingale to himself.

"Well, what the devil is that?" asked Ezra loudly. "Wee who? What a thing for a parrot to sing." Rising, he stomped to the front of the room. "Sing, you danged son of a seahorse," he commanded, glaring at Nightingale. Neil could not help himself and snorted into his hand. So did Mr. Trent. Serendipity and Eugenia, despite all the tension, or perhaps because of it, began to giggle.

"Sing, you dang-ed son of seahorse!" exclaimed Delight in joyous imitation, climbing from her chair up onto the table.

" 'Hey there, mister,' " rumbled Uncle Ezra's deep baritone. " 'I saw Hiram kiss yer sister.' "

"Oh, my gawd, no, not that," chuckled Wickenshire. "What sort of a thing is that to teach a bird?"

"Never mind. Sing it again. Get him started," ordered Ezra.

" 'Hey there, mister, I saw Hiram kiss yer sister,' " managed Wickenshire, around the laughter in his throat. " 'Down in the shade of the old oak tree.' "

" 'Hey there, mister, I saw—Hiram kiss yer—sister,' " sang Nightingale enthusiastically. " 'Down inthe—shade—of the oldoaktreeeeee. Hey, theremisterit—were-notme—what kissed her. I were—jist awatchin'sir—it were not meeee. Wee WillieWee—Willieeee, go 'wayfrom m'door,' " he added without the least encouragement. " 'I cannotsaywhy— But— I love theee—nomore.' Morning, Nightingale. Awwk! Mrrrrow! Rrrrarf-arf! Knollsmarmer!" he squawked.

"I wish I could remember that Knollsmarmer thing," mumbled Uncle Ezra. "Important, that. Albert told me it was important, but he did never tell me why. So, the bird has sung, Trent," he added, turning to glare at the solicitor. "Pay the boy his money."

"No," Wickenshire interrupted, taking a step toward

his friend, Mr. Trent. "Never mind, William. I do not want the money. Neil may have it. But I should like to keep Nightingale. That will be all right, will it not? He did sing."

"Me? Me, take the money?" Spelling cried, leaping from his chair. "Me, Nicky?"

"No, not you, you rattlebrain," growled Ezra. "Sit back down. The money is yours, Nicholas, all right and tight, lad. You got Lord Nightingale to sing."

"I know," Wickenshire said, "but I cannot accept the money, Uncle Ezra. It . . . I . . . You will never understand, but it is money made from smuggling and—"

"Oh, for glory sakes!" broke in Uncle Ezra. "Who the devil told you that?"

"Well, I guessed it at first, and then Jenkins said—"

"Jenkins? Jenkins is a butler. Your butler. What the devil does he know about Winifred's money?"

"Do you mean to say it is not from my husband's share of the—arrangement—Ezra?" asked Lady Wickenshire excitedly.

"Damnation! No, it ain't! Came from Winifred's first husband. Invested it in the Funds some twenty years ago, she did, when she married Albert. I helped her to do it."

"But then, what happened to Papa's share of the smuggling money?" asked Wickenshire suspiciously.

"Squandered it. If ever a man was born with beans for brains, it was your papa, Nicky. Why your mama ever saw fit to marry that b-ah-dastard, I cannot imagine. But if you think for one minute that I owe you anything for the years we have been using Willowsweep as a—stopover—so to speak, you can just put that out of your head, boy. Gave your blasted father what he requested. Four thousand pounds ready money. Ain't our fault he spent it. He had no use for this place. Albert and I did. Only right we kept on using it after he died."

"But you are not going to continue using it, Uncle Ezra?"

"No. Found another spot. Sebastian and I agreed upon

it. Do not want you involved, Nicholas. You are not like Neil. Make a rotten pirate. Always be trying to give back the blasted booty."

Wickenshire ran his fingers through his curls and whistled a low whistle. He shook his Uncle Ezra's hand with great energy, strode to the table, tugged Serendipity up into his arms and kissed her wildly upon the lips, setting Delight to squealing, Lady Wickenshire to crying, and Eugenia to laughing gayly.

"Nicholas, you shall have the money after all," managed Serendipity around a great lump of happiness in her throat once he gave her space to speak. "You shall have Lord Nightingale and the money—"

"—and you, my darling girl. And Delight and Stanley Blithe and Sweetpea too. Do not forget them. Oh, what a family we shall make!"

"A most loving family," offered his mama softly.

"An' a big one," squeaked Delight gleefully.

"And a blessed one," sighed Eugenia, smiling.

"Almost had it," Neil mumbled to himself as Wickenshire set about kissing Miss Bedford again, thoroughly. "Came this close," he muttered, holding his thumb and forefinger barely a hairsbreadth apart. "This close."

"An inch is as good as a mile, Neil," chuckled Mr. Trent, his eyes fastened with joy upon Wickenshire and Miss Bedford. "He will have the best of all lives now, Nicky will, and someone to share it with, too."

"Knollsmarmer!" squawked Lord Nightingale, flapping his great wings once and gliding to land on Wickenshire's shoulder, where he proceeded to nibble at his master's hair while his master continued to kiss Serendipity. "Knollsmarmer! Knollsmarmer!"

"I am getting old," Wickenshire's Uncle Ezra commented to Jenkins, who stood grinning like a lunatic upon the threshold. "I cannot remember about Knollsmarmer. Ah, well, never mind. Hire any number of workmen now, the lad can. Use the free time to make love to the girl. About time he got himself leg-shackled.

I will send them three cases of the finest Irish soap for their wedding, Jenkins. See if I do not!"

Jenkins coughed and grinned and said not a word.

"Morning, Nightingale. Mrrrrow. Rrrrarf-arf," Lord Nightingale cried as Stanley Blithe and Sweetpea scampered into the room. "Knollsmarmer!"

BOOK YOUR PLACE ON OUR WEBSITE AND MAKE THE READING CONNECTION!

We've created a customized website just for our very special readers, where you can get the inside scoop on everything that's going on with Zebra, Pinnacle and Kensington books.

When you come online, you'll have the exciting opportunity to:

- View covers of upcoming books
- Read sample chapters
- Learn about our future publishing schedule (listed by publication month *and author*)
- Find out when your favorite authors will be visiting a city near you
- Search for and order backlist books from our online catalog
- Check out author bios and background information
- Send e-mail to your favorite authors
- Meet the Kensington staff online
- Join us in weekly chats with authors, readers and other guests
- Get writing guidelines
- AND MUCH MORE!

**Visit our website at
http://www.zebrabooks.com**

Lord Nightingale's Love Song

And a Happy Knollsmarmer to you all, my dears! Ah, no, that's not right. What does Knollsmarmer mean, anyway? And now that the evil Lord Upton and the nefarious Neil have been put in their places and Nicky and Sera are looking happily ahead to their wedding, what can be left for Lord Nightingale to do? I'll give you a hint; Lord Nightingale's next mission has a great deal to do with Cousin Eugenia and a marquis who has built a solid rock wall around his heart. *Lord Nightingale's Love Song* will be on the shelves next month.

If you would like to take a guess at what Knollsmarmer means before you read book two, or just tell me what you thought of this book, you can e-mail me at regency@localaccess.net or write to me at 578 Camp Ney-A-Ti Road, Guntersville, Alabama, 35976-8301. I promise I'll answer as soon as I can.

—Judith

Thrilling Romance from
Meryl Sawyer

__**Half Moon Bay** 0-8217-6144-7	$6.50US/$8.00CAN
__**The Hideaway** 0-8217-5780-6	$5.99US/$7.50CAN
__**Tempting Fate** 0-8217-5858-6	$6.50US/$8.00CAN
__**Unforgettable** 0-8217-5564-1	$6.50US/$8.00CAN

Merlin's Legacy

A Series From
Quinn Taylor Evans

__**Daughter of Fire** $5.50US/$7.00CAN
   0-8217-6052-1

__**Daughter of the Mist** $5.50US/$7.00CAN
   0-8217-6050-5

__**Daughter of Light** $5.50US/$7.00CAN
   0-8217-6051-3

__**Dawn of Camelot** $5.50US/$7.00CAN
   0-8217-6028-9

__**Shadows of Camelot** $5.50US/$7.00CAN
   0-8217-5760-1

Call toll free **1-888-345-BOOK** to order by phone or use
this coupon to order by mail.

Name _____
Address _____
City _____ State _____ Zip _____
Please send me the books I have checked above.
I am enclosing $_____
Plus postage and handling* $_____
Sales tax (in New York and Tennessee) $_____
Total amount enclosed $_____
*Add $2.50 for the first book and $.50 for each additional book.
Send check or money order (no cash or CODs) to:
Kensington Publishing Corp., 850 Third Avenue, New York, NY 10022
Prices and Numbers subject to change without notice.
All orders subject to availability.
Check out our website at **www.kensingtonbooks.com**

More Zebra Regency Romances